HAMILTON ROBB

REG QUIST

Hamilton Robb
Reg Quist

CKN Christian Publishing
An Imprint of Wolfpack Publishing
6032 Wheat Penny Avenue
Las Vegas, NV 89122

ISBN: 978-1-64119-029-9

HAMILTON ROBB

THE SHERIFF, GLANCING OUT THE FLY-SPECKED AND SMOKE-encrusted window, saw deputy Hamilton Robb ride up. He elbowed his way through the crowd in front of the jailhouse and shouted above the din. "Robb, where've you been? How come you're never around when I want you most? You need to gather up a posse and get after those men."

Robb leaned his arms on the saddle horn and cast a weary eye at his boss. "What men would those be, Alex? You might want to remember that I've been three days away, chasing horse thieves. No way I could know what's been happening here in town."

Even though the noise level had lessened with the arrival of the deputy, the sheriff continued to shout, "Your friend, Chuck Wagon Charlie, robbed the bank, that's what's happened. Him and three others. Shot old Hattie in the process. Taken off to the west with more money than I'm ever likely to have, working with deputies who are never around when they're needed, and with this sorry town hardly paying enough to keep body and soul together."

"Why didn't you go after them yourself, Alex? Might have done you a world of good to get out of that swivel chair for a day or two."

"Don't lip me off, Robb. Remember who's the sheriff here and who's the deputy. I need you to pick a posse and get after those thieves. Time's a wasting and if those boys get out of our county we'll never see them again, or the money either."

Robb stepped to the ground and spoke to the men gathered in front of the sheriff's office, "Hanna, Thompson, Carlyle, get what you need together. Meet me here at first daylight tomorrow. Bring an extra blanket and a warm coat. It's cold up in those hills at night. The rest of you men find someplace else to be. You're making so much noise a man can't hardly think. Take your talk to the saloon; I don't want to hear any more of it here."

The sheriff had started towards the jailhouse door but, hearing Robb speak, he turned around and came back. "What are you talking about, tomorrow at dawn?" he shouted. "I needed you on the road three hours ago. You get back in that saddle and get under way." He came near to sputtering, he was so angry.

Robb passed the gelding's reins to a boy who had been leaning against the jailhouse wall. "Toby, I'll give you a two-bit piece if you'll take Blackie to the livery and care for him. A gallon of oats, easy on the water for now, a manger full of hay, and a good rubdown. Do you think you can do that?"

The boy said nothing. Nodding at the deputy after pocketing the silver coin, he gave a slight tug on the reins and started leading the big black to the barn.

The sheriff continued to shout in anger and frustration,

"I gave you an order, Robb. I want you after those men before they cross the county line. I want you after them now, not tomorrow morning."

Robb pulled off his hat and beat some dust out of each pant leg, returned the hat to his head and stared at the sheriff. "Alex, I've been on the road for three days which means my horse has been on the road for three days. Maybe got six hours sleep in all that time. Neither of us has another mile left in him. And as far as the county goes, the only thing west of here is rocks and sand bordered by the river with the empty Mohave on the other side. No one but a few hold-out Indians live there. If I pick up a man or two out there I can't see as how those Indians are going to complain much. I doubt as how they know where the county line is, or care.

"Now, tell me about the robbery; why you think Charlie was involved and how bad Hattie was hurt."

The sheriff was still angry but he had quit shouting. "Four men stood up the teller and cleaned out the cash drawers, plus that poor excuse for a safe old Bentley is so proud of. I know it was Charlie, mask or no mask, because he was talking to the teller in that ear-damaging squeak of a voice he's plagued with and there's no hiding his clothes or his horse. He ain't got but the one set of clothes and everyone in town knows that horse. No idea who the other three gunmen were.

"Hattie, she's going to be alright, given time. Just shot a bit through her upper arm but I don't expect that bullet is going to sweeten her up any. Danged if that old woman couldn't clabber milk before it's milked out of the cow. If she gets any more…"

He was interrupted by Deputy Robb, "Alright, Alex, I'll get after them in the morning when my horse is rested and I've had a bath, a feeding and a good night's sleep. I'm going to get started at that right now so I'll see you in the morning if you find it necessary to get up and watch us ride away."

Deputy Robb had taken three or four steps when the sheriff asked, "Did you find those horse thieves the Triple-T complained about?"

Robb stopped and turned around. "Found the horses. No thieves. There never were any thieves. Old Therian was pulling a fast one like he does from time to time. I found the horses in a corral, hidden in a small box canyon on the northern edge of his range. When are you going to figure out that Therian is just making trouble? He wants you out of office and he wants his nephew to have your job. But that's your problem. Me, I'm just the deputy that has to do all the riding, miss the meals and the sleep, and get shot at from time to time."

Robb took another couple of steps towards the hotel and then turned around again. "By the way, you might just as well know it now. This will be my last ride with the badge. If I get back in one piece, and breathing, you get the badge back and get to wish me well as I ride off."

The bank robbery forgotten for a moment, the sheriff was stunned by this news. "What do you mean? You can't quit now. Where am I going to find another deputy? And it's a long time till the next election. You can't quit between elections."

Robb smiled at the distraught sheriff. "Alex, it's you that won the election. Me, I just work for wages. I started the job and now I'm going to stop. This is my last ride."

He had intended to pass the deputy badge to the sheriff when he returned from hunting Therian's horses. But with all the shouting and excitement around the small combination jailhouse and sheriff's office when he rode up, it was clearly not a good time to unpin the piece.

At dawn the next morning, the four men rode out of town towards the western hills. The sheriff didn't bother getting out of bed to see them off. They picked up the trail of four horses less than a mile from town. "We'll follow these tracks a ways and see what we can see," Robb told the three men. "Don't hardly think there's been four others out this way since yesterday morning so I expect these are our boys, alright. Charlie, he's no brighter than a man really has to be to survive so if one of the others didn't think to cover their tracks, we'll have easy going."

Carlyle nodded his agreement, leaned over and spat his wad onto a nearby rock, and said, "Sheriff claims you're pretty friendly with Charlie. That going to present a problem when the time comes?"

"Sheriff has that not quite right, like he has a lot of things not quite right. He's an alright sheriff as far as that goes, but I would have to say he jumps to conclusions from time to time. All I've ever done with Charlie is stake him to a meal a time or two. More out of pity than anything else. There's no friendship involved nor could there ever be. Charlie and I are about as different as this black horse and Baillie's goat."

Carlyle nodded his understanding. After a short pause, he asked. "How did Charlie get his name? Never met anyone tagged with Chuck Wagon for a handle before."

Robb shook his head and smiled. "I never worked with the man myself but the story is, that on a round-up or on the trail, Charlie was always the first in line at meal time and was often seen bringing in firewood for the cook and doing other small chores that would keep him close to the grub wagon. Someone called him Chuck Wagon and the name stuck."

Some days later, still in the forested area south west of Brown Stone and short of the true desert by several miles, the posse spotted a deserted camp. The tracks led into a small copse of brush and the recently-used campsite. The small grouping of trees was near the base of a rise of land that was fringed with a good stand of pines. The slope rose about two hundred yards and then leveled out, leaving a small hump of grassed-over dirt and a scattering of rocks for shelter. The three posse men sat their saddles as Robb stepped off the black gelding and touched the campfire ashes.

"Warm to the touch. Doesn't look like much of a camp, but this had to have been their breakfast fire."

Picking up a stick of fire wood, Robb poked around in the ashes. He turned out a few beef bones, two empty sardine cans and a couple of fire-blackened tins that might have held peaches or some other fruit, although the paper labels were burned off so that was purely a guess. Beside a nearby shrub, he found a ratty blanket and a pair of worn-out socks.

"Shows all the signs of a hasty departure. Might have seen us coming. Those boys are lazy, as well as careless. They could have been miles from here if they'd half tried."

Two rifle shots followed this short speech. One shot missed the deputy by bare inches before taking the big black gelding square in the head. The poor beast stood for a heartbreaking moment, its knees trembling, as dead as it would ever be, and finally crumpled to the ground. Two of the posse members dove off their horses and scrambled into the bush surrounding the campsite, then rolled behind some rocks. The third posse member grabbed his shoulder and fell to the ground, his horse skittering and running off a ways. The other two horses followed, running a short distance before dropping their heads to graze.

Robb dove behind his dead horse. He lay still for a moment, waiting for more shots. When none came, he removed his hat and very carefully rose on one elbow. His head clearing the horse just to eye level, he looked up the slope in the direction of the shots. Seeing nothing of the shooters, he lay back down and looked around at the posse. Hanna was lying out in the open, his shirt soaking in blood. Robb called to the two hidden posse members, "You two drag Hanna into some shelter and see what you can do for that shoulder." He then reached over the top of the horse and slid his carbine from the saddle scabbard.

He shouted up the hill, "You men! You've got nowhere to run, just nowhere at all. Stand where I can see you and walk down to me. Leave your weapons on the ground." There was no answer.

Robb lay back down behind the horse and checked the ammunition in his pistol and then in the carbine. He talked quietly to himself about what had to be done, "Dang fools. They'll likely end up dead and I sure as shooting could end up the same way. If there's a crazier way to make a living I don't know what it would be, for them or me either."

He lay there picturing in his mind what he had seen of the hillside. "The safest route would be up through the trees. Not many trees though. Lots of open space. If those boys are intent on shooting someone they're sure enough going to get the chance."

Thompson called out from behind the rocks, "You talk'n to us, Robb? Speak up, can't hardly hear you."

"Pay me no mind, boys," he answered, "I'm just talking to myself. I've been doing that more and more lately. Reckon I need to spend more time with folks and less with my horse. You look after Hanna as best you can. I'm going to root these fellers out."

Starting up the hill through the well spaced-out trees, using as much shelter as the hillside offered and expecting a shot at every footstep, Robb ran from tree to tree, pausing often to look around.

He wasn't exactly sure where the two ambushers were. But unless they had run off, hoping to escape, they shouldn't be too hard to find if he somehow managed to live that long. The hilltop was covered in sparse bunches of grass and a bit of prickly pear. The trees stopped well short of the rim.

Robb crouched down behind a stunted pine, turned his back to the trunk and waited while he caught his breath. He wiped his sweat-soaked hands on his pants and then used the sleeve of his shirt to dry the grip on the carbine. He told himself that the slight tremble in his hands was from the effort of running up hill and had nothing to do with risk and hot lead. He didn't really believe it.

He had been keeping a careful eye out for the men but he spotted their horses first; two horses loosely tied to some shrubbery, perhaps one hundred yards to his right behind a copse of brush. He carefully made his way through the trees towards the horses. When he got close he squatted, sitting on his heels, and remained still and silent for five minutes. When there was still no sign of the men, he stretched his wait into ten minutes and then fifteen.

Finally, ignoring the risk, Robb got to his feet and glanced around. Trying to look in all directions at once, he made his way to the first horse, a bay mare. The animal watched his every move, ears up and alert. He tugged the reins loose. The second animal, a black and white pinto gelding, pulled back on his reins, snapping off a part of the shrubbery and neighing as he did it.

Someone shouted, "The horses, they're after the horses."

Robb grabbed both sets of reins and ran down the hill, all efforts at silence forgotten in the crash of broken branches and tumbling rocks. Three or four wasted shots from the hidden fugitives hurried him along. He reached the campsite where the posse men were still hunkered down behind the small grouping of sheltering rocks. Pulling the horses behind the rocks and tying the reins to a shrub, he asked, "How's Hanna?"

Thompson, his carbine pointed up the slope, spoke from behind some brush, "That's a nasty wound and he's lost blood. We've done what we could but he needs a doctor. We figure Hanna's a sight more important than that bank money. We've voted to head back just as fast as our horses will take us. Maybe Hanna can make it if we get him some help."

After a quick look at Hanna, Robb agreed that the wounded posse man had become the priority. "Alright, you men get him fixed up and ready for the saddle. Pull my saddle off the black and get it onto that pinto gelding. Then you stay hidden for just a bit. I'll be right back."

He started back up the hill through the trees, climbing as quietly as he knew how. He still had no clear idea of where the two fugitives were. They had probably moved since taking the shots. The only thing he was sure of was that they would not have tried to escape on foot; there was absolutely nowhere to go without their horses.

Stopping at the edge of the trees, he looked up and took a guess. If the men were directly ahead, over the lip of the slight rise or behind the rocks, attacking straight on was to invite death. Off to the left, the tree line grew higher up the slope, wrapping around the lip of the rise. To the right was scrub brush and cactus. The men could be anywhere. It was also possible they were circling around, hoping to recover their horses.

Robb chose to stay with the trees. He climbed to his left as quickly as possible without making noise. Ten minutes later, he was crawling through the underbrush, stopping behind a fallen log. Now he was above the lip of the knoll; not much higher, but enough. He scraped dirt and debris from beneath the log so that he could see under it, not being willing to lift his head over that bit of security.

At first, he could see nothing. Then, looking more closely, he saw a foot and a part of a leg, the toe of the boot pointing downward as if the man was on his knees staring down the slope. The distance was perhaps two hundred feet, less than ten seconds running distance away. But a gunman can do a lot of shooting in ten seconds. Could he make it to the men before they saw him? Or was this a foolish thought? He preferred to take the thieves alive, but was this the time to play fair? Was an arrest going to be possible? If he called out for the men to surrender, what would they do? Remembering the ambush that brought down Hanna and the black horse, the question answered itself. And then there was the need to get Hanna to town as quickly as possible so time had become an issue.

Stealth forgotten, he leaped to his feet and started to run, his Winchester spitting fire with each step. There was little chance of hitting anything but that wasn't his goal. He wanted to shock the men into surrender. The leg disappeared and a man stood, hunched over, and charged through the brush and down the slope away from the shooting. The second man stood, lifting his carbine to his shoulder. Robb dove to the ground, rolling. The bank robber fired, the bullet striking a rock and ricocheting off. Robb brought his carbine into firing position. A bullet struck his arm, burning a shallow furrow almost to his elbow before burying itself in the sod behind him.

Ignoring the screaming pain in his arm and the dripping blood, Robb pulled himself back into firing position. Another shot lifted dirt and pebbles, spraying his hands and the carbine with dust, drawing more blood where the pebbles struck. He blinked away the dust and pulled the trigger. His first shot took the fugitive in the thigh and as he started to crumble to the ground, Robb's second shot took him full in the chest.

Robb pushed more cartridges into the carbine and jumped to his feet. Leaping over the dying man, he ran after the second fugitive. He dropped to his belly and peered over the edge of the knoll. Grass and shrubbery shook, marking the path of heedless, frantic movement through the brush below. A man burst into view and stopped, looking up the hill.

"Too easy," thought Robb as his finger tightened on the trigger. The sound of the shot was loud in the still morning. A startled camp robber jay flew up with a squawk. The man fell over backwards, flinging his carbine into the brush.

Robb stood and looked all around, seeing no further movement nor did he expect to; the two tied horses almost surely meant that the other two thieves had gone on alone.

He turned back and knelt down beside the dying man who looked at him with half-closed eyes.

The robber's shirt and upper pant leg were sodden with blood. A tear fell from the corner of his eye. He looked pleadingly at the deputy. Finally, he spoke, so quietly he could barely be heard, "Stupid. That's what we all were. We're not so desperate that we needed to try a daylight robbery." He was silent for a moment and then begged, "Don't leave me out here. Can't stand the thought of the critters gnawing on my bones."

"I'll not leave you here if you tell me your name and where the money is."

The fugitive gasped a couple of times and whispered, "Name's Galen Roberts. Half the money's in the saddlebags on those horses you led away. The rest is with the others. Thought if we split up we'd be harder to find. Stupid! The whole thing was stupid!" He gasped twice more, his final two breaths.

Robb rose to his feet and wearily started down the hill.

The uninjured posse men carried both bodies to the campsite.

Robb went through the pockets of the dead men, finding a bit of loose change, a pocketknife and not much else. In their saddlebags, each man had a couple of letters from family that confirmed their names.

They laid the two fugitives together and piled rocks over them. Unless coyotes and buzzards learned how to move rocks, the bodies would be safe enough there. They loaded Hanna onto his horse and saddled up themselves.

Robb spoke to the other men, "You head back the quickest way you know how using that spare horse to spell off the others. Get whatever help you can for Hanna. Give that bag of money back to the bank. Make them count it in front of you. I wouldn't trust Bentley as far as I could throw that iron safe of his. I'm going after those other two. I'll hope to see you in a few days."

He mounted the pinto and swung it around to head southwest, taking one last fond look at the dead black. "So long, pard. I hope you've found a pleasant green valley. I'm looking for one myself. I was hoping we'd find it together."

He gently touched the pinto with the spurs and tugged his hat down tight. "The sooner started, the sooner finished."

It was almost a week later that Robb saw the smoke of a campfire showing itself against the shadows cast by the setting sun. He had left the pine forest behind three days before and was now in an area of rocky desert with huge piles of large boulders scattered around. There was the typical desert growth; prickly pear in abundance, plus saguaro, cholla and mesquite, and an array of smaller shrubs with just enough grass to keep the pinto from starving.

He swung the weary horse toward the camp and pulled his Winchester. "Pinto, let's hope this is them. I've about had it with these desert hills. Expect you might feel just about the same. Still, we'll take a little rest here."

Robb shook his canteen for the fourth or fifth time that day; it had been empty since the day before. It was still empty and would be until he found water, an unlikely prospect in this sun-baked wasteland. He wondered idly if the heat and thirst were making him irrational. He frowned, hung the empty container back on the saddle horn, took a deep breath of the hot desert air and stepped to the ground. Whether he was suffering more from thirst or hunger was a toss-up. His horse was staggering with weariness. It sometimes seemed to Robb that he had been hungry, thirsty, and exhausted ever since he had pinned on the deputy badge three years before.

He tied the pinto to a mesquite and hunkered down behind a boulder well out of sight of the camp.

For reasons that Robb couldn't get his mind around, there was an almost steady stream of murderers, hold-up artists and desperados of every sort hoping to escape into the garden of sand and rock to the west of Brown Stone, Arizona Territory; the area he had signed on to protect. It was a brutal country with endless miles of inhospitable sand and rock. Water was only rarely available and difficult to find. If a man didn't die of thirst or heat, there was always the risk of being set afoot which was the same as dying, but doing it slowly. And, of course, there were the Indians who had never found a good enough reason to like or trust the men who had intruded into their territory. The desert offered an abundance of ways for a man to suffer and die.

Robb didn't like the desert. He often drew pictures in his mind of gently rolling hills; green hills with flowing streams every few miles, nothing but well-broken horses to ride, and dinner on the stove served up by a smiling wife when his day's work was done. It was a nice dream to hold onto but the plain fact was that he had a job to do first and there was not a green hill or a smiling wife in sight. Those two images were little more than vague dreams to hold against an uncertain future.

There were no clouds and no shade other than the bit of shadow cast by a mesquite that was struggling for survival. It was hot as it had been every day of the hunt.

At an inch under six feet, Robb wouldn't be considered a big man. But he had the broad shoulders and slim waist of the typical rider plus a determination that seemed to overshadow everything he did. He was strong and confident in his movements, handling horses, cattle or men with ease. He admitted to himself that he had no concept at all about handling women, although he doubted that handling was exactly the right word but he couldn't think of a better one. He liked women and enjoyed being around them but he was awkward and seemed to have trouble finding words. He sometimes thought he was learning how to talk to a girl but he also knew he had much yet to learn.

Twenty minutes later, Robb climbed into the saddle and spoke to the pinto, "Step up now, boy, we've got a job of work to do." He started the horse up the small hill towards the camp smoke using every bit of cover the rocky terrain provided.

He'd never felt quite right about taking another man's life even though it was occasionally a part of the job. The two fugitives lying under the rocks a few miles back had haunted his sleep ever since the posse had laid them out. He had no desire to add to the number of bodies. He swung off the pinto and tied it securely behind a grouping of desert brush before taking off his spurs and hanging them from the saddle horn. As quietly as he could, he crawled toward the camp. His first task was to make sure who was settling in for the night; to draw down on an innocent traveler was no part of his plan.

It took but a matter of a few minutes to crawl to an opening in the brush that gave him a clear view of the fire. Robb recognized Chuck Wagon Charlie right off. He was lying on his bedroll while his partner was sitting by the fire with a cup of coffee. There had been no water for miles in any direction and the sight of that coffee set the deputy's mouth to watering. He saw a canvas water bag and two canteens so the fugitives had come well-prepared for staying a while. With difficulty he dragged his eyes off the canteens and the steaming coffeepot.

Holding his carbine in firing position, Robb shouted loud enough to be clearly heard, "Charlie, this is Deputy Hamilton Robb. You're under arrest, both of you. Throw out your guns and stand up."

Both men dove for the bush. Robb got off one shot. Charlie made it safely into the bush and dropped down behind some scrub that surrounded a small rock outcrop. His partner fell headlong into a large clump of prickly pear, his life blood being soaked up by the dry desert. Robb swore under his breath, not liking the outcome.

"Charlie, you're alone now. I got the other two some days back. Stand up and come out. If you fight me, I'll shoot you dead. I don't want to but I'm really tired of all this. I'm riding for home in a few minutes. You can be sitting in a saddle or draped over one. It's up to you."

There was silence for a few moments and then Charlie

hollered, "I got no life back there, Robb, living like I do. Just no life at all. A man shouldn't have to live like that. I'll take my chances here."

"There's no life out here either, Charlie. Where did you think you were going? There's no escape out of here in any direction."

"We weren't trying to escape, Robb. We were just hiding until the heat was off and the posse went home. Then we were going to Tucson. I tried to tell Davey and them that there wasn't no quit in you but they wouldn't listen. I guess you could say that cost them. But I'm still not coming out. I've got a gun, too, and you've got it to do, Robb."

"Dumb as a sack of hammers," Robb said just loud enough to hear himself, looking at Charlie's knee sticking above the rock he was hiding behind. He took careful aim and pulled the trigger. Blood and bone flew through the air and Charlie screamed in agony.

Robb stood and slowly walked towards the two men. The one was for sure dead and Charlie was offering no resistance. He writhed on the ground, screaming in pain and shock, most of his knee blown away with blood running freely. He looked up at Hamilton and moaned.

"That was just downright mean, Robb. Mean. Never would have thought it of you. What am I going to do with just the one leg?"

Robb knelt beside Charlie. "You won't be doing anything at all if we don't stop that bleeding. I'm going to cut your pant leg off and tie it as a tourniquet; maybe save your worthless life. But first I want your guns. Don't you move while I gather them up or you won't need anything else ever again."

Robb lifted Charlie's six-shooter from its holster and

threw it behind him. He then reached for the carbine that lay on the grass, forgotten by Charlie.

He pulled his knife and cut the bloody pant leg off above the knee. Tying it around the badly damaged leg, Robb picked up a short piece of mesquite branch and, using it as a lever, wrapped the bandage tightly enough to slow down the bleeding. Charlie screamed until he finally passed out.

Robb rummaged through the two men's saddlebags, pulled out the cleanest shirt he could find and wrapped it as a bandage around the knee. "It's filthy but I don't see as I've got much choice."

On the way to get the horses, Robb stopped at the fire, pouring himself a cup of coffee. He then drank most of a canteen of water. He poured another canteen of water into his hat for the pinto.

They were a long four-day ride from town by the most direct route Robb knew. He didn't want to bury another body in the bush so he slung the dead bank robber over a horse. Charlie rode upright, his leg dangling. They made only one short camp along the way. By the time they rode down the main street of town, the horses were staggering, Hamilton was more than ever determined to turn in his badge, and Charlie was delirious with fever and infection.

Robb rode directly to the doctor's office. A shout from someone on the sidewalk started a crowd gathering.

Robb looked at the townsmen with bleary eyes. "Some of you men get Charlie into the doctor's and take this other one to the shed out back. And those horses have been bad used. Someone take care of them."

He rode to the livery and left the pinto with the hostler. "Treat him well, he's done some work."

Robb staggered to the hotel where he kept a room and fell onto the bed. He needed a bath and some food but that could wait. After sleeping for twelve hours without even taking his boots off, something he had never done before, he got up, ate a huge breakfast and went back to bed.

At noon the following day - rested, bathed and overfed - Robb walked into the sheriff's office and placed his deputy badge on the desk.

The sheriff picked up the badge and held it in his hand. "You really going to do this, Robb? You'll miss the pay and be back here within a month, looking to be taken back on."

"Don't you count on it. I'll not miss the pay, and I'm not wanting any pay that I haven't already earned which means you owe me money just up to today. Write a chit for the bank and I'll be getting along.

"Did you run down the names of those three robbers? Maybe there's a reward for some of them. There's no reward for Charlie so far as I know. How is Charlie, by the way? And how's Hanna?"

The sheriff tapped the deputy badge on the top of his desk and looked at Robb, wondering how much to tell him. He was momentarily tempted to keep the rewards for himself. Finally, he laid it all out, everything he had learned by telegraph to the territorial capital.

"Charlie died this morning. Sorry about that; I know you did your best to get him back for doctoring. He was mostly a harmless fool. Too bad his old pards found him. Actually, there's a reward on him and the other three, too. Seems they did this kind of thing before down south. Tucson and Nogales. Around there.

"Anyway, I've never known you to change your mind so the banker already has your pay chit and the reward chits, too; five hundred dollars on each man, plus the five hundred the banker put up. Quite a haul for you on your last day. I never seen you spend anything you didn't have to either so I expect some of that money you recovered for the bank was from your own savings account. You'll leave here with enough to keep you in feed and shelter for a while. Hanna's going to have some stiffness in his shoulder, but he's alive and likely to stay that way."

Robb listened to that information and then asked, "You sure about Charlie? Seems hard to believe. I guess you never really know about a man. Never would have guessed. But some of the reward goes to the posse; we'll have to split that up."

The sheriff shook his head. "No, the men decided it was all yours. They said you did all the catching and, with you leaving and all, they wanted you to have a road stake. You go get your money and luck to you.

"Any idea what part of the country you'll be heading for?"

"I only have two things in mind. I don't want to use my guns anymore and I want out of the desert. I'm heading east until I see green grass in every direction, and where folks don't know what a red rock hill looks like nor the Mogollon Rim from a wagon wheel rim. I'm done with the desert and with law work.

"I know you're not happy with me but will you shake anyway?" Robb held out his hand.

The sheriff gripped it and said again, "Luck to you. Ride careful."

Robb walked to the livery and saddled the pinto. "I guess it's you and me now, Paint. You just keep your tail pointed at this town. We'll find us a green valley by-and-by."

2

"WELL, LOOKY WHAT'S A-COMIN!"

The excited, foghorn shout drew attention from every direction.

"If'n that ain't a sight, then I never seen one!"

The excited shouter turned to the man standing next to him on the boardwalk. "You ever seen such a thing, Robb? Looks like one of them there paa-rades a body hears tell about, like when the circus comes to town. Ain't never seen a real circus my own self nor a paa-rade; neither one, but I heard tell."

Smokey Dillabough always had something to say but only seldom did his words make any sense at all. Smokey, the Canyon View town character, thin as a fence rail with a tangled gray beard hiding the age-generated wrinkles on his face, was harmless and sometimes entertaining. Mostly he kept out of people's way, existing on handouts and the modest wages he earned from a grave-digging job the town had given him. He often sat on a ladder-back chair in front of the general store and talked nonsense to anyone who would listen, telling of Indian wars he hadn't fought in, Civil War cavalry charges he didn't ride in, and great fur-trapping adventures that ended before he was born. No one paid him much heed.

But Smokey's grating, growling voice had taken on a sense of wonder and awe that caused Hamilton Robb to turn from his chosen path and look to where the town character was pointing. Then he realized that everyone on the street was looking in the same direction and that the saloon and the retail stores were emptying out, spilling both patrons and clerks onto the sidewalk.

Hamilton had to step around two ladies whose hats were big enough to shadow the boardwalk like a cloud that had drifted into place and then hovered there. Making his way to the edge of the walk, he was finally able to see what Smokey was so excited about.

"Whoo-ee," shouted Smokey. "Ain't that just a sight? Pride on a stallion. That's what that is. That's just exactly what that is. Pride ride'n a stallion."

Hamilton looked over the group of riders and wagons parading down the main street of Canyon View, casually wondering who they were. He knew that before long everyone would have the answer. There were few secrets in a small community.

He had taken a step or two towards the general store when he spotted the young lady holding the reins of the team pulling a covered spring wagon; the most beautiful girl Hamilton had ever seen. Maybe the most beautiful girl anyone in the territory had ever seen.

He stopped dead in his tracks and stared. He saw nothing else and didn't hear the shout beside him.

"Pride riding a stallion," Smokey hollered again, "Whoo-ee."

The arriving cavalcade couldn't help but hear the shout.

The proud rider leading Smokey's 'paa-rade' was

followed by the two ladies in the spring wagon; the younger, beautiful girl plus one older lady who could only be her mother, judging by looks. Following the wagon were two young men on horseback, four covered freight wagons, a chuck wagon and fourteen tough looking cowboys.

Big Bob Stanton had left just a skeleton crew of riders to deal with the Circle S cattle and loose horses, wishing to have as many cowboys as possible bringing up the rear of his personal parade.

He had set out to make a show of his arrival and, judging by the attention he was getting, he was successful at that venture. He made sure to expand that attention by gently heeling his stallion while pulling its head up causing it to sidestep and prance proudly.

The entourage rode right down the middle of the only business street in Canyon View, making a show for the townsfolk. The Texas-proud rancher had no objection to being seen or talked about as long as the talk was positive and complimentary.

Big Bob looked neither to the left nor the right as he sat pompously astride his black stallion, fifty feet in the lead of the wagon that trailed him.

The wagon held his wife and daughter. The two women sat back in the spring seat, purposely looking at nothing but the roadway before them. Wanda gritted her teeth behind her pasted on half-smile and spoke so quietly that only her mother could hear her. "I've never been so embarrassed in all my life. This is ridiculous."

Mrs. Stanton, always supportive of her husband, withheld her personal view. But she was hunched back in the wagon seat with the brim of her bonnet pulled far forward as if trying to hide behind it. She studied her daughter sitting up straight and tall, gathering the attention of the townsfolk, men and women alike. "I must say, you don't look all that embarrassed. Perhaps you're more like your father than you know."

Wanda tipped her Stetson back as if daring anyone to criticize. Just the fact that she was wearing the traditional men's hat branded her as an independent young woman. And there was no denying that the white hat set off her blond curls in a most attractive fashion and accented her golden tan. "Mother, Father is who he is and we aren't going to change him. I hate this attention but as long as we're with Big Bob Stanton, we might just as well get used to it.

"I don't know as I would wave to the crowd but sitting up and looking like you're happy to be here probably wouldn't do you any lasting harm."

Mrs. Stanton remained huddled behind the brim of her bonnet.

Big Bob's two sons followed the spring wagon while the freight wagons and the cowboys who were not needed to drive the herd brought up the rear of this small cavalcade.

Bob swung his eyes from side to side, at least as much as he could without turning his head, appraising all he saw. Not much of a town but the country around grew good grass and that's what his animals needed after surviving on mesquite beans and dust all winter. "Wonder if there's any real cattlemen in the territory? Well, there's one here now. No one needs to doubt that!"

The drovers were herding the forty head of loose horses and fifteen hundred head of mixed Longhorn cattle on the western edge of the town, stirring up a turmoil of dust and cattle droppings.

As the Stanton family reached the fork in the road a half mile beyond the livery barn, Big Bob turned to the left, following the road off to the west towards the foothills. He was admiring the green of the spring grass when his two sons rode up beside him.

Benjamin, the older of the two, asked, "How far from here, Pa?"

Big Bob pointed towards the foothills. "The R/R is about twelve miles out this way. We'll ride on to the ranch and get the women settled in. The cattle will have to overnight somewhere along here, wherever we can find water."

Big Bob had purchased the ranch formerly owned by long-time resident, Rusty Randall. The R/R had been an early pioneer fixture in the Canyon View community for over twenty years. But everything eventually comes to an end and the very eventful life of Rusty Randall had come to an end in the dust and horse droppings of a corral when he was pitched from the back of a wild bronco that he was determined to break and ride.

Rusty's widow, who at the age of sixty-three was looking forward to a life of less work and more ease than a pioneer ranch allowed, announced her intention to move to Denver to live beside her daughter, son-in-law, and her three grandchildren whom she barely knew. She had always hoped for more children and more grand-children.

She and Rusty had built a large ranch house complete with wraparound deck and gingerbread trim. In their younger days, they imagined it filled with happy voices and growing youngsters. They had raised one beautiful daughter but the other bedrooms had remained empty. Those empty bedrooms cast a shadow of disappointment over their lives and the widow would be happy to see the old house for the last time.

The widow Randall had let it be known that the ranch was for sale and somehow the news got down to the Texas panhandle where the Circle S was fighting a losing battle against drought, debt, and an overcrowded range.

Within two weeks, Big Bob Stanton was in town, having enjoyed the comfort of the cushions as he rode the rails to Cheyenne. He had telegraphed ahead and an R/R cowboy met him there with a spare horse and guided him back to the ranch. The cowboy spent two days riding to every corner of the R/R with Big Bob and the Texas cattleman liked what he saw. He made an offer; Mrs. Randall accepted the offer and Big Bob went back to Texas to gather up his family, his cows and his cowboys.

He sold off enough of his herd to pay off his debts and provide travel money plus a deposit on the R/R. He claimed title to only the one quarter section of Texas grass that held the Circle S headquarters and, since land was worth almost nothing in that part of Texas, he accepted the low offer from a neighbor. He was left with fifteen hundred Longhorns and a loan at the Canyon View bank.

Now, after a long walk, those Longhorns were in Canyon View in the shelter of the Eastern Slopes of the Front Range and within a single day's drive of their own green home.

3

DURING THE SIX YEARS SINCE HE HAD PUT LAW WORK BEHIND him and purchased the Double-D cattle ranch, renaming it the H-R, Hamilton Robb had come to be known as a hard-working rancher, a good cattle man, a helpful neighbor and a reliable friend. He never talked about his past and, true to the spirit of the times, no one asked although most knew he had once been a deputy sheriff.

Popular with men and women alike, the bachelor rancher was known mainly for raising white-faced cattle and breaking wild horses. He had brought the cattle in by rail at considerable expense, each year replacing a few of the Longhorns that had always populated the ranch. He kept the two breeds separated with fencing to prevent cross-breeding and, after five years, there were no more Longhorns on the H-R.

The horses he caught himself, deep in the high-up hills out back of his home place.

His foothills ranch had become an example of hard work and competent management.

Usually full of good cheer, smiling his way into the

social structure of the Canyon View district, and with considerable interest in someday changing his matrimonial condition, he nonetheless had avoided involvement with any particular young lady although opportunities abounded. He was twenty-eight years of age, just less than six feet tall, and husky through the chest and shoulders. His long blond hair which he paid the barber to cut twice each year - once in the spring and once in the fall - was sun-bleached to a light gold where it escaped his hat and hung over his collar. He was always well-dressed when he came to town, sporting a clean shirt and having dusted off his boots.

After his days enforcing the law, Hamilton had ridden east looking for a fresh start in life. He found it in Canyon View and the Double-D Ranch.

On the day of Smokey's paa-rade, Hamilton stood on the boardwalk, his mind blank and his eyes glazing while he watched the ladies' wagon roll by. He couldn't have told how many horses there were or how many cowboys. He couldn't have remembered the number of freight wagons or the colors of the teams. He noticed none of these things. But he could have told that the girl in the wagon was about nineteen years old with golden ringlets of hair falling from beneath a Stetson hat which sat at a delightfully stylish angle on her head. He could have told that the girl wore a dusty, once blue, high-collared traveling dress that was designed to conceal the wearer's femininity although there was little chance of success at that goal.

He noticed that the dress had a long row of mother-of-pearl buttons and a gray collar. He admired the way she drove the wagon with authority with one foot braced on the wagon's dashboard, showing a black high-buttoned shoe and just a bit of ankle, while also seeming to cower before the stares of the citizenry and the loud exclamations of Smokey Dillabough.

"That's Mrs. Hamilton Robb, only she don't know it yet." Unaware that he had spoken out loud, Hamilton was oblivious to the stares from the two women standing beside him.

The young owner of the H-R watched the wagon disappear into the dusty distance and then got on his horse and headed for home in a slow walk, his mind blank of every thought except the spring wagon girl. He was well out of town before he remembered that he had not made the purchases he had ridden in for. He decided to do without rather than ride all the way back and face the hoo-rawing of the good old boys who spent their time whittling and gossiping, sitting in the cane-back chairs in front of the general store.

Within three miles he caught up to the Circle S herd. The drovers were holding the Longhorns on a small creek that made its way into the bottom lands below Robb's H-R. He pulled up at the sight and then slowly walked his horse towards a group of riders who were in the process of making coffee over an open fire.

"Howdy, boys. I take it you're heading to the R/R. I'm Hamilton Robb. Looks like we're going to be neighbors."

Three riders, showing more belligerence than the occasion seemed to call for, were silent for a long thirty seconds. Finally, a man looked up at Hamilton and spoke, "I would guess a good Texas rider can go wherever he wants without having to explain himself. But it happens that this is the Stanton herd of the Circle S. We've taken over what you call the R/R. Ain't no more R/R. Ain't nobody's business but our own anyway."

Hamilton took a slow, obvious measure of each man one by one, and then grinned at the speaker as if calling his bluff. "Always found it easier to just get along, friend, but you have it your way. It makes no never mind to me. But if you find yourselves in need, why don't you just drop by the H-R and I'll see what I can do. My place is easy to find, just up the road a piece here."

"Don't hardly see how the Circle S will need anything from any of the shirt-tail ranchers around here."

Hamilton grinned again. "You just never know. You can't never tell until all the tellin's done and it's all wrapped up."

With a touch of the spur, the gelding stepped out for home. An empty cabin, a cold stove and a tail-wagging dog would make up his welcome. That and a cow to milk, followed by a quiet evening by himself.

Of course, being Saturday, the evening would include a bath in the tin tub that he kept in the bush out back of the cabin; hidden against the off chance that an unexpected visitor would catch him with his dignity at risk.

On Sunday morning, Hamilton arose early to get his chores done, ready for a trip to town. No matter how self-sufficient a man is, a bachelor ranch can be a lonely place. So Hamilton had joined the choir at the Canyon View Community Church, more for the singing and the visiting than because of any firm devotion.

On his way to town, he stopped at the end of his lane to watch the Circle S herd amble past. Crouched on one knee and chewing a stem of grass, his horse nudging his shoulder, he made a rough count of the animals as they made their way along the dirt road.

The surly rider from the evening before rode over and stopped. "I see you count'n. Ain't a bit of your business how many beeves there are. I'd advise you to stick to what's yours. The Circle S don't appreciate nosy neighbors."

Hamilton smiled at him and watched him ride off. "Right neighborly," he said to his horse. "But if I'm ever going to marry that girl with the blond ringlets it would be best if I don't let these riders goad me into a stupid fight. Anyway, it's a beautiful Sunday morning and I'm off for the singing. Might get an invite for lunch if I'm lucky."

Since his first visit to the Canyon View Community Church, Hamilton and the Rev. Josiah Brockton had become fast friends. Although he never talked about his past, most people knew that the Rev. Brockton had not always been a man of the cloth. The fact was that he felt his past was best forgotten. Hamilton was one of the few he had shared it with.

"After rambling around for far too many years, I rode - broke and tired - onto the Tumbling T in central Oklahoma, hoping for a job or at least a meal if there was no job to be had. I got the job and, over the next year, I won the hand of Sarah, youngest daughter of Hoss Tibault, patriarch and owner of the Tumbling T.

"Hoss is a devout man and Sarah holds firm beliefs herself. One thing led to another and I found myself liking who they are and how they lived. Made a few changes myself and before I knew it Sarah and I were married and I was sitting in a classroom studying the Scriptures. Never once thought I would end up back in school. But I liked it and I like this town and its people and our little church. I sometimes miss parts of the cowboy life but I don't miss the rambling one bit. Nor the trail dust or the cold nights sleeping on the ground with a pouring rain hammering on my tarpaulin. Guess I'm going soft but that's how it is."

Josiah and Hamilton spent many hours together, riding the green hills of the H-R. As often as possible Josiah rode out to a nearby ranch and put in a few hours of work, happy to take a ranch meal as his pay. The H-R was often the beneficiary of this effort although he would have admitted that the meals he and Hamilton put together were sometimes questionable pay.

It was some time before Josiah felt he knew Hamilton well enough to ask, "What's your story, Hamilton?"

There was a lengthy pause before the answer came.

"The folks were big on going to meetings but mostly I just liked the singing. Once I started to gain my growth, I showed more interest in horses and guns than in those meetings. Haven't been inside a church in many a year until just now.

"But living alone gets real quiet sometimes and I found myself singing just to hear a human voice, and hymns are the only songs I know. Kinda liked the sound of the words as they rolled off my tongue so I rode in one Sunday morning and the next thing I knew I was in the choir. Hard to believe, but there it is."

4

Big Bob didn't notice Hamilton on his first visit to town. If he had noticed, the Texan would have paid no attention. He was not in the habit of concerning himself with lesser men, even ones who were close neighbors and whose land actually shared a border at one small, irregular hillside corner.

He shoved his way through the Saturday morning shoppers on the boardwalk and entered the general store with a written down list in his hand. He shouldered his way past two other customers, slapped the list onto the counter and demanded, "Fill this; I'll be back shortly." He then bulled his way out of the store and down the street to the saddle and gun shop. The folks in the store watched him walk out with thoughts in their minds that Big Bob would not have enjoyed hearing.

Mrs. Stanton was visiting with a couple of ladies who had approached the wagon with a welcome.

Wanda was on the sidewalk in front of Miss LaFleur's Ladies Wear Store with instructions from her father to be back at the wagon in one hour. Wanda didn't hear him.

Her attention was fixed on the young cowboy who was just riding up to the hitch rail in front of her.

The cowboy was long and slim with broad shoulders straining a clean but threadbare, sun-faded shirt. Straight, blond, sun-bleached hair rolled down over his collar and pushed out the sides of his going-to-town hat. He had shaved for his trip to town and had wiped the mud off his boots.

He rode up to the hitch rail, nodded to a friend crossing the street, and swung down. His motions were easy and without effort. He flipped the reins around the hitch rail in a smooth, practiced action. Then he looked up and saw before him the image that had taken up most of his mind for the two weeks since the Stanton family's arrival.

In all of Hamilton's twenty-eight years he had never been known to be the least bit clumsy. But with his eye on the wagon girl, with a funny feeling in his stomach and with not a single rational thought in his mind, the young cowboy took two steps towards the sidewalk at the same time lifting his hat off in deference to the beauty before him. Those two steps were alright, but his third step brought him up against the water trough which caused him to lose his balance. He reached out to steady himself but all he found to grab onto was water. One arm went elbow deep into the trough, his feet went out from under him, and his hat fell into the street.

Two loafers, sitting on chairs under the awning, chuckled but Hamilton didn't hear them.

Smokey Dillabough helpfully said, "You went and got your shirt wet there, Robb."

Several people had stopped to stare but Hamilton didn't see them. All he could see was the wagon girl.

That young lady's initial interest in the rancher had turned into amazement bordering on amusement. From her heightened position on the raised wooden sidewalk, she looked down at the cowboy as he struggled to pick up his hat, pull himself out of the water trough and nod an embarrassed greeting along with a quiet "Ma'am" all at the same time.

With a slight smile on her lips and several questions in her mind, she turned and stepped into Miss LeFleur's Ladies Wear Store, leaving the cowboy-rancher to struggle with his hat, his wet shirt sleeve and his bruised ego.

Hamilton stood in the sunshine on the dusty street of Canyon View as Miss Stanton entered the store and realized for the first time that people were watching him. Embarrassed and puzzled, he turned to his horse, untied him, mounted, and rode out of town. He was a mile out when he pulled his horse to a sudden stop. "I've done it again. Forgotten to get what I rode in for. But I'm near out of coffee and I need a box of matches so I'd better go back."

Penny Hatcher, clerking in the general store, placed his purchases in a small paper sack and grinned up at him. "Didn't I see you ride out of town just a bit ago? You're going to wear out that horse, riding back and forth. Of course, it does give your shirt sleeve the opportunity to dry out."

Penny's grin and the mischievous look in her eye told Hamilton that people were talking about him. Embarrassed, he picked up his purchases, turned, and immediately bumped into Miss Granet, the school teacher, knocking her oversized sun hat all askew. He mumbled, "Sorry, Miss," and stepped onto the boardwalk. Penny and Miss Granet watched him go, looked at each other, and then burst out laughing.

The sound of laughter in Hamilton's ears was a shameful thing. He was sorry he had come back. It would have been easier to do without the coffee. At least it was a toss-up; Hamilton truly enjoyed his coffee.

Big Bob was waiting impatiently at the wagon when Wanda finally arrived. He had already sent his sons out to track down their sister. Benjamin, Big Bob's eldest, rode his horse up to the wagon just as Wanda arrived.

Benjamin grinned at Wanda. "Did you find out who that stumblebum of a cowboy was that caught your eye? Seems like as how if you're going to fall for a man it should be one who's able to walk without falling into a water trough. Why, you're the talk of the town, little sister, what with your man making a fool of himself and you asking around all about him." The grin deepened. "Yup, your very first trip to town and already everyone is talking."

Big Bob turned to Benjamin and demanded, "What are you talking about, boy?"

Without waiting for an answer, he turned to Wanda, "What's your brother talking about?"

Mrs. Stanton came to Wanda's rescue while also giving her a quizzical study. "Come on, Father, it's time to go home."

Big Bob threw a hard look towards his son, and again at his daughter. Then, saying nothing more, he led out on his stallion as he always did. Wanda took up her place beside her mother on the wagon seat. Mother Stanton was openly studying her daughter but Wanda looked straight ahead, not inviting inquiry.

Hamilton was placing the sack of purchases in his saddlebags when the Stanton family rode past. He pushed his hat back to provide a better line of sight and folded his arms over the saddle, watching the wagon roll slowly along. He stood there gazing into the distance even after the ladies in the wagon were long gone.

Finally, Smokey Dillabough spoke, interrupting Hamilton's reverie, "What-cha looking at Robb? All's I see over that way is the stables and that ain't noth'n worth star'n at."

He glanced at Smokey, hesitated a moment, swung to the saddle and slowly started home.

Hamilton, by devious inquiry, found out that the wagon girl's name was Wanda, although he would call her Miss Stanton until she gave him permission to use her first name. Wanda was the youngest of the Stanton family and the only daughter. She was fiercely protected by everyone on the Circle S Ranch. Even though several of the cowboys went to sleep from time to time in their rough bunkhouse beds with shameful thoughts of her in their minds, there wasn't a one of them who wouldn't fight to the death to protect Wanda and her good name.

Even though thoughts of Wanda were never far from Hamilton's mind either, he didn't let those thoughts interfere with his ranch work; not too often anyway although it was rumored that Hank Blossom, his closest neighbor, had found him writing a poem. No one really believed the rumor about the poem.

Hamilton had no way at all to know it but he represented everything Big Bob despised. He hadn't given any thought to such things until he and Hank were having coffee one rainy morning.

Hank grinned and leaned across the table in Hamilton's kitchen, pointing with his coffee cup. "I remember the feeling, neighbor, when you see something you think you want more than anything else in the world, especially if that something is topped out with blonde curls and is as pretty as a newborn colt. But think about it from that Texan's viewpoint.

"He struts around with a show of wealth to the community. If you have any excess funds, no one's ever seen them.

"He comes from an old family with a long history of

achievement, or so the story is being told around. You've never talked about your family or your background.

"He holds title to twenty thousand acres of rolling foothills and prairie flatlands. I suspect he shares that title with the bank but he still claims it as his own. This little spread of yours, straddling the Poudre River like it does, is actually a better ranch but that Texan looks down on anything that ain't big.

"He walks with hard heels, daring the world to challenge him. You're a tough, hardworking man, but gentle for the most part.

"He goes armed at all times as do his sons and his cowboys. You've got that old, much-used Winchester carbine hanging over the door there.

"I wish you luck my friend but it looks like an uphill pull to me."

Hamilton drained off his coffee and stood up, showing a lopsided grin. "Thanks, friend. I'm glad we had this visit; I feel much better now."

Hank laughed and reached for his rain jacket. "I'm here to help any time you feel the need. Always glad to help."

5

THE FIRST CONTACT HAMILTON HAD WITH THE CIRCLE S riders happened in mid-June when the early summer heat was just starting to cure the grass on the stem and dry up all but the best of the water holes, giving warning of a hot month or two to come. Hamilton was moving about one hundred head of nursing cows and their calves to his high, north pasture where they could finish out the summer on untouched grass and enjoy the poplar-shaded pool that had accumulated behind a dam he had built on a little unnamed creek. Although Hamilton owned title to this section of land, he had never fenced it. He saw no need of fencing since the pasture was ringed by a rough circle of hills that formed a natural barrier to drifting cattle. The only outside entrance was a narrow draw at the end of a rocky outcrop. No animal would willingly leave good grass to cross that rocky ground. This outcrop was the one place where H-R land adjoined the Circle S. The Stanton cowboys had taken the lack of a fence as an invitation.

As Hamilton rode over a little rise and headed down into the pasture, hazing his cows ahead of him, he was amazed to find three cowboys holding a small herd of Longhorns close against the pool of collected water. Hamilton pulled his horse to a stop and stood in his stirrups. He waved his hat and started to yell but thought better of it. Instead, he settled back into the saddle and set the gelding into a long trot around his own cattle and down towards the water hole.

Hamilton was a peaceful man for the most part but the sight of strange cowboys taking unwelcome advantage spurred him to instant action. He pulled his coiled lariat from the saddle horn and rode directly into the drinking cattle, ignoring the cowboys. He pushed his way through the gathered cattle and administered a sharp blow to the dripping wet nose of a big steer that had just pulled its head from the pool. The steer bellowed and pulled back and Hamilton struck the next steer in line. In only a few seconds he had the cattle pulling back and turning for home in a wild run with their tails in the air. No word had been spoken.

Then one of the cowboys, tired of trying to hold the frightened animals, shouted a warning at Hamilton and spurred his horse angrily towards him. The armed cowboy's intent was not exactly clear but Hamilton could see no reason to take it as friendly. He had been swinging the coiled lariat from side to side at the cattle and as the cowboy lunged towards him, he knocked him from his horse with a sharp rap across the head with the iron-hard, coiled rope. The man fell without a sound and lay still. His horse trotted off a ways and dropped its head to graze.

One of the other cowboys, seeing what had happened, gave a shout and rode towards Hamilton, reaching for the Colt pistol that was jammed firmly into its holster and held in place with a leather thong. Before he could get the gun loose, he too had felt the sting of the coiled lariat and was also on the ground, blood gushing from a smashed nose and broken lips.

He rolled to a sitting position, giving Hamilton a murderous look. "I'll kill you for that."

Hamilton's response was to whack him again with the rope. This time the man fell over and lay still. The third cowboy was busy with the stampeding cattle. Since the Longhorns were running away from the water hole and off H-R land, Hamilton decided it might help if he hurried them along a little.

The H-R white-faced cows were nosing their way towards the water hole, giving a wide berth to the two still forms lying on the grass.

Hamilton hazed the two grazing horses ahead of him and let out a wild yell. The two horses broke into a stirrup-flapping run, following the stampeding cattle for a short way and then turned, doubling back towards the water hole. He let them go. The third cowboy looked behind him in horror as the terrified Longhorns threatened to run him down. He managed to get to the outside of the herd and slow his horse to an easy run just in time to realize that he was off H-R land and back on the rocky outcropping that belonged to the Circle S. Hamilton was close behind, still yelling and swinging the rope. He didn't stop until the cattle were well off his land. Then he turned and trotted his horse towards his home range and for the first time noticed a small group of riders who had just arrived.

Hamilton rode up to the group and demanded, "Who put those cattle on my grass and my water?" There was no friendliness in the question.

A booming voice said, "Those are my cattle but I gave no instructions to drive them off my range. My men did that themselves. I don't appreciate you running my steers in this heat. You ever do that again and you'll answer to me."

"Answer, and be hanged. Those cattle were eating my scarce grass and drinking my even scarcer water. You keep your cattle on your own grass and water. I'll have no man take what is mine."

The voice boomed again, "You talk big. Do you know who I am?"

"We haven't met, sir, but I know who you are. All I care about right now is that those cattle were on my land. And I won't have it, regardless of who you are."

"My name," the voice boomed with considerable authority, "is Stanton. My brand is the Circle S. And I won't have anyone talk to me like that. You keep a civil tongue in your head."

Not three minutes had passed from the time Hamilton rode over the rise to see the strange cattle at his water; three minutes of extreme activity and blood-boiling anger. The anger drained away from Hamilton enough for him to calm his prancing horse and look at the gathered group. He looked at the owner of the big voice and at the other men gathered. It was only then that he realized the rider behind Stanton was a girl, the same girl who kept him awake at night and was responsible for that poem. The poem he would never have admitted writing.

He glanced at Stanton and then at the cowboys. He tried not to look at the girl because he wasn't sure he could look without letting his feelings show.

The initial rush of anger was dissipating in both groups.

Stanton spoke up, "I see two men down. Are they dead?"

Hamilton looked down at the fallen men and then back at

his neighbor. "I didn't shoot them, if that's what you're asking, so I don't expect they're dead. But I hope they're hurt'n a little. I did my best so's they'd understand the situation. My message was clear and they have no more excuse. One of them threatened to kill me. It might be best if he re-thought that. I wouldn't take kindly at all to anyone trying to kill me."

Stanton turned and pointed at two cowboys. "Toby, you and Clem ride down and pick up those men. Bring them back here. Andy, you go catch their horses."

The cowboys started to move out but Hamilton spurred his horse to cut them off. "No, they can get out by their own effort. Let them walk. You and your men need to understand that I will have no animal other than my own eating H-R grass or drinking H-R water. You did it once and we'll say no more about it. But it never happens again. Not ever. I hope you all understand that."

Hamilton glanced at the girl and then at her father. Right at that moment, it seemed an unlikely thing that this big man with the booming voice would ever be his father-in-law no matter what Hamilton's feelings were or how many poems he wrote. Nevertheless, he tipped his hat a little at the young lady. "Ma'am, my name is Hamilton Robb and I'm sorry you had to see this. I'm sorry I had to meet you and your father this way, too, but it was not of my choosing."

He then glanced at Stanton. "I always welcome neighbors and you're welcome, too, as neighbors. You or your family, or your cowboys. If you're neighboring, the coffee will always be on and you'll always be welcome. But leave your cattle at home. Now I have work to do so you will have to excuse me."

Hamilton was turning to ride away when Stanton spoke, "We don't want trouble, Robb, and I will see that my cattle stay at home. But you were hard on my riders. Those boys aren't going to forget that."

That might have ended the conversation had Wanda not spoken up, "Mr. Robb, we are hospitable too. I'm sorry we started out this way. Why don't you come over Sunday afternoon for coffee and a neighborly visit?"

Wanda's father looked like he might choke and her older brother sat his saddle with his mouth hanging open. The cowboys expressed great interest in the ground beside their horses.

If he had taken time to think it through, Hamilton would have said nothing at all. As it was, the words were out before he really had his thoughts under control. Later, he would tell himself that it was the fault of his lack of experience in situations like this; that he had never been comfortable talking to girls. But, of course, no excuse was good enough to get the words back.

"Thank you, Miss Stanton, I would like that very much. And I would also like to call on you personally, with your father's permission."

At this, four cowboys turned their horses and walked away while the older brother whipped off his Stetson and slapped his pant leg with it. He started to say, "Why, of all the ….." His father's bellow stopped him.

Stanton's voice could have shaken rocks loose from the canyon wall. "No two-by-twice, down-in-the-heels nester is going to be calling on my daughter. You come anywhere near her and I'll sic the dog on you. You stay away, you hear?" His outrage was a dreadful display.

Sitting her horse just a little back of her father, Wanda flashed a shy smile at Hamilton. A smile that could have meant "Come over anyway" or it could have meant "You fool."

Hamilton turned his horse and rode back to his cattle.

Riding back to his own herd, Hamilton spoke to his horse, "Spinner, I would have to admit that speaking out like that was one of the dumbest things I've ever done. Why didn't you stop me, turn and walk away, or pitch me into the dirt or something? What kind of a friend are you anyhow?"

The horse bobbed its head up and down several times as if in agreement.

"Ya, well I see that you agree but it's too late for you to help me now. But I'll tell you this, Spinner; I would make a darn poor politician. Always seem to say the wrong thing at the wrong time. If ever someone were to talk me into running for office, like that sheriff tried to do back in Arizona, I'd do nothing but make a fool of myself. Then I'd need all the friends I can find, horse or human, just to repair the damage."

6

THE FOLLOWING SUNDAY MORNING WANDA DROVE THE TOP-buggy into town, her mother sitting beside her, to attend the Canyon View Community Church, Rev. Josiah Brockton presiding. They made their way into an available pew and took their places, nodding to a few other worshippers as they entered. The church hall, usually and traditionally silent before the service, broke into a gaggle of muffled whispers as the good ladies of Canyon View took note of the two newcomers, the younger of whom would obviously be serious competition for their own daughters in their search for a suitable life mate.

The men did their best to ignore the interruption but the good ladies felt the need to share their thoughts with other Canyon View matrons. This was followed by a goodly number of sly glances aimed in the direction of the Stanton ladies.

"My, my," whispered Mrs. Stanton to Wanda in a some-what wondering tone of voice as she glanced up and noticed the many heads turned her way, "I'm not sure that I enjoy being the center of attention."

Sharply at 10AM, Mrs. Walter Howard, the sheriff's wife, took her place on the bench of the foot-driven pump organ and struck the first notes of a medley of familiar hymns; a medley she had put together herself and was quite proud of although she would have balked at the use of the word "proud".

Sheriff Howard graciously gave up the privilege of church attendance, allowing as how the safety of the town was more important than his own selfish enjoyment, alleging that he must be ever vigilant and constantly available to uphold the law, and to keep the peace in their small village.

As the notes from the wheezing organ gratingly filled the small sanctuary, the Rev. Brockton entered from the door on the right of the hall while the choir entered from the door on the left.

The choir took their places and turned to face the gathered worshipers. Mrs. Stanton heard Wanda take a deep breath and then, a short moment later, expel a small explosion of the held air. Mrs. Stanton dared a quick glance at her daughter and couldn't help noticing that Wanda was chuckling to herself behind her lace-frilled handkerchief.

At her mother's questioning glance, Wanda leaned into her ear and whispered, "The man on the right is the neighbor that drove Daddy's cattle off his land and put down two of our cowboys."

Again Mrs. Stanton said, "My, my," and took a careful study of the young man.

At the conclusion of the service, Mrs. Stanton and Wanda spoke for a moment with Rev. Brockton, said hello to a few ladies, and went to their buggy. They were just settled in for the drive home when a voice said, "Good morning, ladies. I saw you in the congregation and was hoping to speak with you and introduce myself in a more satisfactory manner than the last time we met."

Hamilton strode boldly up to the side of the wagon and continued, "You must be Mrs. Stanton. I'm Hamilton Robb. We're neighbors by a few miles. I met your daughter very briefly some days ago. The circumstances were somewhat trying at the time. I'm pleased to have this better opportunity to say hello again. I'm hoping that we can overcome the incident of our first meeting and be at least good neighbors, if not good friends."

Wanda gave him a mischievous grin. "Good morning, Mr. Robb. It's good to meet you when you are not whacking cattle with a rope and beating cowboys into the ground." If she hadn't smiled as she spoke, Hamilton would have been devastated.

"My, my," said Mrs. Stanton. "Did you do those things, Mr. Robb? You sing beautifully and I would have hardly thought you capable of such actions."

"Oh, he's very capable of those things, Mama. You should have seen him. Why, I have never seen Daddy so upset or holler so loudly. Of course, the real excitement didn't come until Mr. Robb asked Daddy's permission to come calling on me. I must say, that did catch Daddy off guard. The whole thing was really worth seeing, Mama. I'm sorry you weren't there." The mischievous grin was still on Wanda's lips.

Hamilton had absolutely no idea where to try to lead the conversation and he couldn't see a positive ending coming from the direction it was now on. Remembering the last meeting where he had spoken out of turn, he feared that he had muddied the water to the point where the whole thing couldn't be fixed.

Mrs. Stanton saved him from saying anything else that might have dug a deeper hole. "My, my, Mr. Robb, did you really do that? We've been here just a few weeks and you are the second man to so upset my husband. The first was a cowboy who apparently fell into a water trough, although how that can happen I can't imagine. And, of course, I wouldn't have known about it except that there is talk all over town and it managed to get to my ears. I somehow can't rely on my daughter to tell me these things."

"That was also Mr. Robb, Mama."

Mrs. Stanton took a closer look at Hamilton. "Mr. Robb, I hardly know what to say. I do so very much dislike seeing my husband upset. And there is little in this world that upsets him more than something that affects his family, especially his only daughter. Perhaps you should try to get to know Bob as a neighbor before you make any further grand pronouncements." Her small smile saved whatever was left of the meeting just as Wanda's had a moment before.

Having no idea what to say next, Hamilton doffed his hat again. "Well, thank you for speaking with me, ladies. Perhaps we'll speak again soon."

Hamilton stepped away from the buggy and Wanda slapped the reins on the horse's back.

As the two ladies drove away Hamilton stood, watching them go. He was still standing there after the road showed no further sign of the buggy.

"She's gone," said a female voice. "You might just as well stop looking."

Hamilton turned to see Penny Hatcher grinning at him. "Good thing I hadn't set my cap for you Hamilton or I would have been devastated watching this little show."

Hamilton let his shoulders sag. "Am I being a bit obvious? I'm afraid watching an empty road is becoming a habit."

Penny was still grinning. "Just a little bit obvious perhaps."

When they were out of sight of the town, Mrs. Stanton turned to look at her daughter. She stared until Wanda could no longer ignore her.

Wanda turned to her mother with a small giggle.

"And what am I to make of all of this, young lady?"

"I like him, Mama. He's very well-respected in the town and his ranch has apparently prospered with his white-faced cattle. And he certainly knows what he wants. And you admitted yourself that he sings very well."

Mrs. Stanton mumbled, "My, my," and turned back in her seat.

THE COUNTY WAS LIVING through a chilly, late spring rain when Hamilton rode into town, bringing along a piece of wood for whittling. The Canyon View whittlers, spitters and checkers club, an unofficial but well-attended group, met on Saturday evenings, weather permitting. The men met in the saloon while the ladies shopped and visited with friends.

After losing his third checkers game in a row to town sheriff Walter Howard, Clark Ransom pushed his chair back and looked over at Hamilton who was shaving the last small pieces from the wooden block he had been whittling on.

"Somth'n I been thinking about, Hamilton. There's been a lot of foolish talk and gossip among our womenfolk about your matrimonial condition. Now, if you were to choose a bride and settle down to the drudgery that most of us live with, that foolish talk would mostly stop. And it would mean that the other girls who were not given the opportunity of enjoying your questionable attention for the rest of their natural lives could take the opportunity to have another look at our other young men.

"On the other hand, I will admit that the goings on among our female gender, most of them wishing to play the leading role in the change to your marital condition, provide a considerable amount of entertainment."

Hamilton grinned at his grizzled, rancher friend. "If I'm not concerned, why should y'all be? Seems as how you've got troubles enough of your own to deal with without you trying to fix whatever ailments you see in my life."

The sheriff, ignoring Hamilton's prostrations, finished laying out the next game before he added his wisdom to the question at hand. He looked over the gathered men, puckered his lips as if trying to figure out the correct words to use, twisted the ends of his overgrown mustache, took a further study of Hamilton, and began: "There are, by actual count, exactly seventeen eligible young ladies within a two-day ride of our fair village. That's not including a few younger ones that are wishful of appearing older than what the actual facts will support. That number presents a sizable problem of culling out."

Tiny Shaw, who stood six-foot-three and weighed two-hundred-fifty pounds, guffawed at this short speech. "I don't hardly think "culling out" is a proper term in this situation, Walter. And anyway, how do you know there are seventeen available future brides? I didn't even know you could count that high."

The sheriff was unaffected by this contrary opinion and continued right on, "It's the sheriff's job to know who resides in the community and I say there are seventeen youngish ladies. Now I did say "culling out". And proper term or no proper term, anyone would have to admit that the situation is going to have to be addressed, soon or late, if the foolishness that has overtaken our lady folk is to be brought under control.

"Seems maybe that we should strike a committee and help you make a choice, Hamilton. Haven't thought about that before but, now that it's been said, I seem to feel that it's the thing to do."

Hamilton, still grinning, had nothing to say.

Jimmy, the bartender, who had been watching the games and listening to the banter, spoiled the fun by saying, "The reason Hamilton has nothing to say is because you're all way behind the times. If there were seventeen eligible young ladies before, now there are eighteen and our young friend Hamilton has already made his choice. I would say that he's done like a Christmas goose. There's simply no help known to mankind that can bring a man back from the condition our young rancher friend finds himself in."

This information brought a series of exclamations and questions from the gathered checkers players, all of which Hamilton ignored.

7

THE POSITION OF THE SCORCHING JULY SUN TOLD HAMILTON that mid-afternoon had arrived. His shirt was soaked through with sweat. His hair, matted beneath his battered "work-hat", was also soaked. The rag he had used to mop his brow and neck, leaving streaks of dusty grime in its wake, could hold no more water. He had spread it on the mower frame below the metal seat hoping it would dry a bit before it was needed again. The team of blacks glistened with sweat. Both he and the horses needed a rest and a drink. He would stop as soon as he reached the other side of the hay field; the closest access to some sparse shade provided by a small grove of aspens whose quaking leaves rustled in the slightest breeze and whose feet were watered by a slow-running stream.

As Hamilton guided the team into the last turn before the run down the long side of the hay field, he was surprised to see a horseman sitting a-saddle in the shade of the aspens. Hamilton did not recognize the man but seeing who it was would have to wait.

When the mower reached a spot roughly across from

the shade trees, Hamilton called 'whoa' and the horses came to a stop. It was but a few moments work to unhitch the team. Leaving the mower where he had stopped it, he walked the horses across the already mown hay towards the shade and the much-needed water.

As Hamilton neared the side of the hay field, he recognized the rider. It was one of Big Bob Stanton's sons. He was sitting his saddle with one foot in the stirrup and the other pulled up in front with his knee hooked over the horn. He had a casual and friendly look on his face. They had never met and Hamilton didn't know his name but he saw no threat so he led the team to shade and water, ignoring the man until that task was completed.

Turning towards his visitor, Hamilton wasn't quite sure what to say. He knew this was one of Wanda's brothers and multiple questions roared through his mind as he waited for the man to speak. As he studied his visitor up close for the first time, he realized that although he had the broad shoulders and thick chest of Big Bob, he had the more relaxed and smiling presence of his mother. He was smiling now.

"You said one time that visitors were welcome for coffee. I've come to see if that's true or not. My name is Samuel Stanton although I prefer just Sam anytime Ma is out of earshot."

Dropping his foot back into the stirrup, he reached back and touched a saddlebag. "I feared I'd find you working with no coffee ready to hand so I bottled some up in a Mason jar and brought it with me. Probably getting a mite cool by now but it'll still be wet. Brought some cake, too. Baked fresh this morning. Do I get down or do I pour the coffee from up here?"

Hamilton gave the man a tired grin. "You might spill

most of it if you pour from up there so I expect you'd better step down."

When Sam reached the ground, Hamilton stepped over to him with his hand outstretched. "Good to meet you. I'm Hamilton Robb and visitors are always welcome. Never had a visitor bring his own coffee before, or cake either for that matter, so I don't quite know how to deal with that."

He pointed out at the hay meadow. "I'll have to get back to finishing this field pretty quick but the horses need a rest so your timing is perfect. Let's pull up some of this nice soft ground and sit down."

Sam grinned at Hamilton and pulled a towel-wrapped jar of coffee from a saddlebag. He passed it to Hamilton along with two crockery mugs and then went to the other saddlebag where he had carefully placed the fresh cake.

When the two men were seated, Hamilton opened a small wicker basket that he had stowed in the shade and pulled out what was left of a brown-paper-wrapped loaf of bread. Next from the basket came a few slices of roast beef and some cheese.

He indicated the bread and beef to Sam. "Help yourself. I try to keep some lunch for midafternoon. It's been in that basket all day so it's bound to be dried out a bit but you're welcome to what you want."

Sam helped himself to a half slice of bread and a bit of meat. He then poured mugs of coffee and the two men leaned back against the aspens they sat beneath. "Quite a picnic we got going for ourselves here."

Smiling at Hamilton, he continued, "So, you're wondering why I'm here. Don't blame you, I'd be wondering too. The pure fact is that you've been getting considerable attention and discussion over on the Circle S and I got curious. Got to wondering if any of the talk was true or if none of it was. I came to find out."

Hamilton chuckled a bit. "Well, the coffee is good, no matter why you came. But my experience tells me that most talk and speculation is just that: talk." Hamilton placed some beef on a slice of bread and took a bite. He chewed for a few moments while he thought about his visitor. "I'll tell you whatever I can to set your mind at ease if you'll tell me what the talk is and what you need to know. As far as that goes, I've been ranching here for a good many years and most folks know me. There's no real secrets."

"We don't know many locals to ask so we're pretty much in the dark. But as to the talk, I guess I could say that, according to Little Sister, you're best known for whacking cattle with coiled lariats, beating men into the ground, falling into horse troughs, and generally being quite interesting and entertaining. There was also some remark about being handsome." He looked at Hamilton and chuckled. "I'd have no opinion on that. Just none at all.

"And then, according to Mother, you sing very well and dress like a gentleman although she seems to see some threat just the same."

He paused as if gathering his thoughts. "Big Brother's first opinion was that anyone who would fall into a water trough had to be a stumblebum but he came to doubt the truth of that after having a better look at your ranch and cattle, what little can be seen from the road anyway."

He seemed to be enjoying dragging this litany of opinions out for as long as possible. He shook his head as if expressing sorrow.

"Father, on the other hand, thinks that you should be horsewhipped for running his cattle in the heat and for what you did to his cowboys. And then, of course, he's convinced that you should be hung for even looking at Little Sister. He does admire the way you look after your ranch and cattle but he would choke before he told you that."

"Is that all?" asked Hamilton. "That doesn't seem like so much. Nothing that a couple of lifetimes of hard work might not correct." The two men laughed together over that image.

Sam gathered his thoughts again. "That's all except, of course, that a couple of our cowboys want to shoot you and the rest are eager to be there to watch when it happens."

"Oh, well, when the list gets that long, what's one or two more things? Are you sure I'm not responsible for your milk cow drying up?"

Hamilton looked at Sam and they both laughed.

"It does seem like quite a list considering that we've only been in the district for a few weeks and none of us have really gotten to know you. I hate to be responsible for spoiling all the rumors and talk but I thought I'd ride over anyway. Bring some coffee as a peace offering. See what I could find out."

Hamilton grinned again. "The coffee's a pretty good peace offering but that cake might be a better one. Don't ever make a cake myself. I'm looking forward to you unwrapping that one."

Sam opened the brown paper wrap to expose two generous portions of chocolate cake with a rich, creamy icing on top. Some of the icing was stuck to the brown paper. Sam gently lifted one piece of cake off and passed the paper to Hamilton. Hamilton, in turn, lifted the baked treasure from the paper and then fingered the icing from the wrapping.

Licking off his finger, he looked over at Sam. "I want you to thank your mother for me; I haven't tasted baking since the last community supper several months ago."

"Well, I could thank Mother I guess but then Little Sister would carry on something fierce, upsetting everyone around, and you have no idea what that does to our household. Little Sister baked the cake, sliced it and wrapped it, and insisted that I bring it along."

Hamilton took a long look at Sam, trying to see if there was a message here that he hadn't seen at first. "I do appreciate the thoughtfulness. You thank her for me. Tell her how much I enjoyed the treat."

The cake was eaten in silence.

Sam drank off the last dregs of his coffee and turned the lid back onto the jar. That done, he pointed at the hay field. "What are you going to do with all the hay? Seems like a big field and a lot of work in this heat. You being alone and all."

Hamilton stood up and went to his horses. "This here is the small field. There's a bigger one down the way a piece."

Sam looked across the field. "Ranch seems awful cut up. I'm surprised you don't get lost going from one part to another. I nearly gave up looking for you. Finally heard the noise of that grass-cutting machine and followed it to here, easing through the bush and wading two streams. Didn't see the trail until I was almost here."

"Your Circle S is a bit further out from the hills where the land flattens out. But the H-R and the other foothills ranches all have portions cut off by forest and rock outcroppings so the ranch is a mite cut up. The added elevation makes for a little longer winter, too. But we're never short of snow run-off and the grass stays green longer than down on the flats. And there's several streams, some of them pretty small. But it's all water and we always need water. I've had to build a few bridges over streams and a couple of trails through the forest but I like it. The folks who owned the ranch before me did a sight of work that I'm benefiting from so, overall, it's a pretty good situation."

Sam turned in an arc and looked over the land before him. "Someday I'd like to ride the H-R with you. It's completely different from the spread we left in Texas or even from the Circle S. We've always ranched on big dry-land acreage so I'm having a bit of a problem seeing what you see. But one thing I do see for sure is a lot of work on that hay field."

"I actually only do the mowing alone. I have a crew coming here in a day or two to rake it up and haul it to the yard. I couldn't do that alone. What I need now is a good week of sunshine. The country always welcomes rain but I don't want it this week."

"Well, Pa wouldn't agree with you. We're running short on grass and water and it's still only July. Won't be August for several days yet. The fact is, we have too many cattle but Pa won't listen. He bought another small herd last week that sets fair to crowd out the range that's left. Pa and my older brother Ben think they're still in Texas with free-range grass all around."

Hamilton was leading his horses towards the mower with Sam walking along beside. "With all those cattle, you had better hope for a good hay crop; this first cut and then another next month if we get rain at the right time."

Sam pointed with his hand to the northeast. "There's no hay cutting planned on the Circle S. Pa set one lower field aside for winter graze and the rest has already been grazed off. Can't convince Pa of the need for hay. Right stubborn about it."

Hamilton was hitching the team to the mower. "Well, I expect that by next spring he'll have had ample chance to rethink that. I wish you all luck but I'll keep cutting hay. I've been here a good many years and have never once been sorry for my haystacks. Come each spring, I've never had much left over from a year's cut either although I try to stay the most of a year ahead on supply."

"How did you manage to get a year's supply ahead?"

"At the start, I had a much smaller herd. Didn't really need the feed but I went ahead and made all the hay the ranch would allow anyway. Left to grow and lay down under the snow, it's a fire hazard come spring. So, I just kept making hay. Never found a reason to regret it."

Sam was studying the mower. "I've never handled one of these contraptions. How does it work?"

"It's pretty simple, really. The mechanism is driven off that wheel with the cogs on it. That shaft and the gearbox turn the circular motion into a back and forth motion driving the bar. The moving bar acts against the stationary bar like a pair of scissors and the grass is laid over as slick as you please. I just have to keep it well-greased and the cutters sharp, and watch out for rocks."

Hamilton swung up onto the mower seat. "Great piece of equipment, great invention."

Sam said, "There's two like this in our wagon shed but Pa won't even go look at them."

"He will next year," predicted Hamilton as he picked up the reins. "It's been good meeting you but right now I have to get this work done. Thanks again for the coffee and cake. Come again if you're of a mind to."

Sam stood and watched as Hamilton drove the team down the field. As the tall grass fell into a rich, green swath behind the mower, he thought of the grazed-off fields on the Circle S. Something like a premonition, a feeling he couldn't identify, ran through his mind and he didn't like the feeling. He watched a moment longer and then walked off. He swung into the saddle and waved from the edge of the field.

8

Two days later, Hamilton's bottom meadow was alive with cooking fires, children running and playing, dogs barking, horses tethered in every available corner, and hide teepees being raised. His haying crew had arrived just after dawn. Indian women were cooking breakfast while the men were putting harnesses on two teams of rangy-looking, half-wild horses. Two other men were leading one of Hamilton's heavier teams up from the pasture. The animals Hamilton had worked the day before were in the barn having earned an overnight rest and a liberal feeding of oats.

Hamilton had waved to the group on his way to the barn and his milking chore. The milking done, he was in the hen house gathering what eggs were available when he heard a thunder of hooves on the ranch road. He stepped out of the chicken coop in time to see what looked like the entire Circle S crew riding full-tilt into his yard, waving their carbines and shouting warnings.

They pulled up at the sight of Hamilton. He stood there

holding the basket of eggs with the milk pail on the ground at his feet.

Big Bob himself was leading the group. He pulled up sharply and sat his prancing stallion while he tried to catch enough breath to address Hamilton.

"Lucky one of my men spotted those red devils sneaking down that back road into your place just before full light and shouted the warning back at the ranch. It looks like they've broke from the reserve and intend to settle on your land; pitching their tents and all. Most likely left a trail of death and destruction getting here, sneaking around at night.

"What you just standing there for? Get your gun; we'll hold them off for you until you get back." Excitement blazed in his eyes and transferred itself to his eldest son, Ben, and the rest of the crew.

Sam, the younger son, had not pulled his carbine nor did he look excited. He held up his hand as if to speak to his father but Hamilton spoke first, hollering to be heard.

"Now hold up there just a minute. I don't know where you think you are but this is peaceable country and those Indians are friends of mine. In fact, they work for me. That's my haying crew that has you all in a knot. Settle down and put those guns away before you hurt someone."

Sam spoke up, "Pa, someday you're going to have to learn to listen. I tried to tell you. Even in Texas the Indian threat is several years past. Now you got everyone all riled up, nearly wind broke all these horses getting here in a hurry, and there's no telling what trouble you might have caused if you had actually fired that Winchester."

"That's enough, boy. All the Indians I ever saw was fixing to take a shot at me. I disbelieve that these will be any different, given opportunity."

Hamilton shook his head at the stubborn rancher.

"Either step off those horses and come meet my friends or turn around and go home. I appreciate your willingness to help but you're about to get into a world of hurt if you go down to that hay field waving those weapons. Those men were mucho-warriors not long ago. I'd hate to see them regress but they aren't about to take any guff from the likes of you Texas riders. So, you make up your mind but do it fast; we have hay to gather and sunshine to take advantage of."

For once, Big Bob seemed to have nothing more to say although he alternated a hard look between Hamilton and the Indians.

Sam spoke again, "I don't know about the rest of you men but I'm going to let Robb introduce his Indians. Pouch those weapons, men, and either step down and come with me or head home."

Benjamin scowled at his younger brother. "Sam, you're just not in any position here to tell anyone what to do. No one is going to listen to a kid anyway." Ben agreed with his brother about the lack of a threat but he wasn't about to give up his privileged, elder sibling position.

Hoof beats had announced a new arrival a few moments before and now a new voice broke into the debate, "Someone had better start to listen or I'm liable to come up short a father or maybe a brother or two. I'm sitting here looking at a pack of fools. It's time you all admitted it. Sam said to put the weapons away. That was real good advice. There's days I'm just not proud to owning up to being a Stanton. This is shaping up to be one of those days."

Big Bob stared around at his daughter. "What are you doing here? Don't you know any better than to put yourself in danger? You go home and help your Ma. This is men's work."

"This is fool's work," responded Wanda. "All of you are the ones that should go home. If there's danger here, it comes from you and this crew of idiot followers."

Turning to Hamilton, she asked, "Will you walk me down, Mr. Robb? I would like very much to meet your Indians."

"Now see here….," started Big Bob at full volume. But Wanda wasn't listening.

"That's another fight you misjudged, Pa," said Sam with a bit of a grin. "Little Sis is pretty much a full-grown woman. I doubt as how you can get your way with a raised voice. Not anymore, anyhow. She can listen less than just about anyone I know."

Wanda and Hamilton made their way past the garden fence. From there the view over the acres of the H-R was striking. Wanda stopped and exclaimed, "Why it's beautiful. I love the mountains and look at all that green grass. You have meadows and rock outcroppings and streams and woodlands. It's beautiful. And your log house is cute, too. Did you build the house and barn?"

"No, I'm not much good with hammer and saw. I've built a goodly amount of wire fence and a couple of small bridges across streams but the ranch buildings were pretty much as you see them when I bought the place. And, of course, we can thank God for the mountains and the meadows and everything in between."

Wanda turned her face to study Hamilton as if she was trying to figure out what to say next. After a few moments, she turned her eyes back to the sight before her. "Beautiful," she said again and started down the slope.

Hamilton, looking back at Wanda, said to himself, "Beautiful," but he wasn't referring to the land.

Big Bob let another holler follow Wanda. If she heard, she didn't let on.

Hamilton passed the milk and eggs to one of the Indian women and started to make introductions. Sam walked up in time to catch the last couple of names. Hamilton glanced around to see that Big Bob and his crew were dismounted and watching the proceedings.

After a few minutes, one of the Texas riders spoke to Big Bob, "What do you want us to do, boss? We left the ranch pretty early. I expect the cook will be about ready to throw out the breakfast fixings." Pausing, but receiving no answer, he continued, "If it's all the same to you, boss, I'll ride back, take on some feed and then get back to my regular work.

"Perhaps we can fight Indians another day but for right now I'd say this shindig is about over. Anyway, I fought Indians once. The experience wasn't just exactly like it was advertised. Cost me considerable dignity and one good friend who we buried under a live oak that I could never hope to find again. Just as soon not repeat that."

Big Bob just waved his hand as if to say, "Go then."

Most of the crew stepped into saddle and turned for the ranch road, leaving Big Bob, Benjamin and a couple of crew riders watching the happenings at the Indian encampment.

Benjamin spoke, "You want to walk down there, Pa?"

Big Bob was a long time answering, "We'll walk down. But we'll watch each other's backs. Any sign of trouble and we shoot first and sort it all out later."

"No, Pa. This time I agree with the others. We go down there with Winchesters showing, they'll be carrying us back up here on the flat of a door. We leave our guns here and we keep our mouths shut tight. Else we go home."

Big Bob passed his Winchester to one of the crew. "You stay here and keep a close watch, especially on Wanda. Any sign of trouble, you know what to do."

Benjamin took the carbine out of the rider's hands. "Go home. You and these other two also. Get some breakfast and go to work."

The Stanton sons rarely contradicted their father. Big Bob was shocked to hear Ben say, "Pa, you're just bound and determined, aren't you? Call me a fool all you wish but I see no danger here. I know Robb got himself wedged sidewise in your mind but we have no reason to believe him a fool."

Ben took a deep breath to steady his thoughts. "Now we either walk down there peaceably or we go home. Make up your mind. If we go, we go without guns. In fact, take off your sidearm and leave it here, too. I'll do the same. There's been a lot of graves dug with the barrel of a short gun. I wouldn't want you or me, either one, to have that said about us."

Big Bob looked at his son. "Be foolish to go down there totally unarmed. Wanda's down there with that stumblebum and he's unarmed, too, so he can't even protect her."

"Now, Pa, you only read books slowly but you count pretty good. You take another look and count up the Indians in that field. I would say that they have the edge in numbers by a wide margin. And I remind you of what I said about lying on the flat of a door."

The rancher passed his sidearm to his son without further comment and started down the path, his shoulders hunched and his hands balled into fists.

Hamilton and Wanda were talking to a tall, well-built young man who was dressed in typical ranch work clothes but with an eagle feather worked through the braid of his long black hair.

"Miss Stanton, I would like you to meet my friend, Johnnie. He has a much longer Indian name but I can't seem to get my tongue around it. Johnny, this is my neighbor Miss Stanton and her brother Sam. They wanted to meet you and your people."

"How, Miss San, Stan, Stant, me Johnnie. Glad meet friend Robb's girl. Much good look. Robb very happy with girl."

Hamilton's face glowed with embarrassment but he finally started to laugh. "Johnnie, drop the dumb Indian routine. Say a proper hello to Miss Stanton and her brother Sam. You might want to say hello to her father and older brother, too. This is Bob Stanton and his eldest son Benjamin."

Johnnie shook hands with Wanda and then her two brothers. Big Bob reluctantly accepted the offered hand but was clearly unenthusiastic about it. He shook and then unthinkingly wiped his hands down the sides of his pants.

"I'm pleased to meet you all and I'm very glad you chose not to shoot us. I didn't know you had new neighbors, Hamilton, and such a very beautiful one at that. I can see that you two are ideally suited to one another. I predict a long and happy life for you together."

Big Bob was about to explode but Sam cut him off.

"Tell me about this dumb Indian act you tried to lay on us, Johnnie. You talk like a college graduate. Why the dumb act?"

"Sometimes the dumb act keeps me safe until I see the lay of the land. There's still a lot of folks around who can't accept an Indian with an education. I wait to size things up. And then, too, a dumb Indian can say things that an educated one can't because folks don't expect any better. How else could I say that your sister is very beautiful and that she and my friend Hamilton look very good together?" He said all of this with a dazzling smile.

This time, there was no stopping Big Bob, "You watch

your tongue. I'll have no dirty savage talking about my daughter no matter if he's been to some school or not. And as for this down-at-the-heels neighbor, we're only here because we were told the ranch was under attack. There's nothing more to it. Certainly nothing that includes my daughter. Now you owe her an apology and, by thunder, I'll see that she hears it!"

Johnnie smiled again at Wanda, seemingly not in the least intimidated by the volume of Big Bob's voice. "Why certainly. Miss Stanton, if you were somehow offended by me telling you that you are very beautiful or that you look fine standing beside my friend, then I apologize."

Wanda and Sam both laughed. Wanda said, "Pa, I'm perfectly capable of knowing when an apology is needed and it's not now. But, Johnnie, I would like to know more about you and your group. Most Indians are restricted to the reserves. How is it that you're here, and where did you get your education?"

"We're not really here. Not officially anyway. We have a good system worked out to the benefit of all of us. We pretend to be on the reserve, sitting uselessly, waiting for the next government handout, and the Indian Agent pretends he didn't see us leave. That's why we usually travel at night. Some folks aren't as accommodating as Hamilton and the Indian Agent. It's a great system. We do some work and make a bit of money so our womenfolk can visit the trading post, and Hamilton and a few of his neighbors get their hay put up. Great system.

"I admit that most of us would rather be hunting buffalo or maybe Sioux or Blackfoot. But the buffalo are gone and the great father in Washington gets very upset if we hunt Sioux or Blackfoot. We do the best we can. Perhaps we can put your hay up for you when we finish here."

Big Bob just couldn't keep quiet, "God put the grass in the ground, not in big piles. There'll be no haying on the Circle S. And if there was, I guess we'd not want Sioux-hunting savages doing it. I've a mind to talk to that Indian Agent about this situation."

Wanda looked at her father in surprise. "You'll do no such a thing, Father. It's ridiculous keeping these people on reserves. You'll butt right out and so will we all."

Benjamin held a hand up to stop his father's coming outburst. "When exactly did you start giving orders in this outfit, Little Sister?"

"When the men all took leave of their common sense."

Wanda continued, "Johnnie, you haven't answered the education question yet."

"There's not much to tell. My father turned to the white man's God many years ago and when the opportunity came for me to go to mission school, he dressed me in my best buckskins and sent me off. I learned your language and picked up a bit of the rest of the teaching. I struggled pretty much with numbers but I learned to enjoy reading books. From that I started to understand that the world is much bigger than any of the tribes had ever understood. And I made up my mind to try to share some of that learning with my people.

"When I was old enough, the missionary took me to a college in St. Louis and convinced them to take me on. I studied to be a teacher. I graduated two years ago and came home to my own village. All winter I teach school and in the summer I look for work for the men."

"And never leave the reserve." Wanda smiled.

"We're not allowed to leave the reserve." There were grins all around except for Big Bob.

Big Bob had been looking around carefully as Johnnie was talking. Finally, he spoke, "I'm led to believe you travel armed. I don't know as how I can find much trust for an armed Indian, college or no college. Where did you get the guns? Does the army know about the weapons?"

Johnnie directed a tense smile at the rancher, all the lightheartedness of the previous few minutes gone. "Have you seen any guns? I don't see any guns."

Big Bob waved his arm at the rising teepees. "I think I should take a look in those tents and maybe under the loads on the wagons. I'll be wanting to see any weapons removed before I decide whether to talk to the army or not." He took a step in the direction of a wagon while his two sons gasped and were about to stop him. They didn't get the chance.

Johnnie stepped in front of him and several Indian men moved closer to their wagons, fierce looks on their faces. Johnnie placed the palm of his hand on Big Bob's chest and looked him full in the eye. "Mr. Rancher, you would be wise to go about your business and leave us to go about ours."

This was a completely different Johnnie than the one who just moments before was talking about mission school and teaching tribesmen. The look on his face scared Wanda and even brought Big Bob up short. They decided that this was not a man to be taken lightly in spite of his normally smiling demeanor.

Ben stepped between his father and Johnnie. "I apologize on behalf of my father and our family. This is all pretty new to us. We've never met Indians up close before and we have much to learn. I think we will all go home now and let you get on with the haying. But you have to try to understand. Trust comes hard after years of conflict. I expect that's true on both sides. But we'll give it some time; see how it all works out. I'm hoping that you're true to your word."

Hamilton entered the conversation, "We have a hay crop to stack and no guarantee this sunshine will last. Johnnie, the men have the teams and wagons ready. I think we need to get at the work."

Johnnie's smile wasn't quite as broad as it had been before. There may have been a tinge of sarcasm in his voice, "Nice to meet all you Stanton men and the very beautiful Miss Stanton but Hamilton is right. We have work to do. Perhaps another time we can visit longer."

Big Bob was in danger of bursting again when Sam said, "C'mon, Pa, time to go home."

Hamilton said, "Thank you for coming, Miss Stanton, and you too, men. I know you meant well and I appreciate it. Come again after the hay is up and we'll put the coffee on."

"Call me Wanda."

Hamilton blushed right through his deep tan. "Wanda. I'll remember that, Miss Stanton."

Wanda looped one arm around Sam's and her other around her father's for the walk up the hill. She had to tug just a bit to get her father moving.

She turned to Hamilton and smiled. "See you Sunday."

Hamilton swallowed and lifted his hand a bit in a farewell gesture but was unable to respond with words. Johnnie clapped him on the shoulder. "You're a lucky man, my friend, a lucky man."

"I'm not sure you have the straight of that."

"God gave me good eyes. You're a lucky man."

Hamilton got the men started raking and loading hay. One of the Indian's broomtail, half-broke teams was hooked to the hay rake, the horses stamping and prancing the whole time. Hamilton cringed as he watched the rig race across the field, fearing his hay rake wasn't up to the challenge. The two horses seemed to be in competition with one another and the driver looked like he was enjoying the erratic ride. Hamilton wondered idly if the Indian was reliving his buffalo running or Sioux hunting days. As long as the rake held together and the hay got stacked, Hamilton couldn't see any harm in the Indian's imagined adventure. He grinned a bit before turning away.

He gathered up the reins of his mower team and swung onto the back of one of the big blacks who didn't seem to notice his weight. He walked the team the half mile to the field that still needed cutting. He had a start on the field but there was still a lot to do. He figured three more days of cutting and, if the sun continued to shine, the grass would be dry enough for stacking by the time the Indian crew worked their way there.

The women butchered and dressed a fat steer that Hamilton had kept in a corral for them. To women who had spent years dressing buffalo after the hunt, one steer presented no challenge. A couple of the warriors had suggested turning the steer loose so they could run it and bring it down with arrows.

Johnnie had just smiled, looking at the fattened animal, and tried to picture it running anywhere except to the feed trough. "Maybe another time."

In ten days, the hay was dry and in giant stacks, stored close to the winter feed and bed grounds, ready for the needs of the feeding season. The stacks were a little ragged, showing that there was still much to learn for the workers but Hamilton didn't figure it would make much difference. There was still a goodly amount of hay remaining from the previous year plus a few older stacks scattered in the further corners of the ranch. But Hamilton slept better knowing he had enough, and more. They kept the stacks close together so they could be fenced off.

He paid the Indian men and thanked the women for

their work. The crew was due at Clark Ransom's ranch next and the thunderheads building up over the Rockies were causing concern. Clark had been down to check on the crew the day before, hurrying them along, so taking down the little village and saying goodbye was kept to the shortest time possible.

Wanda had been over to watch the haying several times and had become friendly with the women although there was a considerable language barrier. Somehow she knew they were ready to leave and showed up to say goodbye. Sam was with her. She walked through the gathered women and spoke to each one. She then went to the men and shook each of their hands. Sam did the same.

Johnnie watched from a distance, chuckling to himself. When Wanda came to him, he said, "In their hearts those men are still warriors. They aren't familiar with women speaking to them openly. But even Indians can recognize a beautiful woman, and a beautiful woman can get away with almost anything if she smiles.

"You go easy on my friend Hamilton. He knows he's a gone goose but he's still not sure what to do about it. You go easy on him until he figures it out."

Hamilton looked around as if he was trying to find a hole to crawl into.

Wanda could think of no good response so she wisely kept quiet.

The wild-eyed team that had been on the rake was now pulling a wagon loaded with women, kids and rolled up hide teepees. They left the yard at a full run with the kids screaming in excitement and the driver urging the animals to even more speed.

9

THE HAYING AND FENCING DONE, HAMILTON WAS FREE TO address other tasks. But before he could get to them the storm hit. The lightening came first; cracking and crashing, rending the sky with brilliance and filling the air with the not unpleasant odor of ozone. The lightening display was followed by thunder that seemed to roll down the hills, gathering momentum before landing on the flat lands below with a glorious cascading of sound. Soon the lightning flashes were overlapping each other and the roll of thunder was almost continuous, rattling the window glass in Hamilton's log house. Then the rain came; a cloudburst of rain, a deluge. It was as if the heavens had opened all their gates and the downpour was let loose.

The ranchers might have preferred a gentler rain, a rain that the thirsty earth would have time to take in; to nourish the precious grass roots and moisten the rich black soil, holding the excess for the needs of the days to come. But the land in the shadows of the Rockies is a land of extremes.

The storm continued to blow with the rains pounding

the roofs of ranch buildings, shredding leaves from the quaking aspens and soaking the land surface, then going on its way filling every creek and stream to overflowing and, further east, blowing itself out until eventually becoming just another forlorn, delayed hope offering no respite to the farmers tilling the soil of the dry eastern flatlands.

As welcome as rain always was, the ranchers still working on their hay crop lamented the timing of the storm. The cut hay would have to be turned once the sun came out to allow for thorough drying. That was a lot of extra time and work. But the extra work was balanced by the knowledge that the ground would soak up at least some of the moisture and the roots would drink it in, pushing the grass into another growth spurt before summer's end. The rain that the earth couldn't absorb rushed downhill to fill reservoirs and creeks. For two days, the Poudre River came close to overflowing its banks before finally settling back down as the rain gentled off.

One of Hamilton's dirt dams gave way on a small unnamed stream. He noticed the extra silt flowing downstream as he was checking his herd. He drove a wagon through the drenching downpour, carrying his digging tools to the location of the break. He spent several hours gathering rocks and placing them in the torrent of the creek, backing the rocks with clay dug from the hillside.

Finally, soaked to the skin and satisfied he had done all he could, and watching with satisfaction as the water again started to gather behind the dam, he threw his tools onto the wagon bed and turned the team towards home. He stalled the team, gave them a brisk rubdown and a pail of oats and went to the house. He spent the next couple of hours wrapped in a blanket beside the blazing cook stove, reading a book.

After rebuilding the dirt dam, Hamilton used the remainder of the first day of the storm to rest and do some house cleaning. The haying had been almost three weeks of nonstop work and the time of rest was a welcome respite from the never-ending ranch chores. Once the kitchen was set in order he took his cup of coffee onto the porch and watched the rain come down, thankful for the porch roof the builders had included in the construction of the log house. His dog tracked muddy footprints onto the porch floor and nuzzled Hamilton's leg, seeking attention. Hamilton placed his coffee cup into his other hand so he could scratch the dog behind the ear and talk to him.

When he had drunk as much coffee as he thought he should, he moved to his rocker at the table with paper and pencil. He was halfway through the writing of a poem when he got up and dropped the bar into its slots on the door. Neighbors often just walked in unannounced the way Hank Blossom had a few weeks before. Although he had put the paper away as quickly as he could, Hank saw what he was doing.

Hank, always the thoughtful one, didn't mention it at the time. But as close-mouthed as his neighbor was, it seemed he had let something slip to his wife who had mentioned to her fourteen-year-old daughter how nice it would be to have a man who wrote romantic poetry. The daughter knew her mother was not talking about her father and, remembering that her father had visited Hamilton that day, put it together in her youthful, romantic mind. She whispered the news to a girlfriend at school and it was soon all over town.

Hamilton would rather take a whopping with the double of a rope than have that happen again.

Taking full advantage of his opportunity to rest, Hamilton even went so far as to have a siesta nap. Years before he had placed a cot on the porch. He slept out there on warm nights and he napped there that afternoon, listening to the rain on the roof. By evening, boredom had set in.

Hamilton took the second day of the storm as an opportunity to visit some neighbors. Saddling a sure-footed horse and donning his rain gear, he set out on the muddy roads.

Hank Blossom, looking from the open barn door, saw him coming and waved him inside. "Get yourself down and we'll go find some coffee. Might find an oatmeal cookie, too, if those kids haven't eaten them all up. It's a caution the groceries those kids can put away. Keeps me busy buying supplies and my wife busy at the stove."

The two men hunched their shoulders against the rain pounding on their yellow slickers and mucked their way to the house. Hank swung the door open and had one foot on the kitchen floor when he was met with the business end of a broom held by his very determined wife. "You take one more step, Mr. Blossom, and you'll find yourself on your hands and knees washing this floor. We happen to have a perfectly good roof over that porch to leave your boots under. You might want to use it or go back to your barn."

Hank stopped so fast he nearly lost his balance. He grabbed the door post and pulled himself back onto the porch, purposely exaggerating his actions. His three youngest children sitting at the table with milk and cookies, shouted in glee, "Daddy got the floor muddy; Daddy got the floor muddy…."

"Sorry, dear. I don't know how I forgot that."

"You've had a lifetime of practice at forgetting so I imagine it's coming natural by now."

"I'll take off my boots but you're going to give Hamilton the wrong impression of our domestic bliss, you waving that broom around and all. And just when he's come for a visit, too. If he had the idea of inquiring of us about the making of a happy home, he's probably changed his mind. Seems a shame to have lost this opportunity." He was trying to hide his grin.

Mrs. Blossom had put the broom back behind the stove. "Welcome, Hamilton. I see you already have your boots off. Comes from being a bachelor and having to clean your own house. As far as inquiring after marital bliss goes, I expect that collection of misfits down at the saloon have you so confused by now that nothing I could say would help.

"But I hid a few cookies from the kids so come on in and set yourselves down. You kids get on out of here; let the men sit down."

Like most of Hamilton's neighbors, the Blossoms were good friends. In ranching country, a neighbor might live many miles away and be seen only once or twice a year but they were taken as friends until they showed themselves to be unfriendly, a situation that happened only rarely.

After the coffee and cookies and a short visit, Hamilton went on to call on two more neighbors and then made his way back home. He didn't often feel the emptiness of his house but this evening he did and he found himself longing for company. He had a firm opinion on who that company should be.

Like all storms, human or natural, this one finally ran its course and the ranchers returned to their normal work.

Constantly striving to improve his ranch, Hamilton cleaned out a couple of water holes and dammed up a few small water runs to create more collection pools. Even in this foothills country there was never more water than what the ranchers wanted and often less than what was needed. The cattle were constantly tramping down the banks of the dugouts and streams. It was a never-ending chore to keep them in good usable condition.

The streams running across Hamilton's H-R dumped their water into the Poudre River just before leaving his property. Damming them had little or no direct impact on his neighbors. It was a serious matter for a rancher to dam a flowing stream that a neighbor depended on, and it was a matter for hard feelings on the rare occasions when it had happened.

He drove a wagon up into the hills where he dug up a load of tree seedlings. Over the years he had dug up several hundred two and three-year-old seedlings as well as some larger saplings, replanting them along the edges of the two main streams that worked their meandering way across his land. His hope was that in a few years those transplants would grow into shade for the water and animals alike as well as stability for the creek banks. Strictly speaking, it was not the prime time of the year for planting but Hamilton planted anyway, hoping for the best.

The Eastern Slopes was good country, suitable almost anywhere for cattle or sheep. In small pockets, the ranchers were able to plow some ground and plant a crop. But early frosts were a constant concern so Hamilton restricted his planting to a fifty-acre field of oats for his horses.

As important as the breed and quality of his herd animals were to his ranching success, Hamilton knew that the real wealth came from the land and the grass it produced. So he did everything he knew to do to protect the water and grass and wished he knew more.

Being alone all week in his solitary bachelor cabin meant that by Saturday evening Hamilton was ready for a woman-cooked meal at the hotel dining room, and then a visit with the whittlers and checkers players that regularly gathered in Murphy's Saloon.

Arriving later than usual on one August evening, Hamilton found the men deep in discussion. It was impossible not to notice that the conversation stopped as he approached.

"Evening, men. Did I disturb something? Seldom ever hear so much silence from y'all. Don't mind me and don't hold back on your talk because of me. I'll just sit here quietly and marvel at your wisdom."

He pulled up a chair and sat down, taking out his pocketknife. "By the time I whittle through this piece of wood I brought along, I expect my mind will be bursting with new information that will prove advantageous to my success in life and the general well-being of the community."

Clark Ransom gave Hamilton a light slap on the shoulder. "You got here just a few minutes too early." The old rancher wasn't given to smiling but he offered a half-hearted grin.

"We were just narrowing in on the solution to all your problems. Now you went and broke our train of thought and who knows if we'll ever get it back. It's a waste of good thinking is what it is. All that deep thought just gone to waste. I'm losing faith in you, Hamilton. Seems a man should know when to leave his friends to their contemplations. How're we going to make good decisions for your future without being able to give adequate time to the problems at hand?"

"I wasn't aware that I had problems that required the gathered intellect of Murphy's checkers club for their solving."

Clark shook off Hamilton's doubt. "See, that's just what I mean. How are you going to come up with the right solutions when you don't even know what the problems are?"

The sheriff stood up and pushed his chair back. "I'd better take a walk around town. Never know what tribulation might be approaching. And anyway, it's clear our bachelor friend doesn't respect the hard-earned knowledge of his married neighbors so I might as well go where I'm needed."

The saloon wasn't very large and the men were sitting close to the bar where Jimmy the bartender could participate in the banter. "You run into any real desperados out there, Sheriff, you give us a holler. We'll come and give you advice."

With the sheriff gone, there was room for Hamilton to sit at the table. He slid the chair back a bit to make whittling easier and looked over the checkers-playing men. "How's your water supply holding up, Clark? That last rain do it for you?"

"Well, it certainly helped but that's the most of a month ago. And it's been hot since. My upper creek that feeds down from the high hills has gone bone dry. First time that ever happened before so I rode up onto the open range pasture to take a look. Never saw so many cattle, most of them carrying a Circle S. Creek banks are all trampled down and what little water's left is all silted up.

"That Texas neighbor of yours just doesn't seem to understand that he don't own that whole mountainside. His scrawny Longhorns have just about taken over that entire area. Don't know why he went to the trouble to drive those culls all the way from Texas when he could have bought better cattle here for a fair price. Sure hope all my cows caught from my own bulls before I drove them up there. One thing I don't need is calves from his bulls.

"And then, if that's not bad enough, someone built a dirt dam across the whole waterway. I suspect the Texan again but I have no real proof. Gathered up a small pool behind that dam but now that's almost gone, too. No water at all getting out to the lower pastures. At first I was fit to be tied but it's about time to move my critters off that section anyway. I'm heading up the first of the week to gather up my bunch and bring them home.

"As for other water, the creek from the Watkins' spread is still running but not by much. We need rain again pretty soon. Whatever snow pack is left in the high-up hills isn't enough to feed the entire Eastern Slopes. We need rain before long."

Hamilton studied his friend for a moment. "How many head you figure the Circle S has on the public range?"

"More than the R/R ever put on it, that's for certain sure."

"There's trouble brewing if the Circle S doesn't pull in its horns," said Amos Watkins. "Could be that someone should have a talk with that Texan. Tell him this isn't really open-range country even if that one area is shared."

Clark responded, "I tried that. Met him in town one day and asked about the number of Circle S brutes on that grass. Told me not to butt into his business and said if I wasn't man enough to compete with a real rancher maybe I could get a job clerking in a store."

Amos shook his head at this. "That don't sound friendly, don't sound friendly at all."

"Well, I let it go since he had three or four of his crew backing him and I promised the wife some time ago that I'd avoid any more fights. She's always worried that I'll show up dead after some run-in but I kept telling her that hadn't happened yet."

"I bet that comforted her," Hamilton said, laughing.

"Sometimes it's just easier to go along, especially where the wife is concerned. She can get decidedly narrow in her thinking and I pay too high a price for that. So I made the promise."

After a short pause, he finished his thought, "Might be better all the way around."

"Might," agreed Amos. "But that don't answer the question about that dirt dam. Seems to me if he's done it once he'll do it again. Pretty much all our water gets its start up on that high plateau. Wouldn't do at all to go to damming any of it up."

Clark had more to say. "The real problem is much bigger than that one dirt dam. The problem is the Texan has no regard for our range tradition or for any of his neighbors, nor for what grass the land is able to produce. We've been sharing that range for many a year with no issues coming up that I remember. The Circle S hasn't shown much friendliness but it could be that one of us has to try to talk sense to him. Before it all blows into an old-time range war, I mean."

Clark tipped his chair dangerously onto it back legs and looked over the gathering. "I fought through a range war up in Wyoming a long while ago. Maybe you'll remember me talking of that before. Back then I was just a thirty-a-month rider doing another man's dirty work.

"Us riders didn't even really know what it was about; we just did as we were told. The whole thing was senseless. At the end of that shindig, four cowboys and both ranchers were dead, their cattle stolen and driven off. I'd hate to see it come to that around here.

"If it came to that, there's no telling what the outcome might be. Or how much trouble I'd be in at home if I got involved. Like I said, I pay a high price for any discontentment at home."

Tiny looked at his friend and laughed. "Would that be the same range war old Smokey fought in?"

"You can laugh all you want but there was precious little to laugh about at the time." Clark sounded a bit unhappy at the challenge to his story.

Hamilton, trying to lighten the mood, pointed his whittling stick at Clark. "Well, now. You've all been wanting to enlighten me on the pros and cons of the matrimonial condition. Could be that hearing the details of your home life would be a forward step in my education."

"You don't need details. Just know that sleeping in the barn is the least of my troubles."

The men laughed until Clark was forced to put on a small smile himself.

Amos said, "Seriously, Hamilton, you've met the Circle S more than any of us. How about you talking to them?"

Hamilton considered that option but almost immediately the probability of driving even more space between himself and his hoped-for father-in-law caused him to hesitate.

"You're the one to do it, Hamilton. There's just no other option," Clark urged.

Hamilton stopped whittling and looked at his friends. "Since his dirt dam nor his cattle, neither one, is bothering me, Big Bob would know that y'all put me up to it. Don't rightly see any advantage in that for me or any good outcome for the rest of you."

Clark chuckled a bit and continued, "Well, now, that's a right selfish attitude neighbor. Never known you to talk like that before. Or maybe it ain't so much selfish as it is fear. Fear that you'll upset the young lady if you push a bit against her pa."

Hamilton stopped his whittling again and looked around the group. "I ain't likely to see Miss Stanton if I was to ride into the yard. They see me coming, they'll lock her in the root cellar till I'm gone. Anyway, since I don't put any animals on the public lands, the Circle S would know I was talking on your behalf and they would rightly wonder why you weren't speaking for yourselves."

Amos leaned back in his chair and looked around the circle of friends. "Well, the summer is about gone. Not much more harm to do anymore. That plateau grass isn't about to grow any more this year and as soon as the cattle are driven to home grass we can go up and dig that dam out. Worry about it next spring."

That seemed to put an end to the discussion but several minutes later Clark brought it up again, "Big doings at the hall next weekend; supper, dance and all. Maybe you can soften up that Texan with an extra slice of that sweet ham you always bring, Hamilton. Kind of ease into a talk about the plateau."

Hamilton just glanced at him and went on with his whittling.

The men fell into serious checkers playing and wood whittling and nothing more was said about the Circle S or the dirt dam.

10

THE FOLLOWING FRIDAY EVENING THE SCHOOLYARD WAS A maze of buggies, wagons, and tethered horses. There was no discernible pattern to the parking. Whole families arrived in wagons; the kids in the back along with covered pots and plates of food, the parents sweltering in their dress clothes riding the seat. Some childless couples arrived in single-seat buggies while the unattached men rode horseback. Hamilton, carrying a cooked ham still in the roasting pot and too hot to hold, decided to put his buggy into service.

He never missed the occasional town dances where he freely shared his time and dancing skills with as many girls as possible. He found that he enjoyed dancing and had become good at it.

The twice-a-year community dinners were especially popular with the men, Hamilton included, who never found a reason to refuse good food. The dinners had evolved from the traditional box socials into buffet-style affairs after Tony Spiro, the perpetual town bachelor and long-time mayor, won the pre-packed lunch prepared by Agnes Whippel in exchange for three dollars and seventy-five cents, cash, several years earlier. The boxed dinner had proven to be almost inedible and Agnes almost impossible to avoid for several months following that sad event. Tony had put his considerable political skills to work and the town never again risked the uncertainty of a box social.

The ladies had the tables set and were arranging the food on the big serving tables when Hamilton arrived. He passed the ham to the first lady he saw who was wearing an apron. He turned towards the door, telling himself that only the one woman had noticed him and she was busy heading into the small kitchen with the ham. But before he was safely out the door, several of the mothers and a few of their daughters were gushing over him and the ham which they had neither seen nor tasted yet. He tipped his hat and smiled and made it to the door.

The men, as usual, were gathering out behind the schoolhouse. Amos Watkins was there and, although he had brought some samples of his homemade product, he had left it in his wagon since daylight was lingering and the children were still around, yelling and playing and seeing how high they could push each other on the school-yard swings.

The conversation soon turned to range conditions, the need for rain, the size of the hay crop, and cattle prices. That was the world these men lived in and they had very little interest in any other.

The Circle S showed up in strength. Big Bob had left his stallion stabled for the evening in favor of sharing the spring wagon seat with his wife and Wanda. Except for the ranch cook and a couple of men who had no interest in dancing, the entire crew arrived, all on horseback.

Big Bob selfishly pulled his buggy right up to the schoolhouse door and stepped down. One of his men quickly unhitched the horse and took it to shade, tying it to the fence rail. Big Bob helped his wife and Wanda to the ground and turned to stomp into the building, leaving the ladies to follow along.

Mrs. Stanton called him back. When he turned towards her, she hooked her arm through his and said quietly, "It would be nice if you would wait for me."

Wanda looked around her and called her two brothers over. "I need help getting this food into the hall. And then, why don't you two push this buggy out of everyone's way? Father has made it nearly impossible for anyone to get into the building."

After carrying the food into the hall, Wanda called her brothers again. Hands on hips, she said, "Let's move this buggy."

Benjamin started to refuse but Sam spoke up first, "It's a bit awkward placed where it is, isn't it? Pick up those shafts, Ben, and I'll push. Do you think you can steer this thing or should I holler for help?"

Benjamin didn't appreciate the sarcasm from his younger brother but he picked up the shafts anyway.

Big Bob was soon back outside having quickly noticed that the room housed only women. He stood on the entry landing and gazed out at the yard. Seeing only his own crew, he rightly assumed that the district men were out back. Wrongly taking for granted that the district men would be impressed with his presence, his arrogance blinding him to the truth, he strode around the corner and approached one of the small gatherings. The conversation stopped at his arrival and he couldn't help noticing the sudden coolness in the air. He pressed on nonetheless. "I haven't met all of you men. I'm Bob Stanton, Circle S. Bought out the R/R. Can I assume that you're all neighbors and district men?"

Clark Ransom took his time drawling out, "Can assume anything you want. It's a free country."

Big Bob's hackles immediately rose and did battle against his better judgment. "What the Sam Hill does that mean?"

Again, there was an uncomfortable silence. Finally, Clark spit a brown wad into the tall grass at his feet. "I guess partly it means that we've always had a right friendly community around these parts. Kind of look out for one another, if you get my drift. Always shared the free range. Shared the water. Hate to see that changing." Clark's approach to the subject was the exact opposite to what he had asked of Hamilton. The other ranchers stood in stunned silence.

Big Bob was beside himself with anger. "This is a man's world. If you're going to live among men, you have to act like a man." He turned and left.

Angry to the core, Big Bob stomped back into the building and over to his wife who was visiting with some neighbors she had just met. Wanda was close by, visiting with some of the young ladies she had met at church.

"Get your wrap. We're going home."

Mrs. Stanton looked her surprise. "Why ever in the world would we do that? Bob, I would like to introduce you to some neighbor ladies."

"Another time," he said gruffly. "I said get your wrap. We're leaving. I'll get the rig; you and Wanda gather up your stuff."

Wanda stepped up to her father. "You leave if you wish. I'm staying. I'll see you at home later." She turned back to the group she had been visiting with.

"You'll do as I say," Bob said with more volume than what wisdom would have asked for.

"When I was a little girl, Pa, I always did what you said. I still do when you're right. But now I'm an adult and you're wrong so I'll see you at home later." The girls Wanda had been visiting with were staring at the floor, embarrassed to have overheard this family quarrel.

Mrs. Stanton hesitated and then, finding courage, turned to her husband. "I'm also an adult, Bob, and I know of no reason for leaving. And there's certainly no reason for raised voices. I wish to meet more of the neighbors and I can't do that if we leave. Let's go find a seat. Supper will be served shortly."

Probably no one in the world could have a calming effect on Big Bob except his wife. In spite of all his roughness and the volume of his voice, he loved her deeply and wouldn't purposely do anything to hurt her although he was often unaware of the results of his actions until long after the fact. "There's no place for us here. I see no welcome at all."

"Well, my dear, we have to be welcoming if we expect to be welcomed."

Big Bob had no comeback for that so he followed her to a table along the wall and sat glaring around the room.

One of the women raised a window in the kitchen, leaned her head out and hollered, "Supper time!"

As if by magic, the men's conversations stopped. "I'm ready," several said in unison.

As soon as the men had gathered inside, Mrs. Ransom, Clark's wife, who had the habit of taking over anything she was involved in, hollered loud enough to hush the many conversations in the hall. "Hamilton, Rev Brockton said he would be along later but this food is ready now. Since he isn't here, how would you like to say grace for us this evening?"

Hamilton took off his hat as he stepped to the center of the floor and said, "Let's give thanks together."

After a shuffling of feet by the men as they moved away from the door to let the stragglers in, they removed their hats and bowed their heads. Some appeared to be distinctly uncomfortable but they followed the example of their neighbors anyway. Big Bob neither stood nor removed his hat. Mrs. Stanton tugged at his arm until he stood up. Showing no sign of intending to remove his hat himself, she whispered, "Hat."

Big Bob responded, "I doubt the Lord hears the prayers of down-at-the-heels squatters."

Wanda linked her arm into her father's and smiled at him. Then she reached up and lifted his hat off and passed it to him.

On the cattle range or in a fight of any kind, Big Bob was totally at home and not intimidated by anyone. But standing between his two women he was like a bird with a broken wing, uncomfortable and more or less helpless, and with no idea at all what to do about it.

In any case, he stood silently while Hamilton gave thanks. The two women glanced at each other at the end of the prayer. Wanda smiled and looked intently at Hamilton. Mrs. Stanton took a long study of her daughter and finally said, "My, my."

When the lineup for supper began, Big Bob would have shouldered his way to the front but his two women had a strong hold on his arms. Mrs. Stanton whispered, "We're not so hungry that we can't allow the others to go first."

Wanda said, "Be nice, Papa."

Bob sat down and perhaps the rumble from his chest

would have turned into words at another time but this time it stayed as a rumble.

Eventually supper was over and the serious visiting began as a few women cleaned up in the kitchen. Most of the pots and bowls were carried out to the wagons and buggies to be cleaned later when the families arrived home.

One of the girls from church sought out Wanda and gushed breathlessly, "Did you try that honey baked ham? I do believe Hamilton is a genius at doing honey baked ham." Her excitement seemed to be well beyond what was appropriate to the situation.

Wanda merely confirmed that she had tried some and it was delicious. As the girl walked away, Mrs. Stanton looked puzzled. "Am I missing something here?"

"Nothing important, Mama."

The meal completed and the dishes dealt with, the hall was made ready for dancing and visiting. The sun was going down but, before full dark, the families with small children brought in blankets from their buggies hoping the littlest ones would settle down and sleep. The men attended to their animals, taking turns pumping water from the yard well and putting out a bit of hay.

The tables and chairs were moved to the outer rim of the floor and three men were soon arranging one corner of the room to their satisfaction, making space for a guitar, a fiddle and an accordion. The trio was well known in the district for music that was more energetic than it was melodic. But it was danceable and in this small village that's all that was expected, or mattered. The fiddle player stomped his foot to pick up the beat, counted one–two–three, and the trio of musicians struck up the first piece more or less together.

The men who saw dancing as a somewhat questionable

activity returned to the outside to visit. These men who could sit the saddle of the rankest horse, throw a loop under the feet of a running steer, and who's every movement on the ranch was completed with agility and athletic grace somehow developed two left feet on the dance floor. Men who had never quit on anything else in their working lives had quit on dancing. It had become a source of combined humor and embarrassment. They would spend the remainder of the evening visiting with friends, some of whom lived so far away they seldom saw them.

The children were back on the playground screaming and running every which way.

Amos Watkins and a few close friends found their way over to his wagon where they formed a tight circle, keeping prying eyes from seeing things that were best not seen. The men knew better than to overindulge. Their ride home would be woodenly silent and stress-filled if they were to do anything displeasing to their womenfolk on this social occasion.

The Circle S cowboys hung together as a group, not knowing any of the locals by name and not being especially welcomed. Figuring on maybe indulging in a nip or two from a bottle stowed away in a saddlebag, they made their way into the yard and gathered around the Circle S buggy. They planned to return after the dance got well under way. A couple of the riders had been bragging about their dancing abilities and the others were determined to at least try, assuming they could entice some young lady away from the locals.

Dalton, the Circle S rider who had threatened to kill Hamilton after the incident with the coiled lariat, was working himself into a fighting mood, spurred on by his buddies and the three nips of the bottle that had been making its way around. The fact that Hamilton had been asked to say grace was just the capstone to push his anger over the limit.

Dalton was a tough, seasoned rider hardened by years in the saddle and more than just a few saloon and bunkhouse brawls. He had never considered himself as more than just average with a six-shooter but he had great confidence with his fists or in a rough and tumble affair. Broad in the shoulders and stronger than most men, he was apt to brag and swagger after taking a swallow or two from the bottle. He was feeling the effects of those swallows now.

"That would-be rancher, down-at-the-heels nester, sucker punched me with that coiled lariat; else he never would have been able to get it done. I made him a promise that we would meet again. And now he's in there smiling at the ladies and saying grace. It's enough to put a man off his feed."

Randy Hanna, his riding partner, a tough enough man himself and inclined to be a bit reckless, encouraged him. "I didn't notice as how it put you off your feed too much at supper but, as to the other, maybe you've waited long enough. Best you get at it and there's no better time than now. Be good to have these nesters and small-time ranchers see what a good old Texas boy can do. Kind of liven up the party, you might say."

One of the other Circle S riders shook his head at this talk. "Yup, and it might also get you fired and then you'd have a long ride back to Texas with winter com'n on. And those of us with you here might get given our pay, too. I don't know as how breaking up this here party is just quite the right thing to do."

Homer Plantz, the saddle maker and gunsmith, stood up. "Couldn't help but overhear, boys. Not poking my head in where it's not welcome but my friend Jasper and I were sit'n right here shaded up from the set'n sun when y'all gathered around this buggy. Guess you didn't see us." He leaned on the buggy, casting Dalton a serious look. "I would urge caution on you, young man; in fact, while it's still light outside, I'd invite you to go for a short walk with me. Got something in my shop you should want to see."

"You got nothing I want, old man, unless it's a silver mounted saddle with black leather that costs ten dollars."

"Ain't no such a saddle here nor anywhere else, son, but why don't you take that walk with me anyway and bring your partner with you. Only take a few minutes and you'll never be sorry."

Randy Hanna slapped Dalton on the back with an arrogant grin on his face. "What could it hurt? Let's mosey on over to his shop and see what he finds so interesting."

One of the other Stanton riders spoke up, "We'll all go."

"C'mon then," said Homer.

It was only a five-minute walk to the saddle shop. Homer inserted his key and opened the door. As he walked to the back of the counter, he tapped the glass above a set of holsters and guns. "Take a gander in that glass case, boys, and tell me what you see."

"What I see is the same thing I saw when I was in here last week," said Dalton. "The nicest two-gun rig I ever did lay eyes on. A bit scratched up and showing considerable use but still a nice rig. I don't have the coin or I'd make you an offer on it."

"Wouldn't do you any good to make an offer. Rig's not for sale. In fact, I don't own that rig. Belongs to a man who asked me to hold it for him."

"So why haul us all the way over here to see something that you don't own and can't sell?"

"The reason is because you need to take a close look at that rig and understand who does own it."

"Somebody we might know?" asked Randy Hanna suspiciously.

"That rig belongs to that would-be rancher, down-at-the-heels nester you good old Texas boys were so almighty anxious to tackle tonight. You might want to give it all a second thought."

Dalton was speechless for a moment. Finally, "Are you telling me that nester is a gunfighter? I find that hard to believe."

The saddle maker leaned into the glass case and withdrew the rig, laying it on the counter. "Everyone in town knows about this rig and what it used to mean. They also know how the toughest fight its owner ever had was taking it off and starting a new life. He's been pretty successful and I'd hate for you boys to do anything that would cause him to walk in here and pick up this belt again. Be bad for you, too. There's just no way any of you cowboys are up to the challenge."

"How come we never heard of him? Seems a man like that would have a reputation and word would get around."

"You boys are from Texas and my guess is that none of you have been away from Texas until you came here. Now, if you was to be from Arizona, say around Prescott, you would surely know the name."

"I think you just might be lying, old man, to protect a nester that can't protect himself."

The gunsmith smiled at Dalton. "Way I heard the story, that nester as you call him, faced up to three of you boys and you armed with both sidearms and saddle guns and him with just a coiled lariat. Did he appear too worried about anything while all of that was going on?"

The Circle S men stood silently.

Homer leaned his elbows on the counter, his scarred leather-worker's hands laid out before them. His shirt was pulling apart at the front where it stretched over his corpulent waistline. Shaggy, uncut hair hung down over his ears. When he pushed his hat to the back of his head, the hair fell forward nearly blocking out his vision. He smiled up at the Circle S riders and pointed with his chin towards the gathering at the dance.

"Here's the truth of all this, boys. Hamilton's a good man and he ain't no nester. He's a solid citizen with a good ranch and the best breed of cattle around these parts. He lives peaceably and is friends with most folks. Were I you, I'd forget all this fighting nonsense and start to get to know your neighbors. There's good folks around here and they'd show you a welcome given half the chance.

"But even if you decide to not be good neighbors, you take an old man's advice and leave Hamilton alone. You just ain't in no way up to facing what he can dish out, fists or guns. You listen to an old man who's seen it all. I've seen gun-handy folks going back more years that I can tell about and Hamilton can stand with any of them. No sir, you leave him alone."

It was a quiet group of Circle S riders that walked back across the street.

Dalton, thankful for the gunsmith's warning but not wishing to admit it and feeling foolish about what he had almost done, wondered how to put the past half-hour behind him. "Might just as well take in the dance. Saw a couple of young ladies in there that might rate a second look."

Happy at the change of direction in their talk, Randy Hanna laughed with relief. "What makes you think any of them would take a second look at you? While I'm here, I mean. Just seems natural that they'd look my way given half a chance."

The mood of the group began to lighten, talking about

the girls and the dance. Poking fun at Randy, one of his riding pards said, "I ain't ever seen you on a dance floor, Randy. I seen a cow trying to walk on ice one time though."

Another said, "You hopeless cow nurses, either one, find a girl dumb enough to dance with you, I'll eat my hat."

The men put their anger at Hamilton behind them for the moment, partly sobered by what the gunsmith had told them but also by the knowledge of the tribulation they would bring upon themselves if they ran crossways of Wanda or her mother and embarrassed the Circle S.

The music had barely started when Hamilton stepped up to Wanda and asked, "Would you do me the honor, Miss Stanton?"

"I'd be delighted, Mr. Robb."

Big Bob, sitting where he could hear, again kept the rumble in his chest from becoming words. It took more self-control than Big Bob usually was noted for.

Mrs. Stanton looked at the two young people whirling their way onto the dance floor and whispered, "My, my."

Hamilton and Wanda were the first dancers on the floor. They seemed to fall into a rhythm that complimented each other's efforts. After a few moments, Wanda said, "You dance beautifully, Mr. Robb. You sing and dance and whack cattle and men into the ground with coiled lariats, and hire Indians to make your hay and have the best cattle around here and have all the girls a-tizzy over you and, golly, I don't know what else. Is there anything you can't do, Mr. Robb?"

Hamilton laughed. "Well, I can't seem to get you to call me Hamilton and I can't seem to make peace with your father and, right now, those are the two most important things I can think of."

"I will call you Hamilton when you call me Wanda."

"OK, Miss Stanton, it's a deal. I'll call you Wanda. Now, how do I make peace with your father?"

"Let's forget my father for a few minutes and enjoy the music."

Wanda looked around and let out a small giggle. "Do you realize we are the only ones dancing? Everyone else is just standing like statues."

"I hadn't noticed. Not sure I care. Just so long as we're dancing together."

Mrs. Howard, the sheriff's wife, leaned over from the next table and whispered to Mrs. Stanton in a voice that could be heard through most of the small hall, "They dance beautifully together, do they not?"

This time the rumble in Big Bob's chest came near to escaping.

Mrs. Stanton looked at the young couple and again mumbled, "My, my."

A circle of young ladies had gathered in one corner, staring out at the dancing couple.

A cowboy who was sweet on Heather Phillips slid over towards her. Holding out his hand, he bashfully asked, "Would you care to dance, Heather?"

She looked at him and then back at the whirling couple on the floor. Hesitating a second or two, Heather took a deep breath, held it and then, the breath escaping and her shoulders slumping, she turned her eyes from the dance floor to the cowboy. "I might just as well."

The cowboy looked hurt. "What does that mean? You don't have to dance if you don't want to."

"No, I want to dance. Let's go."

"I know I'm second choice Heather, or maybe even less, but I really like you and I enjoy dancing with you. I'd like to call on you, too, given half a chance." He had never been that bold before.

Heather glanced again over at Hamilton and Wanda. After a slight pause, she smiled at the young man. "I'd enjoy having you call on me."

The young man's smile was likely to split his face as they stepped to the music, now being joined by other couples.

Wanda's two brothers had come to the dance with specific goals in mind and the accomplishing of those goals was surprisingly simple. Sam was whirling around the floor with Miss Granet, the school teacher. Benjamin, not as quick on his feet as his younger brother, had already stepped on the toes of Penny Hatcher who he had seen clerking at the general store.

Self-consciously, Benjamin said, "You should either have picked a better dance partner or worn big boots to protect your feet. I do pretty good a-horseback but somehow the dance floor has always gotten the better of me. Do you want to quit?"

"I'll let you know when I want to quit, Mr. Stanton."

Benjamin smiled down at her. "Alright then. Until you start crying out in pain, I'll just carry on enjoying my time with you."

Penny's response was to tighten her grip on his hand just a little.

Across the floor, Sam and Miss Granet were having a grand time, whirling and stepping. Sam appeared to be completely at ease on the dance floor. If the truth was to be known, Benjamin was just a bit jealous of his younger brother.

After bobbing and ducking several times to avoid Miss Granet's hat brim, Sam started to laugh.

"Is my dancing that comical, Mr. Stanton?"

"Your dancing is marvelous and not a bit comical, Miss Granet. But avoiding your hat brim has become a bit of a challenge. About two more swipes and I'm likely to have to explain myself when the crew sees my cut-up face in the morning." His smile helped him through this potential minefield of misunderstanding.

"Lead me to my table, Mr. Stanton, and we can fix that. I should have done it before." At the table, Miss Granet reached to the back of the hat and withdrew a pin that was just short of being a serious potential weapon. The hat was soon safely placed on the table.

Sam looked at the pin and then at Miss Granet. "Now that I know you have that pin available on quick notice, I will have to watch for signs that you intend to reach for it."

"I won't reach for it without being given clear cause."

"That means I can probably relax a bit more when you aren't wearing a hat."

She wove the pin back into her hair and smiled mischievously. "I always wear a hat, Mr. Stanton, or at least the hat pin."

Sam grinned and the happy couple swung back into the fray.

Wanda danced with just one other young man during the evening. The opportunity arose only because Hamilton insisted he had to check on his horse. He was back before the next tune started and again he and Wanda were dancing together.

Big Bob had moved hardly a muscle since the dance started. He just sat and stared out at the dance floor like a man in a trance. Mrs. Stanton had watched him when she was able to tear her eyes from Wanda and Hamilton. Finally, she leaned over and whispered to her husband, "You can't control everything in this world, Bob. You're going to have a seizure if you don't relax. Why don't we dance?"

Big Bob barely looked at her. "Don't want to dance."

"We used to dance well together. Don't you remember?"

Her husband remained silent so Mrs. Stanton leaned back in her chair and watched the dancers.

As the evening started coming to a close, Hamilton hesitated in his thoughts but finally spoke, "I have my buggy here this evening. May I drive you home?"

Wanda nodded towards where her parents were seated. "I've never seen a volcano but I did see a picture of one once. It seemed to be causing a lot of damage to the land around and it was puffing great clouds of steam into the air. Best we leave well enough alone and not push Pa any more than we already have."

"I had completely forgotten about your father," Hamilton lied.

"Sure you have." Wanda laughed. "Let's make this our last dance. I have really enjoyed our evening but I don't suppose I have made even a single friend among the girls, monopolizing you all evening. Not that I really care too much."

Then, mimicking the voice of one of the town girls, Wanda said, "But I do declare, you make the very, very best honey baked ham in the whole wide world. Why, I declare…"

She was stopped by Hamilton. "Hush, someone will hear you. And you have no idea how tired I get hearing that."

They both laughed.

"Actually, your ham is really quite good. What else do you cook?"

"That's for another time. The dance is going to end and I want to thank you for the best evening of my life. I look forward to doing it again. And I really would like to call on you as I told you so undiplomatically that time on the range."

"Let's leave that for a while yet. Pa's under enough pressure without us adding to it. I'll see you at church and we can visit a bit. Right now, I want to get Pa onto the dance floor for this last dance. He is really quite a good dancer but there he sits like a lump, acting foolish. Wish me luck."

"I do and, again, thank you for the evening."

11

Amos Watkins looked over at Walter Howard at the meeting of the whittlers and checkers players. "Whatcha hoping that stick will look like when you call 'er quits on the carv'n, Sheriff? Ain't never seen you whittl'n before. Scares me a bit watching you handle that knife. I thought about moving my chair over a mite just for safety, you understand, but I know how easy your feelings are hurt so I sat here and toughed it out."

Jimmy, the bartender, couldn't resist. "Sheriffs don't have feelings, Amos, you ought to of known that without I had to remind you."

Clark Ransom reached over and slapped the sheriff on the back. "Yep, Jimmy, you got that right. Right as rain. Cold, these lawmen, almighty cold. Lock their own mothers up for jaywalking."

The sheriff tried to look serious and managed it but for a slight twitching of his mustache. "Jaywalking ain't no laughing matter, what with the town full of families in wagons and rowdy cowboys racing around. Can't ever be too careful."

Homer Plantz joined the ribbing. "I don't agree with that thing about no feelings. Why, just last week I saw our very own sheriff helping the widow Jamison across the street, him carrying her purchases, too, and stowing them in the back of her buggy. Looked almighty caring to me. Mind you, he looked over his shoulder a time or two towards his own house. We'll never know for sure but he might have been watching for his missus."

The men all burst into laughter with Homer finally finishing the story. "Of course, the widow Jamison is a fine-looking woman. I expect a lot of men would have helped her with her carrying if Walter hadn't been so quick on the draw."

Hamilton figured it was a good time to change the subject. "Not much left of the summer, men. Up on my higher ground there's a for sure nip in the air most mornings. Fall com'n soon with frost and snow and cold on the way. I'm pretty much ready. Got some garden to get out yet and that field of oats to harvest out. I've got it stocked and ready. Stanke is a little late with that harvesting machine of his this year but it's only a good day's work to get my little patch done so I expect it'll all work out yet."

Amos Watkins couldn't resist offering some advice. "That thing with the garden, Hamilton. Rightly that's woman's work. Don't hardly seem right you having to do that. Now I've been considering...."

But he was interrupted by Jimmy the bartender, "How many times do I have to tell you boys? Hamilton's a gone goose. Has been since spring. You all should ought to know that. It's way too late for your scheming."

Clark acted as if this little interlude had never occurred. He nodded in agreement to Hamilton's earlier statements and spit in the general direction of the brass spittoon. "Seems I spend all fall splitting firewood, fencing in haystacks, and patching up wind damage on the roofs. Got too danged many roofs. House, barn, shed, smoke-house, tool shop, outhouse. Too danged many roofs to keep up, what with the wind pulling at the shingles the way it does. Come fall, I seem to spend half my time up on a ladder."

Jimmy offered to get a work party together to take off a couple of the roofs to lighten Clark's workload, maybe tear down a building or two to eliminate the need for roofing.

Clark gave the bartender a withering look. "That might not be altogether the best solution."

Tiny Shaw entered the conversation, "Alright year for hay. Got mine up in pretty good condition in spite of the rain. I ran down kinda tight this last spring. I need a short winter this year to maybe have a little left over for next year. I don't like running right down to my last stack."

Clark looked over at Hamilton. "You're a full year ahead on hay. Good position to be in. I haven't been over your way for some time. How did the haying go for the Circle S?"

"They didn't put up any hay. Don't see as how it's necessary."

The gathering of whittlers fell silent in wonder, looking at Hamilton.

Finally, Clark spoke into the silence, "Well, it'll take a miracle but I hope for their sakes that we have a mild and open winter. Wouldn't plan on it though. Only saw one completely open winter in the sixteen years I've been here. Some winters are easier than others but mostly I plan on snow and cold."

Tiny seemed to speak for the group, "Their problem, I guess."

Clark wasn't finished with his thoughts, "Mighty big problem with that many cows on the range."

Again, Hamilton changed the subject. "I'm driving a wagon up to Stovall's place in a few days to load up on coal. Might make two or three trips. A few of us could go and work together if any of you had a mind to."

Clark reluctantly acknowledged that he needed coal. "Ain't exactly my favorite task of the year. Still and all, one wagon of coal is as good as two or three wagons of wood and I don't have to cut and split it. Just dig'er up and there you go."

Other neighbors would join in on the trip when the news got around.

Tiny grinned over at Clark. "You going to take a stick or two of dynamite with you? Might lessen the digging chore."

Everyone laughed at Clark's expense, remembering his single effort at working with the explosive.

Jimmy stopped laughing long enough to say, "I hear tell there's still rocks and stumps flying around up there. You got to be careful and be ready to duck."

Clark suffered through the remainder of the laughter, knowing these same men would offer fierce protection if any stranger were to laugh the same way.

The coal wasn't right on Stovall's land. He had stumbled on the outcrop when he was exploring the foothills behind his ranch. Each fall, a steady passage of wagons carried men with picks and shovels intent on laying in a load or two of the black gold, knowing it made for a hotter and longer fire than split wood.

A couple of men from town had tried to open a coal mine a few years previous but there weren't enough customers to keep it going so the coal was available to anyone with a wagon and a shovel.

Walt, the livery man who had so far remained silent,

asked, "All you boys got your herds driven up to your wintering yard?"

There was general assent around the table that the biggest portion of the cattle was on close-in grass.

Clark said, "We'll have to take another ride up the mountain to get the stragglers off the public range. Never seen the beat of how those critters can lose themselves in the brush up there. Can't hardly ever be really sure that we haven't missed some. I'll be wanting to dig out the last of them before we make the drive to market."

It was left to Hamilton to organize the run for coal and to Tiny to organize the annual market drive to the railhead at Cheyenne.

Tiny sent a message down to Cheyenne asking when cattle cars would be available. When the answer came back, he made a circuit of the ranchers who intended sending animals down and arranged a date for the drive.

Rancher Russ Skidmore agreed to have his gather-ready but then asked, "Given any more thought to using the siding on the Denver line? Those loading pens are two days closer than Cheyenne."

Russ brought up this discussion every year and the answer was always the same. "There's no buyers there and no stores. We get the best prices when there's two or three buyers in competition. Anyway, I wouldn't want to be the one to try to tell the ladies that we weren't going to the big city. They take that as being close kin to a matter of life and death. Don't fully understand that myself but I'm not going to be the one to challenge it."

WHEN THE DAY for the drive arrived, there were just over four thousand head gathered from eleven ranches held on grass on the outskirts of Canyon View. Most of the cattle were driven in the day before and had been held close, ready for a sunrise start. A couple of herds would join along the way as the travelers passed neighboring ranches.

Jody, the banker's eleven-year-old son, looked over the dinner table at his mother. "Pa says it's alright with him if I go on the drive. All the other boys are going."

"Your Pa said that, did he? I may have a thing or two to say to him when we're alone. Anyway, I hardly think that every single boy in town is going. Is Hector going?"

"Ma, Hector can't do anything or go anywhere. That old maid aunt of his is worse than a prison guard. She's got 'no' coming out of her mouth before the question is even asked. But the other guys are going."

Jody's father came to his rescue. "There are a lot of boys going, dear, and it isn't like there won't be adults along. As far as that goes, there's still time for you to go along on a wagon and help with the cooking. You could even do a little shopping in Cheyenne."

"I can do my shopping right here."

Jody waited another few moments. "So, I can go, Ma?"

His mother said nothing and he took her silence as permission. He jumped up. "Excuse me from the table please." Not waiting for an answer, he was out the door with a whoop.

The next morning after fidgeting and half-listening through the expected final lectures, the town boys saddled up their mounts, screwed their hats down tight and made their way to the gathering. Jody was surprised to see his friend Hector ride up, grinning till it looked as if his face would split. "You coming with us? What happened?"

"I don't rightly know what happened. All's I know is that I saw your pa talking with my aunt on the street last evening and this morning she said I had better take some warm clothes and to be careful."

The boys rode together to the herd, barely holding in their excitement.

The Circle S didn't add any animals or riders to the sale herd although the invitation had been carried to them by Pastor Brockton.

The sale herd was too large and unwieldy for a long drive and the fences along the way would force the animals into a long, narrow line. But for the few miles involved it could be handled. The years of the roundups and the long cattle drives were long past. Now all the land was fenced and many ranches had no hired cowboys at all, the owner and his family being able to manage their herds themselves.

A crowd came out to watch the spectacle. As Tiny lifted his hat into the air and raised his booming voice, hollering, "Mo-oove 'em out," a cheer arose from the gathered watchers.

The men held back a bit, allowing the boys to raise the herd off the bed grounds. The drovers urged the boys on, remembering the excitement of their own youth.

One of the drovers looked over at the Reverend Brockton. "You coming, Rev?"

"Always do, Earl, always do. Someone's got to come along and keep y'all from falling into temptation."

"You might have noticed, Rev, that my wife is riding the chuck wagon. She takes that temptation thing as a solemn duty. But you might want to keep an eye on Hamilton. I do believe he has a wild side barely hidden from view."

They both laughed at that idea.

Town men stood with their wives and kids as the drovers moved the cattle off the bed grounds. Given half a chance, several of the men would have saddled up and gone along but their town jobs and businesses didn't give them that much freedom.

Along the single street that outlined the west side of Canyon View, the women held lace-fringed hankies over their noses to ward off the dust. The little girls copied their mothers while the younger boys ran, whooping and hollering, along beside the drive, worrying their mothers who feared for their safety while causing their fathers to smile in remembrance.

They stretched the drive into three slow days, letting the cattle graze the fence lines along the way.

The distance for the first day's drive was a short eight miles, ending when they reached a small bulrush slough that some called a lake, the only source of water for many a mile.

THE LADIES who were determined to see the lights of the big city, clutching shopping lists and hard-earned dollars in their pocketbooks, worked together to load several wagons with food and bedding along with what they needed for their personal comfort. They set out an hour earlier than the herd to avoid the dust and traveled faster so they had no trouble being prepared for the drovers when the herd arrived at the lake campsite.

Mrs. Ransom had again taken charge. "I'll dig a fire pit over there. Back those two grub wagons up here and then get those teams out of my kitchen."

Hours later the meal was eaten, bedrolls laid out, and an evening of visiting enjoyed.

Tiny brought his coffee and sat down beside Hamilton. "Your stuff looks good, Hamilton. What's your count?"

"I culled the herd a bit more deeply than I did last year, sorting out the dry cows and a couple that had failed to hold their weight. I can't afford to feed animals that don't perform. With those and the fed steers, there's just over five hundred. I kept back the best of the young heifers as replacement stock."

"Some of those heifers going to be available?"

"I'll sell maybe half of them. Are you thinking of moving into white-faced animals?"

Tiny waved his coffee cup in the general direction of the herd. "It don't take a genius to see that those animals of yours are better in every respect. I'd have to be a fool to not consider it. I'll come down next week and we can bargain a bit on those heifers."

Hamilton had arranged for the shipping of two new bulls from a breeder back east, the delivery of them to match the timing of the fall drive.

Seventeen-year-old Adam Blossom was driving one of Hamilton's teams, pulling a high-sided grain wagon which had been rigged out for hauling the new bulls back to the H-R.

The drive was uneventful until the afternoon of the last day when one of the boys somehow managed to spook a Longhorn steer. With a rattling of horns and a good bit of bellowing, the herd took off running. The men swept in and pushed the boys to the sides and to safety before taking after the cattle.

Looking on from his position in the drag, Clark leaned over and spit on the fore-hoof of Amos Watkins' horse. "Danged Longhorns seem to spend most of their lives looking for something to frighten thairselves with. I suppose we better catch up, seeing as how your and my animals both are in that bunch."

Hamilton's short-legged, white-faced animals were in no mood to run and were soon left behind. The boys gathered around them again while the men took after the wilder Longhorns.

The herd had only been about one mile from the stock

pens when the animals started to run. The men were content to keep them heading in the right direction and let them go. A shout at the pens had men rushing to swing gates open and then dive out of the way. The cattle ran right into the pens and milled around in the dust as if they were wondering what had happened.

After the gates were swung closed and the dust started to settle, the railroad foreman lifted his hat and scratched his head. "Never seen it just exactly like that before, boys, but I must admit you got 'er done."

A half-hour later, the boys slowly drove Hamilton's gather into another pen. With the pen gate closed and their work done, they sat on their hipshot horses trying their best to look like what they thought a cowboy ought to look, thumbed their hats to the backs of their heads and grinned at each other. There never was a happier bunch of boys.

Hamilton rode over to them. "Well done, men. You did it just exactly right. You took good care of my animals and I want to thank you."

The boys beamed with deserved pride. Hamilton gave them each two silver dollars and turned them loose on the town. He expected there'd be a hard run on the ice cream parlor.

The cattle were soon in rail cars and headed across the Wyoming and Nebraska plains. Prices were a little better than what had been expected. Several of the ranchers listened as the buyers put a value on Hamilton's white-faced brutes. It was considerably better than for their long-legged Longhorn crosses. Several ranchers were seen glancing at each other as if questioning why they were still raising Longhorns.

There was time enough left in the day to see some of

the sights of Cheyenne and to make some purchases. The ladies wasted no time heading downtown.

The next morning, finishing up breakfast before the sun was fully up, the crew rigged out their horses and harnessed the wagon teams readying for the trip home. The ride back would be spread over a leisurely two days. The men would visit, talking of cattle and range conditions, while the boys would ride on ahead reliving the adventure, their stories becoming more exciting with each telling.

Backing the wagon up to one of the loading chutes, a few of the men helped Hamilton load the two new bulls and tie their halters securely to the wagon box. He would be at least three days getting back to home range with the cumbersome load.

Clark sat his horse a few feet away. "Never seen the like, giving a bull brute a ride in a wagon. Don't know as how I'd want a yard full of bulls that can't walk down a road on their own four feet."

Hamilton looked down from the height of the wagon. "I didn't buy them for their walking ability."

Tiny glanced over at the gathering of women and boys who were listening. "We could probably discuss that more in-depth some other time, boys."

Tiny then addressed the gathering. "That was a good ride and a good drive, men. The animals got here in fine shape and so did we thanks to the ladies who went ahead with the grub wagon and fixed those great meals. And you young fellows made yourselves and your folks proud the past few days. Don't forget to share some of that hard rock candy I see bulging out your saddlebags.

"We'll leave Hamilton and his bull wagon behind now though. It's a long ride but there's still no reason we can't be home and in our own beds tomorrow night. So my thanks to everyone again. Why don't you lead us out and set the pace, Clark?"

Adam was just gathering the team's reins on the bull wagon when Rev. Brockton rode up. "I wouldn't mind getting out of this saddle for a few hours. Mind if I join you for a bit? I'll have to get back in the saddle later if I'm to catch up with the others but that wagon seat sure looks welcoming." The reverend had learned long before that there were many ways to influence a man. Making friends was a good start.

"Glad for the company," answered the young man.

HAMILTON HAD HIRED two other Blossom kids, fifteen-year-old Johnnie and fourteen-year-old Clarissa, to milk his cow, gather the eggs and generally keep an eye on his place. He was rather enjoying the leisurely fall ride although everyone was wary of the nip in the air and the fresh snow they could see on the highest peaks off to the west.

Clark was the first to enter the general store after depositing his check in the bank. He wasn't a man given to smiling much but he smiled at the storekeeper and waved a blank check at him. "Pull that account book out, my friend, and let's settle up. Cattle prices in Cheyenne were a bit better than I expected. It'll feel good to get this account and a couple of others in town dealt with. You'll probably have a bunch of checks to deposit today or tomorrow when the boys get around to settling up."

IN TOWN AS WELL AS ON THE RANCHES, GARDENS WERE harvested and stored in Mason jars or in root cellars. Winter woolens were brought out and aired on the clothes lines to rid them of the odor of mothballs. New, warm clothing was purchased for the older children, the younger ones scrambling to get their pick of the pass-me-down pieces. Canyon View was readying itself for winter.

Several ranchers rode up to the community pasture intent on digging out the dam the Circle S had built. The shortage of graze had forced most of the ranchers to drive their cattle home the previous month, weeks earlier than they did most years. But each year a few critters managed to avoid the riders, finding shelter in the brush, necessitating another trip for the men.

Amos Watkins cast a sad look over the dry creek bed and the surrounding grasslands. The dugout behind the dam was nothing more than sun-dried, hoof-marked clay with no water in sight. The grass had been eaten almost to the roots. "Don't know for sure that this will even recover next spring. We may have to lay off this graze for a season.

What kind of a fool would do this to the land that feeds us?"

Clark pulled his gray gelding up beside the dam and looked at the dry creek bed and its crumbling banks. Folding his hands on the saddle horn, he leaned forward and spat a brown stream into the dust. He was starting to get mad and he didn't like the feeling, knowing where it could lead. "Might just as well round up the few critters still left up here and take them home, else they're liable to starve down to hide and hair. No water, not a blade of grass. Never saw the like. Best we drive them out before they paw up the roots."

Amos stepped to the ground and untied his shovel from behind the saddle. "Come on, Tiny, grab your shovel and give me a hand. The rest of you boys see what cattle you can find. Do me some good to shovel for a bit. Might work off some of my mad."

As the riders spread out to search for cattle, Amos and Tiny went to work. After a half-hour of digging, Tiny leaned on his shovel. "Ain't rightly much of a dam or much of a creek when you really look at it altogether. And when you consider how much this little bit of water means to the animals down below, it's a bit worrisome how easy it was for one man to change it all. Were he of a mind to that Texan could make a real nuisance of himself."

Amos good-naturedly threw a shovel full of dirt on Tiny's boots. "What worries me is that you're leaning on that shovel talking while I'm alone here working up a sweat. Ain't no more water coming down this creek till spring. We'll deal with it then."

A few hours later, the dirt dam was gone and the other riders had returned with thirty-five or forty head of stock. There were brands from several ranches represented including a few Circle S.

Clark's anger had grown with every mile he rode seeing the dried out and devastated grassland. "These poor brutes have been gnawing willow bark. There's no grass left that's worth talking about. We'd better come up again tomorrow and do a more thorough search. A cow critter ain't smart enough to come home by its own self. They're more likely to stand in the dirt and beller till they starve.

"But we're going to drive this bunch home through the Circle S even though it's the long way about and we're going to have a talk with that Texan. We'll keep it peaceable but he needs to understand that this doesn't happen again. He's taken full advantage of our neighborliness but that ends today. He has to be told that."

The gathered men looked at each other. Knowing Clark Ransom, they weren't so sure it would stay peaceful.

Two hours later, a Circle S rider hollered over to Big Bob, "Cattle coming in, boss."

Several men stopped their work to look. Big Bob and Benjamin came from the barn, walked to the end of the corral and watched the cattle being driven into the yard.

"What's the meaning of this?" hollered Big Bob.

The men remained silent until they were even with the corral and then Tiny spoke out, hoping to keep his friend Clark out of a fight. "Got the last of the critters from off the mountain including a few of yours. Were you to open that gate we'll cut out the Circle S for you."

When those few animals were safely in the corral and the gate closed, Clark heeled his horse forward until Big Bob tried to move out of the way. Clark's animal cut him off like a runaway calf. He urged his horse forward until it had shouldered Big Bob hard against the corral rails. The Circle S owner was so angry he could only sputter.

Finally, Benjamin stepped over angrily. "Hold up there, mister. What do y'all think you're doin?"

Clark gave him a withering look, leaned over and spat, and said, "What I'm doing is trying to get his attention. We need to talk about land, and water, and cattle, and neighborliness, and he's going to listen."

Big Bob managed to say, "Back off. One word from me and you'll be shot out of your saddle. Back off, I say."

"You set your riders to shoot'n, mister, they'd better do a good job. You simply don't want me and the boys here hunt'n hide. I've hunted hide more times than you ever will and sometimes I miss the action. Now you shut up and listen."

Big Bob had never really looked at Clark before. Now he did. What he saw was a tough old man half again his own age, honed down by wind and heat until just the rawhide was left. His nearly bald head was covered with a misshapen hat that might once have been white. His wide shoulders were encased in a sun-faded shirt; one pocket weighed down with a bar of chew. Canvas pants were tucked into run-over boots with big-wheeled spurs. He held his reins with his left hand, his broken knuckles showing, while his right hand rested within inches of his Colt. Big Bob looked into his eyes and didn't see an ounce of back-up or an ounce of mercy.

Benjamin and the crew didn't know what to do, seeing that this could end with a lot of hurt if they pulled their sidearms. Most of the visiting riders were also armed.

Dalton, one of the Circle S riders, thinking he was hidden behind a horse, pulled his Colt and tried to sidle up to Clark's horse. A single step from Tiny's roan placed him within arm's length. The big man reached down and wrapped his hand around the gunman's hand, gun and all, and squeezed. Dalton gasped in pain and fell to his knees. Tiny continued to squeeze.

Sam and Wanda arrived about that time, running from

the house, their mother walking fast several steps behind. Wanda looked over the gathered riders as if she was looking for one man in particular. Not seeing him, she continued her hurried walk to the corral.

Sam stepped up to Clark's side and pleaded, "Please back off, Mr. Ransom. Whatever this is about, you've made your point."

Clark glanced at Sam and then at Big Bob. He eased his horse off a step or two and Big Bob sagged to the ground gasping for breath, mixed anger and fear showing on his face.

Clark stepped out of his saddle as Benjamin and Wanda rushed to their father's side. He squatted on his heals so close to Big Bob that their noses could have touched. He pushed his finger into Big Bob's chest. "Now, mister Texas big shot, you're going to listen."

No one could have misunderstood Clark's message. In just a few words he told Big Bob about neighbors, living together and helpfulness. He spoke of water rights and grass and public range. And he talked about the foolishness of range wars. He explained that they had backed off this one summer hoping the Circle S would see reason. He made it very clear that they would never back off again. "You think we're weak because we didn't come at you with guns blazing. Son, I was behind a blazing gun when you were still sucking your thumb and hiding behind your mother's skirts. I ain't forgot nothing I learned back then but I'd just as soon let 'er lie. But you'd be wrong to take that as weakness.

"Now you understand this: No one puts animals on that upper range until the grass comes in strong again. No one. Not you nor me nor anyone else. We'll decide together when the time is right. And then you put no more animals on than what we all agree to. Your range is overstocked by double but you're not going to make it up at our expense, not ever again."

Clark leaned away and spat without taking his eye off Big Bob. "Do you understand all of this or should I go over it again?"

Ben helped his father to his feet and then looked over at Clark. "We heard and we understand. We may have more to say on this later but for now it's done."

Clark swung effortlessly back into his saddle and gathered his reins. Before he turned to leave he said, "Any animals still hiding out in the brush up top ain't going to make it through the winter. A few of us are riding back that way tomorrow to make a final sweep. If one or two of you Circle S boys want to join us, you'd be welcome. If you were to come thinking of more than finding stock, I advise you to rethink it."

He turned to go and the rest of the neighbors moved the cattle out, heading them for their home ranges.

Tiny looked over at Clark. "Sure glad we managed to keep that friendly."

Several of the other men chuckled but offered no further thoughts.

By the time the men had done their ranch chores the next morning and ridden up the mountain trail, the sun was noon high in the sky. They arrived at the site of the dirt dam to find three Circle S riders waiting for them. Clark pushed his horse to the front and made a point of looking at Dalton and the gun resting in its holster on his belt.

Dalton got the message. "We're armed like always but don't you read anything else into that. We're here to hunt Circle S animals, nothing more. You have our word on that. Don't know as how I could do more anyway the way that big gorilla treated my hand yesterday."

Tiny grinned at him. "Another time or another place, you would have been dead."

Clark was leaning on his saddle horn. "Where's your boss?"

"Big Bob and his two boys have ridden further up the hill. Bob always left the herding up to us. He's never seen the upper ranges so he's gone up to take him a look. We'll probably run into them by-and-by."

Clark turned to Tiny. "Tiny, how about you divide us into three groups and lay out the search? Won't do much good if we all cover the same ground."

Tiny made up three groups, placing a Circle S rider with each one. They never did catch up with Big Bob but by midafternoon they figured the twenty-seven head they had were all they were going to find. They met back at the dirt dam site and cut out the Circle S animals. Dalton's group headed home with six sorry-looking Longhorns while the remaining bunch were driven the other way through Clark's home place.

During the mountaintop search, the riders had come within a few paces of Big Bob and the two boys but Bob chose not to be seen. The Stanton men had stepped behind a rock outcropping until the searchers were gone. Bob had seen much on the ride and had it all to think about but he didn't want to answer any questions until he had considered the day's events. When they were alone again, they stepped down from their saddles and tied their horses to some mountain shrubbery. Sam pulled a paper sack of sandwiches from his saddlebag and they sat to eat their lunch. They had little to say while they ate.

Finally, Ben asked, "What're you thinking, Pa?"

Bob was silent for a long time, chewing the last of the sandwich. "I think this is good mountain range. I'd like to have it all for the Circle S."

Knowing what this range meant to the other ranchers and what Clark had told Big Bob just the day before, Sam was appalled by his father's words. He shook his head and looked at the ground but said nothing.

Ben was also looking at the ground, avoiding his father's eyes. "Pretty eaten down, Pa. Don't know how we can avoid taking our share of the blame and Ransom may be right. This grass is going to be a while coming back. And I don't like the looks of those spots of bare earth where the rain started little runs and gullies. Could be considerable damage with the spring snow melt."

Big Bob wasn't in the mood to admit to anything. "We'll see come spring who's to get the use of this land."

Sam couldn't hold back his feeling or his words, "I love and respect you, Pa, but sometimes I'm embarrassed, too. There's some things you just don't understand. Taking care of the range that we depend on for our livelihood is one of them. We ruined the range in Texas and now we're doing it again here.

"Getting along with folks is another."

He stood and stepped into his saddle, leaving his father and brother alone on the grazed-down mountain meadow.

THE YEAR'S FIRST FREEZE CAME ON OCTOBER FIFTH; THE first snow on October tenth. Neither lasted longer than it took to give a taste of what was yet to come but it was a warning. If looking at the calendar hadn't rushed the preparations for winter, the fall of snow did.

Adam Blossom rode up to the barn when he saw Hamilton working there. "Pa says this snow won't last, that we still have some weeks of fall yet to come. I sure hope he's right. I'm not particularly fond of the cold although I will admit that I don't miss the flies or the mosquitoes, either one. They sure disappear with the first frost."

"Most folks would agree with you, Adam. How is the fall work coming over home?"

"Ma's got the most of the root crops dealt with. The potatoes, carrots, turnips, beets and such are all dug up and stored in the root cellar with Pa and me doing all the heavy lifting. Ma's got enough Mason jars filled to feed the entire valley I think but she's bound and determined that we need every one of them."

"She might be right, Adam. I've put up a few myself and that's not my favorite activity.

"How would you like to tie that horse somewhere and hold these animals as I pull off their shoes? I don't need to be feeding these spare horses when they can paw through the snow and fend for themselves. We'll pull the shoes and turn them loose in the barn pasture. We'll do the same for two of the heavy teams. There's lots of grass out there and I have hay for them if needed.

"I'll keep that team of blacks and a couple of saddle horses in the barn. The milk cow, too. The barn temperature will be a long ways from hot but the animals' body heat at least keeps the air inside above freezing.

"I've got to catch the chickens and bring them in before freeze-up. They love the freedom of the barn but the miserable things seem to delight in hiding their eggs. Still, after getting by on frozen eggs most of my first year here, I'd rather do it this way."

HAMILTON HAD SEEN nothing of the Circle S cowboys or Big Bob but he had visited with Wanda and her mother at church a few times. The visits were brief and nothing serious was discussed. The hoped-for invite to the Circle S failed to materialize.

Christmas was a quiet time for Hamilton with no decorating done and just the one gift to purchase. The general store was not noted for its supply of books for sale but Hamilton found a little book of poetry almost hidden under a pile of lady's magazines.

Penny picked it off the counter and smiled. "Can I wrap this a bit special for you?"

Hamilton grinned in an attempt to hide his embarrassment. "Thank you. I'd appreciate that."

At the church Christmas concert Hamilton talked briefly with Wanda over a cup of eggnog. "I got you a little something that I hope you can enjoy. Slip it into your reticule and open it later."

Wanda thanked him with a smile and a very brief but lingering touch on his arm.

The new calendar hanging on Hamilton's wall said it was 1888. Like most folks, he wondered what this New Year would bring for him and the folks of Canyon View. Would there be prosperity or hardship? Would there be health or illness? And most importantly, would there be Wanda or would he still be alone?

The first serious, powdery dry snow started falling on January fifth. As the sun slowly moved across the sky, the snow became heavier and the wind started to blow from the southeast, pushing the snow into drifts. As the winds increased, the snow was driven through every crack or opening in houses, barns and businesses. Parents and children alike were put to work stuffing rags and rolled-up paper into openings in an attempt to block the wind and stop the snow.

In the late evening, the wind swung around to the northwest directly off the Rockies and the snow began falling in earnest. By the morning of January seventh, two feet of snow had fallen. In areas that were not sheltered and where the wind held free reign, the drifts were mountainous. The driving wind piled the snow into madly-sculpted heaps hammered firm enough to walk over if anyone was foolish enough to be out walking. And still the snow fell.

The H-R ranch yard was sheltered just a bit by a stand of trees. The pasture enjoyed no such shelter. There the cleared area was open to the full blast of the storm.

Arriving at the pasture in the early morning to feed his

cattle, Hamilton's eyes and nose were nearly instantly filled with the driven snow. Opening his mouth to breathe, the bitter cold struck his teeth like a hammer blow. Turning a corner in the fence line, the full blast of the wind felt as if it would suck the air right out of his lungs. He tugged his woolen scarf up to cover mouth and nose, making breathing a little easier.

His horse staggered to a stop and attempted to turn back but a firm hand on the reins held him steady.

His short-legged dog ran and leaped and burrowed trying to keep up with Hamilton. "I should have left you in the barn."

The haystacks created just a bit of shelter from the wind. A few animals were bunched up next to the fence in the lee of that shelter. Others were grazing in the few places where the wind had scalped the pasture clear of snow. Most were standing listlessly, tails to the wind with driven snow clinging to their backs.

There is no easy way to count six hundred cows plus an almost equal number of weanling calves. Hamilton wasn't sure if they were all there or not. But an almost covered-over trail through the snow told him that a few head might have wandered off. It took over an hour of brutally hard work to throw hay to the bunch at the stacks and then he went in search of the strays.

He found them crowded up in a fence corner with their tails to the wind. They had pushed three cows into the fence until the poor, suffering brutes had collapsed to their knees.

"No one ever said you brutes were smart. How in all the world am I going to get you out of there, standing in three feet of snow with the wind howling such that I can't even throw a rope?"

Hamilton spurred his gelding through the fresh snow,

making a trail to the huddled cattle. Getting close enough, he managed to reach out and drop a loop over the horns of the closest animal. Turning his horse, he spurred away from the fence line. The red and white brute on the other end of the rope followed stiffly. He pulled until the cow was well onto the pasture and then repeated the process for the other animals. He drove those few up to the feed and then went back for the downers.

It took him the full of an hour to get those three up on their feet and then driven to the feed. He fed them separately, away from the competition of the herd.

He stoked up the remains of the fire in the barrel water heater and added coal. Even with the heater there was ice forming around the edges furthest away from the fire.

When the feeding was completed, he rode his horse to the barn and gave it a good rubdown and a pail of oats.

By the time he was back in the house, Hamilton was exhausted and chilled right through his heavy woolens. It sobered him to think that this chore would be repeated morning and evening for all the months of winter. In past years he had thought a few times about hiring a man but his cabin wasn't really set up for a hired hand and he didn't look forward to the thought of the extra cooking.

Except for longing for the woman he couldn't have, he was really quite content to be alone. The thought of spending twenty-four hours a day with a hired hand didn't appeal at all.

Besides all that, when the weather was reasonably mild and the snow not too deep, Hamilton easily kept up with the work. With the hope that this storm would be a short one, he pushed the thought of hired help to the back of his mind.

That afternoon the temperature began to drop. Even with the wind and the snow the temperature had been fairly tolerable but within hours the land was in a deep freeze, the likes of which the locals had never seen before. Even in the foothills of the Rockies the temperature drop usually comes slowly over a day or two and with moderate wind. On that afternoon, the Arctic air was driven in by a howling, screaming wind carrying falling and drifting snow with it. Visibility dropped almost to nothing as the swirling snow blocked out what little light leaked through the dark clouds. The dropping temperature seemed to have no bottom to it.

People caught outside found themselves blinded by the blowing snow. It was a struggle to keep their directions. The situation was even worse many miles to the east where the land was open prairie and the wind-blocking hills were few.

Many lost their way in the freezing whiteout. Some staggered barely alive into homes or barns or whatever shelter they could find. A school teacher caught by the storm as she walked home buried herself in a straw stack. She was found there, frozen, several days later. Some were lost completely and were not found until the spring thaw exposed the carnage of that awful night but none of that would be known until after the storm broke.

Benjamin and Sam Stanton had gone to town. The trip wasn't an absolute necessity but the women had been talking about being short of some things in the kitchen if they were going to be snowed in for a few days. Ever since the boys had met Penny and Miss Granet at the dance, they had taken every opportunity no matter how flimsy to get to town. They rode in, hoping for a visit with the girls.

Benjamin, a sack of groceries in his hand, turned to say goodbye to Penny.

She turned from looking out the front window of the general store. "Don't try for home, Ben. You and Sam need to put up at the hotel and wait out the storm. You probably don't have any real idea what a Rocky Mountain storm can look like and I've never seen one worse than this. You go get a room."

"That's good advice, young man."

Ben and Sam both looked at the storekeeper.

"It's not but a few miles to home and the folks will be worried. We'll be alright."

The storekeeper leaned on his counter and pointed his pipe out the window. "There's just no way to describe forty below, boys. Unless you've felt it you just can't know. The wind at those temperatures will freeze your lungs and penetrate the warmest clothing as if you were naked. It'll freeze your feet inside leather boots more quickly than you can tell about it. Your hands and fingers will turn stiff unless they're well protected. Bare skin freezes in minutes. Penny's right. You might want to take notice that there's no one on the street. They're all gone home to hunker down for the night."

Sam looked worried but Ben grinned at Penny. "I appreciate your concern but don't you worry about us. It'll take more than a bit of weather to slow us down."

The storekeeper, Penny standing beside him, watched the two young men disappear into the blowing snow.

Nearing the livery barn to get their horses, Ben shouted over the scream of the wind, "We'd better make for home, little brother. This is shaping up like to be a real doozer."

"It's already a doozer. Can't see the length of my arm. Penny's right, Ben. Be foolish to head out home in this. We'd best hunker down and wait it out. I'm going to try to find my way over to the schoolhouse. Those kids nor Miss Granet, neither one, should be heading out in this. They might need help. You go back and get a hotel room. I'll join you there."

Benjamin, still hollering over the wind, pulled his hat down tightly on his head, "No, I'm for getting home. The folks will be worried. You do what you have a mind to do."

"You can't make it, Ben. You can't even see the road. And it's cold, almighty cold. We just aren't set up for this weather. I'm freezing already and we haven't been outside ten minutes. Don't you go, Ben. People are going to die out there tonight; don't you be one of them."

"That's a good horse I'm riding. We'll make out. I'll see you at home."

Sam stood and watched Benjamin heading for the livery. He was lost to sight within a few steps. He studied his own footsteps in the snow and took a direction from there to where the schoolhouse stood two blocks away. Turning to his left, he looked again at the footprints in the snow to reassure himself and stepped out towards the school. He could see nothing but white. The wind-whipped snow lashed every piece of exposed skin and drove snow into his eyes making it almost impossible to look where he was going. Every few steps, he turned and examined his footprints hoping he would be able to tell if he was curving off course. Within minutes, he was so cold he found it difficult to think.

Step by slow step he headed in as straight a line as his senses would allow. Even then he almost walked right past the school building. It was the smell of wood smoke that brought him up looking. A swirling wind whipped around the end of the unseen school carrying smoke with it. It came from his right. Slowly and carefully, he paced off his steps in that direction. He wanted to be able to get back to his original path if he didn't find the building. He was fully aware that if he missed the school he would be into open prairie and he could become one of those unlucky ones that weren't found until spring. That thought brought him up short and he thought of Ben trying for home.

Nothing in their Texas background had prepared them for this. He feared for Ben, with miles to go. He also feared for himself with just a few feet to go and wondered if he could make it.

He found the school by bumping into it, knocking his hat askew and bruising his almost frozen nose. Spacing his two hands wide apart on the wall, he carefully worked his way along until he stumbled over the doorstep, barking his shin. "I'm going to be all over bruises and I ain't done noth'n yet."

Going mostly by feel, Sam found the door knob. As he turned it, a gust of wind blew the door back against the wall, nearly tearing it off its hinges. He stumbled inside, slipped on some blown-in snow and fell to the floor in exhaustion. Miss Granet let out a sharp yelp and several of the girls screamed.

Collecting her senses, Miss Granet ran to the door and tried to close it. It required the help of two of the older boys to complete the task. With the door closed, she bent over Sam and lifted the scarf he had tied over his face. "Sam? What in the world?"

He had every intention of saying, "I was worried about you," but his cold, stiff cheeks wouldn't move and the words came out garbled. His mind quickly flashed to Ben and he knew his brother was in a world of trouble unless he was sensible enough to turn back.

Miss Granet asked again, "What brings you here, Sam? Heaven knows we can use some help but I was expecting perhaps one of the fathers, certainly not you. I didn't even know you were in town. Anyway, come on, get up. We'll get you over to the stove and thawed out.

Miss Granet and the children all had on their coats and

hats even though the wood burner was roaring full out. It was as if the wind was sucking the heat out of the building as fast as the fire could supply it.

Sam stood and stepped over to the stove. He looked around and said, "That's not a very big supply of wood. Is there more outside?"

"There's a whole shed full but I was afraid to let anyone try for it."

"Where is the wood shed?"

"Right outside the back door by about fifty feet," answered one of the boys.

"Just as soon as I warm up a bit here, boys, I'll get the wood if you'll look after the door."

Miss Granet looked worried. "You'll have to be careful. You can't see a thing out there."

"You just get ready to open the door; we have to have more wood."

Sam nearly froze doing it but eventually there was a large pile of fuel cluttering the floor beside the stove, snow melting off it and puddling on the floor. Sam and Miss Granet placed chairs close to the stove and to each other. The kids huddled around, some on chairs and some on the floor.

Miss Granet lightly touched Sam's sleeve and gave him a look that made him feel strange. "Thank you, Sam. We would have been in big trouble without your help. I sent the town children home just as soon as the storm broke over us but I'm glad I kept the ranch kids here. By morning, we'll be chilly and hungry but we'll be alive. I had some serious doubts about that earlier."

14

THE THOMAS JOHANSSON FAMILY'S SMALL RANCH WAS THREE miles north of the Blossom spread and a little east. They were friendly and helpful when needed but, feeling for the most part self-sufficient, preferred to be left alone. They never neighbored and, if seen in town, would offer a friendly enough greeting to folks they met but didn't invite conversation.

Thomas raised cattle and hogs, feeding the hogs with corn he raised himself. The growing season at this elevation was a little tight for corn but most years he managed.

The Johansson kids attended the town school and, although they mixed well enough with the other students, they still swung onto their ponies and headed home as soon as school let out.

On the day of the storm, the family had kept the kids at home, recognizing the fierceness of what was to come.

The oldest child was a son named Olaf who at fifteen showed a lot of responsibility towards the farm as well as to his three siblings. Twelve-year-old Glenda was a beautiful young lady just starting to feel the initial oncoming of maturity and, with it, the modesty that had been absent in her younger tomboy years.

Thomas had instructed his family to stay inside while the blizzard blew through their ranch yard. He had seen blizzards before and knew their danger. His instructions were clear, "No one can survive this storm for more than a few minutes. None of you have any reason to go out. I'll see to the chores and fill the wood box. I've strung the guide ropes so I'll be alright but none of you are to go out." They all agreed.

But when the call of nature was upon Glenda, her newfound modesty got in the way of her better judgments. She looked at her options in the small home and didn't like them. There was little chance of total privacy and the chamber pot would have to be emptied anyway which meant going outside. So she decided that no harm could befall her on the short trip to the outhouse. She would follow the rope and be back inside in just a few minutes.

Her younger sister saw Glenda put on her coat and slip outside. She called her mother immediately.

Mrs. Johansson pulled on her own coat and rushed out, calling to Glenda. The wind took her screams away and the bitter cold dug deep into her, almost immediately. She grasped the guide rope with her bare hand and struggled to the outhouse. The door was still latched from the outside. Frantically, she unlatched the door and swung it open. The little space was empty; no sign of Glenda. She hung desperately onto the rope and screamed Glenda's name until she could scream no more.

Still clinging to the rope, she doubled back to the house and then transferred her grip to the barn rope. With bare hands, no hat and no boots, she was soon unbelievably cold. She hunched her face down into her coat collar and moved as quickly as possible to the barn, calling out to Thomas all the while.

She fell and lost her grip on the rope. Frantically, she swung her arm through the freezing air until she brushed and then gripped the rope. She rose and stumbled forward only to fall again. It took little more than a minute but it seemed like an eternity for the desperate woman to reach the barn.

When she finally released the barn door latch, the wind grabbed the door and swung it open, smashing it against the wall. She fell into the barn and crumpled to her hands and knees, unable to move further.

Startled, Thomas turned from his work and rushed to his wife, knowing only something urgent would bring her from the house. The howling wind made speaking impossible so he fought the door closed and then knelt. "What is it? What's wrong?"

The frantic woman had tears frozen to her cheeks. She was too cold and frightened to speak. She gasped several gulps of air and finally managed to say, "Glenda," while pointing to the outside.

Husband and wife, both on their knees on the barn floor, faced each other. Thomas shook her gently. "What about Glenda? What's happened?"

A few more gulps of air and then, "Glenda went to the outhouse and she's gone."

Thomas leaped to his feet. "Quickly, come with me. We have to get you back into the house. I'll look for Glenda."

Thomas clung to the rope while the two made their slow way back to the house. He eased his wife through the door and said firmly, "Stay inside."

He then started looking and calling for Glenda. To search the ranch yard, he was forced to let go of the guide rope, knowing the risk he took. Calling and walking and finally crawling as his strength left him, he searched. On hands and knees, he groped through every pile of snow in the yard hoping to find his beautiful daughter beneath and yet hoping not to, wishing for a better outcome. But he knew the outcome possibilities were few.

He stumbled into the house once, colder than the human body is meant to endure. He warmed himself for a few short minutes and then was back in the yard covering ground he had already covered, hope gone within him and tears blinding what little sight the bitter winds had left him, his great strong shoulders heaving with sobs.

He searched until all logic was gone. Nothing could live through the storm; no human flesh could survive this long. His Glenda was gone and he knew it but still he searched.

And then he was lost himself. He had turned around so many times he had no idea where the buildings were or the lifesaving ropes he had strung. He was finally saved by falling into the garden irrigation ditch they had dug years before. On hands and knees in the ditch, frantic and numb with cold and exhaustion, he finally figured out by the slope of the land which direction led to the garden. He crawled. Knowing that if he lost contact with the ditch he would join Glenda and the others who would die in this dreadful storm, he crawled. He bumped into the garden fence without seeing it, rose to his feet and staggered along, holding the fence all the way. From the edge of the garden he was able to see just the smallest corner of the house porch. Three lunging steps landed him face down on the porch and he crawled to the door.

Unable to reach the knob and knowing he couldn't make his hands turn if he somehow managed to reach it, in desperation he rolled onto his back and kicked the door until Olaf opened it for him. The boy helped him in without speaking. No words could be heard above the scream of the wind.

He lay on the kitchen floor weeping. Olaf and his mother looked hopelessly at each other. The other children watched, saying nothing.

Finally, Olaf reached for his coat but his mother gently took it from his hands and hung it back up. The young man was trying desperately to hide his tears. "I could look."

Thomas, having risen to sit on a chair, shook his head. "No, son, you are strong and you mean well but this blizzard is stronger than all of us. We will stay inside now."

The family wept and prayed and wept some more; some of the children silently, the mother with great gulping sobs. Thomas sat with his work-hardened hands balled into fists that could have crushed rocks, no sound coming from his locked lips.

And still the snow fell and the wind screamed through the house eves and the temperature dropped even more.

Back on the H-R, Hamilton had floundered in the snow until he had his cattle fed and the fire well-banked to keep the water from freezing. He had then managed, with a great deal of trouble and the help of the barking dog, to lead his spare saddle horses and the other wagon teams from their enclosed pasture and into his small barn. The barn wasn't large enough to stall all of the animals so he had loose-tied them in the alleyway with enough hay to see them through the night.

He could do nothing about the large group of horses he had trained and was holding for sale in the spring. He had no building anywhere large enough to hold them. But the field they were in had an abundance of grass that could be pawed off and nearly fifty acres of bush for shelter. Horses are pretty good at looking after themselves and Hamilton knew they would find their way to the bush. He could do nothing more for them.

He finally had time to milk the cow and then he struggled his way back to the cabin following the rope he had stretched between the house and barn. Stretching that rope was one of the first things he did when the storm blew up, a thing he did every winter as did most of his neighbors. Those ropes had saved a lot of misery and more than a few lives across the district.

Hamilton made himself a meal and then fed his dog. Later that evening, he sat in his rocker beside the kitchen range reading by the light of a coal oil lamp. The coffeepot was close to hand. The dog was curled up on a mat close to the door with his nose pressed into the draft beneath the door as if he wanted to keep contact with the outside world.

There was no twilight, no evening. The sun didn't go down; it simply disappeared. It was light and then it was dark.

The wind and the driven snow were unrelenting. Normally Hamilton checked his animals in the barn before retiring for the night but not this evening. "I think we'll just stay inside, Scruffy." The dog picked up his ears and waited for instructions. When none came, he lay his ears back down as if settled for the night.

Hamilton heard no unusual sound above the wind and the driven snow on the window glass but the dog did. He rose up on his front legs, lifted his ears and let out a low growl.

"What is it, Scruffy, do you hear something?"

The dog gave a short bark and scratched at the door.

"I've never known you to be wrong, boy. Let's take a look."

Hamilton pulled on his hat and coat and lit a lantern.

He opened the door a crack and the dog shot through, growling and barking. Hamilton stepped onto his porch and pulled the door closed behind him. "Someone there?" he hollered. The wind threw his voice back at him.

Holding the lantern up in front of him, he tried to follow the movements of the dog but all he could see was blowing snow. The dog's excited barking was slowly coming closer and finally Hamilton could pick out the shape of a horse. He watched another few moments and then realized there was a man clinging to the horse's neck, his feet encased in snow and seeming to be frozen to the stirrups. Snow was piled high on the man's shoulders and hat. The side of both man and horse that had faced into the wind was layered with white.

"What have you found, Scruffy? Good boy. Let's get him into the house and see who we have here."

He led the animal as close to the porch as possible, tying it to the yard fence and then reached for the man. "You're safe now," he hollered. "Let go of the horse and we'll get you into the house."

There was no response.

Hamilton gently pulled the rider's hands from the horse's neck and tried to get him to a sitting position. With no cooperation from the man, that proved to be impossible. Hamilton worked the rider's feet free of the stirrups one at a time and pulled him off the saddle, dropping him into the piled-up snow. He was far too heavy for Hamilton to lift down gently. Once on the ground, he took the snow-choked coat collar in his two hands and slid the man across the snow into the house. He called the dog in and slammed the door.

After brushing the snow from the fallen man's face, he could see who it was. "Ben? What in the world are you doing out here?"

Ben made no response although he slowly opened one eye and then closed it again. That he had suffered terribly in the cold was obvious at first glance. His cheeks, nose and ears were deathly white. His lips trembled with cold.

Hamilton opened Ben's coat to allow some warm air to penetrate the layers of clothing and peeled off the thin leather gloves. Ben's fingers had started to turn black and some skin came off with the gloves.

There was much more to do for Ben but the horse also needed to get to shelter. Feeling that Ben would be alright for a few minutes alone, Hamilton said, "You hang in there, neighbor. I'll be right back after I care for your animal."

Leaving the dog in the house, Hamilton took the lantern and went back outside. With one hand on the safety rope tied between the barn and the yard fence and one hand holding the reins and the lantern, he led the freezing and exhausted animal into the barn. There was very little room left but Hamilton got the horse inside and unsaddled. He slipped off the bridle, replaced it with a halter and tied the animal to a stall railing. He placed a big armful of hay within easy reach, then wiped the shivering animal down with a rag he had torn from an old saddle blanket some days before. He threw a dry saddle blanket over the gelding's back and patted him again on the neck. "That's all I can do for you, old boy, but you deserve at least that. You done well this night."

Back in the house, Hamilton knelt beside Ben and started to remove his snow-laden coat and scarf. Ben was sobbing although he still seemed to be unconscious. Hamilton saw no reason to intrude or destroy Ben's dignity so he stayed quiet.

When Hamilton opened the door, a blast of cold air had rushed over Ben. After a few moments, he groaned and opened his eyes. He blinked several times and turned his head from side to side to try to figure out where he was and who he was with. Finally, staring through tear-wet eyes he looked at the man beside him. "That you, Robb? How did I get here?"

"I believe you owe your life to that gelding. Would seem so anyway. Why did you come? Is there trouble on the Circle S?"

Ben struggled to sit up. Hamilton helped him into a chair. Ben's lips and cheeks were so cold he had trouble talking. Finally, he was able to say, "I was trying to get home from town. Cold. Almighty cold. I can't feel my feet or my hands. My nose and ears froze hours ago. Couldn't see a thing. I was lost within a half mile of town. Didn't even know the way back. Scared. Scared nearly out of my mind. I don't mind telling you I never been so scared in all my life. Scared to the very core of my being."

Those thoughts seemed to bring on another round of sobs although Ben did his best to hide them.

"When I first realized I was lost, I tried to turn the horse around. But he felt a blast of that wind on his face and refused to go any further. Turned his tail into the wind and slowly started walking. I had no choice but to hang tough and ride. All's I said was, 'I hope you know where you're going, big guy.' Finally, just hung onto that bay gelding and prayed. Don't do much praying but I did this night."

Ben didn't tell Hamilton but at one point on his ride he had done something he hadn't done since he was but a child; he cried. He cried and he prayed and he hoped, not being quite sure who he was praying to or what he hoped for.

"So cold I knew I was going to die, I just let myself go to sleep. I figured death couldn't possibly hurt more than what I was already hurting so I just let go of myself. But I must have hung onto that horse. The next thing I knew I was laying on the floor in your warm cabin. Thank you. Can't say more to you, or that gelding either, than thank you.

After a pause and a moment to gather his thoughts, Ben asked, "What about the horse?"

"He's in the barn and fine for the time being. That's a good animal. I dried him off as best I could and fed him, and it's warm in the barn. No more we can do for him this night.

"Let's get you out of these frozen clothes. I'm going to have to cut your boots off. Sorry about that but your feet are worth more than these boots as pretty as they are. Nothing colder on the feet than tight-fitting, pointy-toe riding boots. Now sit up; we need to first get you out of this coat."

Ben screamed in pain when Hamilton pulled his boots off. His damp stockings were frozen to his feet. Hamilton started easing the stockings off as gently as he knew how but when the blackened skin started peeling off with them, he stopped. "Let's leave those a while."

Ben was shaking in pain, gripping the edges of the chair. He bit his lower lip until it bled but couldn't hold back another scream.

Ben was finally stripped down to his long-handles and seated back in the chair. His eyes were watering in pain and he was letting out little whimpering noises.

Hamilton opened the door long enough to scoop up a pail full of snow. Filling a basin with the snow, he set it on the floor and said, "Put your feet in there, socks and all. We have to thaw you out slowly. Your hands, too. Put your hands in this bucket of snow. I'm going to hold handfuls of snow over your ears. You won't enjoy it.

"Your nose will have to wait until one of us has a hand

free. I'll pour you some coffee, too. You might take a sip from time to time. Warm you a little on the inside."

Ben couldn't hold the coffee cup so Hamilton held it to his lips while the suffering man slurped gratefully.

After that process was repeated three times with a new pail of snow each time and having been given two cups of hot coffee, Ben hobbled to the cot that sat ready in the corner. He screamed in pain and came near to falling when he first put weight on his feet.

Hamilton usually slept in a separate bedroom, but the heat from the kitchen range didn't drift that far and he hadn't bothered to light the Hub Oak stove in that other room. The cot in the kitchen was perfect for cold nights such as this.

"Here's what's going to happen now, Ben. Pretty soon you're going to start to shiver just as soon as your body decides it's worth keeping on living. I'll wrap you in all the blankets I've got but you're still going to shiver.

"And then you're going to start to hurt, really hurt, as the blood starts to circulate again. I expect your ears are already hurting and pretty soon your nose and fingers will be there, too. Your feet are the worst. You're going to need medical help for them but we can't set out for the doctor tonight without both of us risking our lives and the horses', too. You do the best you can tonight and as soon as the wind and snow allow, I'll get you back to the Circle S.

"I have nothing to help with the pain. I don't keep any whiskey on hand.

"This will be a long night for you but you're safe here. That's the best we can do. Might be good if you were to continue that praying you talked about. Even with your troubles you have a lot to thank a merciful God for plus a horse that was strong enough to best the cold and snow."

Ben listened to these words of advice and nodded. "I

have no idea what drew that horse to your cabin but I'm grateful. Grateful to you and the horse both. Don't ever think I'm not. The Circle S has never given you any reason to make us welcome, except Sam a bit and maybe Little Sister. You could have turned me away….grateful…. almighty grateful."

"No one gets turned away when a need is upon us. You're talking foolish. Try to sleep now. I'll be right here if you need me."

Hamilton spent the night sitting in his kitchen rocker, feeding the stove and drinking coffee, dozing from time to time. Just before morning light arrived, the wind dropped and finally died altogether. The sun rose to illuminate an unreal world of clear air shimmering with suspended frost crystals, a maze of broken and twisted branches on the yard trees, and weird swirlings of snow. In places, the wind had scoured the ground almost clear of snow and in other places the drifts were mountainous, reaching the roof of the barn and completely covering the smaller outbuildings.

Hamilton opened the door long enough to let the dog out for his morning run. He took a quick look at the mercury thermometer nailed to the cabin wall. He looked and then looked again. "Minus forty-two," he said aloud to himself. "Coldest I've ever seen it. This will be a night to remember and talk about."

Back in the cabin, he tried to wake Ben up. He stirred a bit and mumbled but didn't open his eyes. Hamilton figured it was perhaps more than just a normal sleep. He didn't know what to call Ben's condition but he was sure he needed serious medical attention.

There were cattle to be fed and a barn full of animals needing attention. Hamilton dressed in his warmest clothing and put his hand on the door knob. He then looked back at Ben and was worried. "Neighbor," he said aloud as was his habit when he was talking to himself, "I wouldn't want you to wake up and decide to feed the fire. I would be real unhappy if you somehow managed to burn the cabin down. If you were to do that, where would your sister and I set up housekeeping? She called my cabin cute. I took that as a good sign. No, I don't want you burning it down. If you wake up and find yourself tied to this bunk, you're going to be a might unhappy but I'm going to take that chance."

With that thought expressed, Hamilton lifted an old lariat off a peg on the wall and threw it around Ben's chest and under the bunk, tying it off so that Ben couldn't reach the knot. "If you don't wake up, you'll never know."

Hamilton stepped outside and headed to the barn, the guide rope not needed this morning. The cold air struck his lungs like a hammer blow and he pulled his scarf up to cover his mouth and nose. His footsteps squeaked in the dry, minus-forty snow, piling up little ripples behind his moccasins as he passed.

The wagon team was stalled in the center of the barn with animals blocking off the space between those stalls and the door. It took a half-hour of shuffling and moving horses for Hamilton to get the team harnessed and outside. The team had fed well over night so they needed no special attention but the horses tied in the runway had to be given hay. This took another quarter-hour. The chickens seemed to be under foot everywhere he stepped.

Hamilton finally had the team hooked to the one hay wagon that he had put sled runners under earlier in the fall. He had started that habit several years before after fighting all one winter trying to drive a wagon on wheels through the snow.

Then he swung the team towards the house and went in to check on Ben. He had left the dog in the barn.

Taking a quick look at Ben, he couldn't see that he had moved so he drove the wagon down the slight grade to the hay meadow, wallowing through one drift and rising almost over the top of another before the weight of the horses broke through the hard packed snow and across to the haystacks where the cattle were clustered. There was so much snow piled around the fence that he had trouble opening the gate. By the time that was done, he was already starting to feel the cold even through his woolens.

He drove the team directly to the water tank and let them drink. There was just a rim of ice on the farthest edge of the tank. "Sure beats chopping ice like I've done for years."

Then, in spite of the cold, he chuckled to himself. "I don't often talk to my horse like some cowboys do but I'd have to admit to talking to myself a considerable amount. Maybe that will stop when Wanda is up in that cabin making breakfast."

And then, talking to himself again, he looked at the cattle and said, "Don't know how you brutes live through this weather. I don't expect you're real comfortable but I don't see any downers. How's about some breakfast for you?"

Fighting the snow away from the stacked hay, he finally got the animals fed and built up the fire in the tank heater. But he didn't fuss around like he normally did; Ben's needs towered over the comfort of the cattle.

He then threw a goodly amount of hay onto the wagon, pulling it from the inside of the stack to avoid the snow, and drove it back up to the house, parking as close to the porch as possible.

Hamilton had delayed his breakfast hoping that Ben might wake up, figuring he'd be hungry. He had put water on to boil for coffee though so it was the work of but a few minutes to have coffee ready. He made his breakfast from leftover biscuits and slices of cold ham. As he ate, he watched Ben for signs of movement and saw none.

Leaving his second cup of coffee to cool, he bent and untied the rope from Ben and threw back his covers. Ben's feet were an awful sight. Hamilton knew he had pulled some skin off along with the frozen boots and socks but those scarred spots were not the worst. The sight of Ben's toes and the bottom of his feet nearly made Hamilton retch. His toes were black and swollen and the bottoms were black and blistered.

The tops of his ears were black as were most of his fingers. His nose had settled down to a bright red, showing signs of blood circulation.

"You're in tough on this one, pard. We need to get you some doctoring help but first I'll need to get you onto that sleigh."

Ben was a big man, certainly weighing over two hundred pounds. Wrapped in blankets, he made an awkward bundle and Hamilton could see no easy way to take a grip on the unconscious man. The task was further complicated by the heavy clothing Hamilton was wearing. He finally decided to try throwing Ben over his shoulder which he accomplished on the third effort by first getting Ben into a sitting position and then draping his arms over his own right shoulder. Slowly shifting Ben upward, Hamilton was able to hold the sleeping man over his shoulder with one arm and grasp a window ledge with the other. He lifted as he had never lifted before. He staggered and nearly fell but finally he was on his feet. He took short, careful steps on the snow-slippery floor and managed to get to the door. He turned the knob and swung the door into the kitchen, grasping the door post for support and balance.

The built-up snow worried him but he stepped onto the porch anyway. What choice did he have? Three careful steps took him to the edge of the porch and another roof post he was able to grab. Counting out the steps to the wagon and picturing in his mind what he had to do, he let go of the roof post and lunged down the two steps to ground level and across the few feet to the wagon. He brought up hard against the edge of the wagon and flopped Ben onto his back in the hay. There was nothing gentle about the way the man was handled.

Ben didn't move. Hamilton decided that he must be in some kind of a coma. He knew nothing that he could do about it.

He went back for all the blankets he could find and carried them to the sleigh, wrapping Ben like an Egyptian mummy. He then covered him with a thick layer of hay and went back into his cabin. He banked the fire, added wood, and drank down the last of his coffee. As an afterthought, he picked up three pairs of moccasins and took them along. His moccasins often wore through the soles before spring so he was in the habit of keeping spares. He purchased them from his Indian haying crew and they were by far the warmest footwear he had ever tried. They might be needed on the Circle S if all they had were riding boots.

Before leaving for the Circle S, he checked his barn animals again and carefully closed the door, not wanting the wind to pull it open while he was away. The calf was in with the milk cow so that chore was dealt with. The dog was sleeping in a manger, seeming to be content with the world.

He had wondered about heading straight to town and the doctor but finally decided that another couple of hours might not matter to Ben and he was sure they would be worrying at the Circle S. They would be wondering about their son.

At the last minute, he thought to grab a shovel in case there were drifts the team couldn't break through. Within one mile, he was down off the sleigh with the shovel in hand, moving snow.

Just a short distance further on, he stopped the team and stared at a mountainous drift before him. He took the shovel and walked onto the drift. His feet barely made a scratch in the packed snow. As hard as it was, he was afraid to try the team and wagon on it. The drift was all of ten feet high and fifty feet wide. Had the horses broken through near the top, he would be in a fine fix. There were no fences in that area so he managed to drive the team and wagon off the trail and onto the prairie, going around the worst of the drift and through a grove of trees, pushing smaller bushes over as he went. He knew he could never have done it with a wheeled wagon but the sled took the grassland and the smaller drifts with little problem.

He was forced to shovel smaller drifts in three places before reaching the Circle S but, for the most part, the team was able to force its way through.

He checked Ben twice in the hour and a half it took to get to the Circle S. He hadn't moved but Hamilton could see he was breathing so he drove on.

15

BIG BOB AND THE WOMEN SPENT THE NIGHT OF THE STORM huddled by the kitchen range or by the sitting room fireplace. The crew stayed close to their cots in the bunkhouse. The windows were covered by a deep layer of frost.

Wanda had carefully scraped away enough frost to allow for a peek at the snow-locked yard. She stared in wonder at the drifts piled to the barn eve and completely covering the small tool shed. The screaming gale had destroyed the windmill during the night. Many corral fences were completely buried beneath the blowing snow.

The unrelenting wind had picked up new snow from across the prairie and dropped it in the ranch yard, creating drifts where none had been just minutes before. The result was a riot of swirls and peaks and hollows. Wanda was reminded of pictures she had seen of wave-tossed oceans except the oceans were blue or black and the yard was the whitest of whites. So white was the snow that even with the darkness of night she was able to distinguish some of the yard features whenever the wind died for a moment or two.

Wanda watched as a couple of horses desperate for relief from the cold and the wind walked over the drifts and out of the corral, finding freedom in the barnyard. Freedom, but no food and no shelter. The Texas horses were numb with cold.

Big Bob finally tired of listening to Wanda describe the activities in the ranch yard. "Wanda, come away from that window. You need to get some rest. Why don't you make up a bed on the couch here?"

"I've never seen anything like this, Pa, and may never again. I can sleep any time but this storm is special."

With morning still a couple of hours away, the wind had mostly died out but the cold and snow remained. The loose animals stood with their tails to the wind and their heads drooping, suffering as they had never suffered before.

No one had gone to bed. The family and crew had all spent the night stoking fires and watching the weather although little could be seen.

As the wind had screamed its way through the mountain valleys and across the prairie and then among the ranch buildings carrying mountains of snow with it, the visibility had dropped almost to nothing. Even as Wanda had stared at the bunkhouse and barn, they disappeared in the white mass.

As Wanda watched, a dark form materialized through the white haze. "Someone's trying to get here from the bunkhouse," Wanda hollered to her father.

Big Bob went to the door and when he heard footsteps on the porch floor, he threw the door open and Dalton stumbled in. "Didn't think I was going to make it," he said.

"I never saw anything like this. Couldn't even see the house."

"None of us ever saw anything like this."

"Thought you needed to know, boss, Randy is missing."

"Missing? What do you mean missing? Seems to me that I was clear; you were all to stay inside. Surely he didn't ride out in this?"

"Didn't ride; walked. His own personal horse is loose in that east pasture behind the barn. He was determined to get it to shelter. He paced the floor and fussed around the bunkhouse all night and finally he pulled on his warmest coat and walked out. We tried to stop him but he was beyond reason. That was a couple of hours ago. We ain't seen him since."

"Maybe he's in the barn."

"No, I checked there before I came here. The blowing snow's covering most everything but in the shelter beside the back door to the barn I saw his footsteps heading into the pasture. None coming back."

"That worries me," said Big Bob. "But we can't go looking for him without some of us getting lost too and that wouldn't do Randy or anyone else a bit of good. We were just talking before you came in that a person could get lost right in the yard and freeze to death.

"There's a big coil of rope in the barn. I've wondered why the R/R had that but I might have figured it out. I'll get on a coat and we'll string that rope between the buildings. At least we can hang on to that if nothing else.

"Then I'd like if you boys would take turns in the barn. Take the shotgun and fire off a shot outside the barn door every five minutes. Maybe Randy will be able to get a bearing and get back. But none of you are to leave the barn looking for him. You got that straight?"

"That's straight, boss. Did the boys get back from town?"

"No sign of them. And that has us considerably worried, too."

As Dalton passed through the open door, Big Bob hollered after him, "See if you can catch those loose horses and get them into the barn."

Dalton raised his right arm in a signal of understanding and stepped off the porch.

The men went two at a time to the barn carrying the shotgun and all the shells they could find. Dalton and a man named Clint were the first to go. Dalton stepped out of the barn door and raised the shotgun. The wind seemed to carry the gun blast away as quickly as it was made.

"Don't see how Randy is going to hear that. Can't hardly hear it right here. But I don't see anything else to do."

Over the next couple of hours, the crew, switching every half-hour, fired off every shotgun shell on the ranch and then started on the rifle and carbine shells. The sound of the shots was whisked away by the wind and lost. Dalton turned to the man with him. "Take a miracle for Randy to hear that over the howl of the wind."

Shot after shot echoed feebly across the whitened ranch land but there was no sign of Randy.

The snow was so light and fluffy that even the dying wind was enough to stir it up. The blowing snow, added to the feebleness of the slowly arriving dawn, made sight nearly impossible.

With the rising of the sun and the slacking off of the wind, they put the guns away. Dalton saddled a horse in the barn and led him out the back door. He knew he wasn't dressed for the conditions but he put on as much warm clothing as he could find and wrapped his head in scarves.

He was back within an hour, walking and leading his horse. The crew, watching from the barn, could see that he had balanced a burden on the horse's back. Seeing Dalton stagger, they ran out to help him. Dalton was too cold to talk. The men stared at the body draped face down over the saddle. It could be no one but Randy.

Big Bob, arriving from the house, hollered at the men walking beside Dalton, "Is he dead?"

"Can't really tell."

"Well, we can't do anything out here. Let's get him inside. And you, too, Dalton. You're about done in."

The ranch yard was completely blocked off from the pasture with drifts of packed snow. The only access from the rear pasture was through the barn. A couple of the crew dug away enough snow to get one of the back doors open. The men entered and led the horse inside. They then repeated the process in the front. With the horse led right up to the house, Randy was carried inside and Dalton was helped up the steps and into the big entry hall.

Big Bob turned to the rest of the crew. "We'll take this from here. I would like if you men would catch as many horses as you can without putting yourselves at risk and drive them into the barn. We should have done it yesterday. That was my mistake and now the horses have suffered and you men, too. I'm almighty sorry about that.

"There's a bit of hay in the loft. You feed the horses as best you can and then get back inside where it's warm. Cook will soon have breakfast on. We'll see what we can do for these men."

"What about the cattle?" asked one of the crew.

Big Bob was slow in answering. Finally, he pulled his eyes off the white horizon and looked at the crew. "That's my mistake, too, men. This is a long ways from Texas and anything I ever seen before. I expect most of them are dead and we can't do a single thing about the rest. The poor beasts must be suffering something terrible. We'll do what we can when opportunity allows."

Wanda lay a padding of blankets on the floor in front of the fireplace and Randy was placed on them.

Dalton was able to pull off his own hat and coat but he needed help with his boots. His feet were already frozen although he had only been out an hour or so. He screamed in pain when the boots were pulled off. His feet were not yet black but they were a fish-belly white and that worried Big Bob. "I don't know a thing in the world about frozen feet but I expect that's what we're looking at here or close to it."

Big Bob turned to the men who had carried Randy into the house. "We've got to get these men out of their frozen clothes and wrapped in warm blankets. You men help Randy. Can you do it yourself, Dalton, or do you need help?"

Dalton, panic-stricken, looked at the women.

Mrs. Stanton caught his worried look and took Wanda by the arm. "Come on, dear. We'll find something to do in the kitchen."

Finally down to his long-handles, Dalton wrapped himself in a blanket and sat in a chair facing the fire. He was starting to shiver and he didn't know if that was good or bad. The women came back in and started to fuss over him but he chased them away. His feet hurt past any hurt he had ever experienced before but he grimaced and refused help.

He accepted a cup of coffee from Wanda and then said, "I'm fine. You look after Randy."

Like Hamilton had done with Ben, Big Bob cut Randy's boots off. His socks came off with the boot along with patches of skin. Again, like Ben, his feet were a terrible sight.

He turned to his crew men. "I can take it from here, men. You go get some breakfast and then see to the horses."

They didn't know to pack the frozen parts with snow so, thinking they were doing the right thing, they wrapped towels soaked in hot water around his feet. Although Randy was still unconscious, he cried out and shook his feet until Big Bob finally said, "Get those hot cloths off. He was more comfortable before we put them on."

The rancher and the two women stood around the frostbitten man, not knowing what to do. Big Bob looked at his wife. "There's just nothing at all to enjoy about a Texas blue norther but at least we were able to deal with them from experience. We are completely at a loss here. This man needs a doctor but I don't see how we can even get to town."

"I have no ideas either," answered Mrs. Stanton. "And I'm worried sick about Ben and Samuel."

"We're all worried about the boys. I've had them on my mind all night."

The front door crashed open and an excited cowboy hollered, "Someone's coming!"

"Someone's coming?" repeated Wanda. "How would anyone get here in this weather?"

Everyone went to the front door and looked out. Big Bob shouldered his way past his wife and stepped outside. He hadn't bothered with a coat but in his excitement the cold didn't hit him right away.

He stepped down off the porch as a team and sleigh pulled up to the yard fence-gate. The driver had his face wrapped in scarves. As a question formed on Big Bob's tongue, he noticed the wrapped bundle covered in hay. He rushed down to the sleigh and hollered, "Who is it? Who've you got?"

Hamilton pulled his scarf down and answered simply, "Ben."

"Is he dead?"

"He's hurting some but he's not dead."

"You men grab hold; let's get him inside."

"Hold on," shouted Hamilton, "This man needs a doctor. His feet are frozen something awful. I only brought him here so you'd know where he was and to see if you wanted to go to town with him. Moving him would be a waste of time. Hard on Ben, too."

Mrs. Stanton asked, "Have you seen Samuel?"

"Seen nothing of him, ma'am, just Ben. Arrived at my cabin well after dark, frozen to his horse. He owes his life to that horse," he said pointing to the horse tied to the back of the wagon. "I'd put that animal in the barn if he were mine. He's earned a pail of oats, too. I had him in my barn all night but he's cold again now."

"My, my," said Mrs. Stanton. "Where in the world can Samuel be?"

She uncovered Ben's face and pressed her warm hand against his cheek. Ben's eyes fluttered and then opened.

"Oh, Ben, you're awake! Mr. Robb is going to get you to a doctor right away. How are you feeling?"

"It really hurts, Ma. I done it up good this time."

"You just hang in there; the doctor will fix you up. Where is Samuel? Did he get lost in the storm?"

"He stayed in town. Went to the schoolhouse to help that pretty schoolmarm. He should be alright."

Mrs. Stanton gripped the side of the sleigh, steadying herself. "That's a huge relief and an answer to my prayers."

Wanda came down the steps hugging her coat around

her. "Mr. Robb, come inside for coffee while the men get ready."

"That sounds like a fine idea, Miss Stanton. I'll do that. We have to get going though. If the wind picks up and makes more drifts, we'll not get to town today or back home this evening."

Big Bob said, "You get your coffee. And we have another man to take to town. We'll be ready in no time at all."

Hamilton bent and picked up the moccasins, passing them to Big Bob. "You men put these on. You just aren't going to make it wearing those pointy-toed boots. Put on some extra socks and put a layer of dry hay on the bottom of these. They'll keep you warm all day."

Big Bob took a doubtful look at the Indian footwear and then carried them inside.

Mrs. Stanton announced that she was going with the men and then Wanda said the same. Big Bob would hear none of it. "You'll do no such a thing, young lady. I don't know as how I can hold your mother back but you're not going anywhere. You stay here and keep the house warm. We'll leave one man here in the house with you and Dalton. He can keep the wood box full. You stay inside and keep warm. We'll be back just as soon as ever we can."

Mrs. Stanton was the first one ready to go. She stood waiting in the warmth until the rest were ready. Big Bob and three of his crew climbed onto the wagon after carrying the injured man out. Hamilton finished his coffee and buttoned up his fleece-lined coat. He turned to Wanda. "Your father told you right. You stay inside. This weather is nothing to fool with and I surely don't want anything happening to you."

Wanda said, "Pa's figuring on going back to Texas just

as soon as the roads are open." She wasn't quite sure why she said that.

Hamilton reached and gripped her hands. "Your pa may be going back to Texas but not you. You're going to stay here with me." He had planned on saying nothing remotely resembling that short speech. He didn't know where the words had come from or what else to say so he said nothing more.

Wanda gave him a look he hadn't seen before and he didn't know what to make of it but there wasn't time to think it through.

"My, my," said Mrs. Stanton, looking at his receding back and then at her daughter

The men had wrapped Randy in blankets and loaded him onto the sleigh. Hamilton looked over the riders and hoped the team was good for the extra load on the long trip to town. "Did you grab some shovels?" he asked.

Big Bob leaped down from the sleigh and literally ran to the barn for shovels. "Sorry, Robb, I should have thought of that, too."

Hamilton saw that the men had put on the Indian footwear. There was none for Mrs. Stanton but she had seated herself beside Ben and covered her feet in blankets and hay so she would probably be alright.

The big hay wagon had a driver's seat fixed high on the front but no one used it. Hamilton stood, handling the reins, and all the men stood balancing themselves against the front of the rack, their backs to the wind.

Hamilton had broken the trail from his ranch so that portion of the trip went quickly. But on the town road they were soon stopped by an insurmountable drift. It took the most of an hour with three men digging to clear a path. They then made another mile before they had to dig again, this time not as much as before.

They had the wagon just under way again when one of the crew hollered, "Someone's coming."

They all looked where the man pointed. The rider was off the trail and the horse seemed to be walking unguided, the rider hunched over the horse's neck.

"That's Samuel," shouted Big Bob. "I'd know that coat anywhere and the horse."

Hamilton kept the sled going until they were up to where the horse had staggered to a stop. Big Bob jumped down and ran to the horse.

"Samuel," he shouted. "You alright?

The rider lifted his head and looked at his father. "That you, Pa? I can't hardly see anything. And I'm cold, almighty cold."

"That's me, son. Can you get down from the horse?"

"Can't see and can't feel my feet or hands."

Hamilton pulled one foot from the stirrup and Big Bob pulled the other. Then together they dragged the young man from the saddle and carried him over to the wagon, laying him beside Ben.

"Spread those blankets around a bit, Mother. We'll take him back to town and get help directly."

"Cover his eyes," said Hamilton. "He's gone snow blind. It'll pass but he'll hurt some. Best you keep him in the dark until the doctor sees him."

Without Big Bob's permission, Hamilton spoke to one of the crew, "We can't leave that horse out here. How about you ride him to my place? It's only a couple of miles. Put him in the barn with some feed and wait in the house. You can stoke up the fire. Just so you don't burn the place down. You'll find some coffee and cold ham on the shelf. Eggs in the barn if you can find where the hens hid them."

The man turned to Big Bob. "That sit alright with you, boss?"

"Fine, but don't run that horse and give it a good rubdown when you get him stalled. He's already shivering with cold. We'll pick you up on the way back."

An hour and a half and three drifts later, the sled pulled up in front of the doctor's small house. Big Bob jumped down but went to his knees in the snow. He stumbled up and staggered to the doctor's door, colder than he wanted to admit.

The doctor had seen them coming and opened the door before Big Bob had even knocked. "What have you got?" he asked.

"Frozen feet and I don't know what all else. We really need you, Doc."

"You ain't the first this day. Any more come, I'll have to build onto the house. Bring them in."

As soon as the men were carried into the house, Hamilton climbed back onto the sled and turned the horses towards the livery barn. Mrs. Stanton ran out the door of the doctor's house. "Thank you, Mr. Robb," she hollered. "Are you going back now?"

"These horses have had enough for one day. I'll put them in the livery and then come over to see how the boys are doing."

"Thank you," she said again.

Hamilton pulled the sled under a lean-to roof beside the big livery barn and unhitched the team. He swung the barn door open and led the team into the dim interior. It was crammed with horses but he found a space in the alley for his team. He hung the harness on some wall pegs and found a large cloth to rub the animals down with. But first he threw down some hay and dipped a pail of water for each animal from a tank the hostler kept inside where it wouldn't freeze. By that time, Walt Trimble arrived.

"Saw you," he said. "But I was just finishing up my lunch

and I figured you didn't need much help. How you making out? That team looks cold. You come from the ranch this morning?"

"From my ranch to the Circle S and then to town. Brought in some frozen feet and Sam went snow blind."

The hostler, a talker by nature, asked, "You bring in just the feet or the rest of the man along with them?"

Hamilton, too cold to see much humor, gave him a long look. "How would you like to get a gallon of oats for each of these boys and then give me a hand rubbing them down?"

When the horses were cared for, Hamilton made his way down the street to the doctor's office. He walked in without knocking. Big Bob and Mrs. Stanton were sitting in the small waiting room. "How are they?" he asked.

Big Bob was sitting hunched over with his head hanging and his hands clutched tightly on his knees. He didn't speak.

Mrs. Stanton was fighting tears, a handkerchief balled up in her fist. "The doctor chased us out. He covered Samuel's eyes with a damp cloth and confirmed what you had said. His eyes will hurt some but they'll get better. But he looked at Ben's feet and grimaced. That's when he chased us out."

Big Bob lifted his head. He took a long look at Hamilton. "We owe you. I can't even tell how much we owe you. We might have lost two sons this day were it not for you. Not to mention one of our crew. We owe you," he said again, and again dropped his head and hunched over.

Mrs. Stanton rubbed his shoulder gently. Her own shoulders shook as she fought to hold back her sobbing.

Not wanting to intrude on this hurting couple, Hamilton said, "I'll go over to the cafe and get some coffee. I'll check in later." Then, feeling the need to say something more, he added, "The boys will be alright. Just take some time, is all."

Entering the small cafe, Hamilton spotted the Circle S crewman that had come in with them. The cowboy gestured for him to take a seat. After hanging his hat and coat on a wooden peg beside the door, he pulled a chair out and sat down.

Hamilton held out his hand. "I don't know your name."

The cowboy shook hands. "Gentry. Will Gentry. We all know your name although you might not appreciate some of the names you've been called around the Circle S. I expect those days are over with."

Hamilton hunched his shoulders and grinned just a bit. "Usually pays to get to know a man before passing judgment."

Hamilton ordered a hot lunch and more hot coffee. Several hours outside with the temperature staying at thirty-five to forty below had chilled him to the bone. "Anything hot sounds good just about now."

He and Gentry didn't have much to talk about until Gentry said, "I've been thinking about the cattle. They were spread all over the range. We held out that big flat to the east for winter graze but hadn't pushed any animals onto it yet. The grass on the rest of the ranch is eaten down to the nub. The poor beasts were practically licking the dirt to get at the roots. No telling where they might have wandered to. We simply weren't ready for this. Had no idea. The animals haven't grazed on good range for days before the storm and now they're doing without entirely. And there's no relief in sight."

Hamilton nodded his head. "We always get enough winter to satisfy most of us but this is the worst I've ever seen. Be hard to be ready for conditions like this."

"You were ready. Cattle bunched, hay to hand, water tank with a heater in it. Sounds to me like you were ready."

Hamilton let the remarks pass. "Guess I'll go see the folks again and then head home. I'll get a livery horse."

"I might just as well come with you. I'm not doing any good here. Perhaps the livery has two horses."

The two men walked to the doctor's house and entered. Gentry said, "How be if I get a livery horse and head back? I'm no help here."

Big Bob looked at the two men and then asked Hamilton, "Are you heading back too? If so, I'd like if you'd stay together. Hate to see one man out there alone."

"We'll go together. Have you talked with the doctor again?"

"Haven't seen hide nor hair."

Just then the door opened and Penny and Miss Granet stepped in. Penny looked at the Stantons. "The news is all over town about the boys and your cowboy. How bad are they?"

Mrs. Stanton answered, "We don't know much. Samuel has snow blindness and some frostbite. Benjamin is worse. His feet are badly frozen and his fingers and ears are bad, too. He would have died except for Mr. Robb.

"Somehow Benjamin's horse found his way to the H-R. It must have smelled wood smoke or something although I don't know how it could with that dreadful wind driving the snow and smoke in every direction. Mr. Robb cared for Ben and brought him home this morning and then into town. Our rider is in bad shape, too, but we won't know any more until the doctor comes out."

Miss Granet said, "You have no way of knowing this then. Sam stayed in town to help the children and me over at the school. He was a godsend. I just don't know what we would have done without him. It's a miracle Sam even found the schoolhouse. The blowing snow made it nearly impossible to see anything even an arm's length away. He went outside in that awful wind and brought wood in several times. And he fed the fire all night.

"When the fathers finally pushed their way through the storm to pick up their children this morning, they were most grateful to find them safe. They couldn't be blamed for thinking the worst during the night. And I am most grateful, as well. You have raised a good son."

Big Bob seemed to not be listening but Miss Granet's words caused him to nod his head just slightly as if in acknowledgement of the compliment.

Mrs. Stanton smiled a weary smile and looked up at the girls. "Thank you for telling us. I know your words will mean a lot to Samuel."

"I have to get back to the store," said Penny. "You tell Ben I asked about him."

"We'll do that," answered Mrs. Stanton. "And thank you."

The ladies turned to leave and as the door closed behind them, Mrs. Stanton looked at her husband with a puzzled look and then back at the closed door. "My, my," she whispered, too quietly for her husband to hear.

Hamilton seemed unsure whether to speak his mind or not. Finally he said, "Feeding's going to be pretty nigh impossible for animals dependent on graze. I've got some hay I could spare if you wanted to put your crew on the hauling of it.

"Longhorns are tough. I'd be willing to bet that you have a goodly number of animals defying the storm, down in the breaks and the bush. I don't have the time to haul hay but you could have the borrow of the sled if you put your own team on it. It wouldn't be easy but your crew could do it. And I'm guessing that you'd save most of your animals."

Big Bob was a long time in answering. When he spoke, he looked up at Hamilton, "I'm not exactly sure why you'd make me that offer but I'll take it. You're sure you have enough and to spare?"

"I try to keep a year ahead so, yes, I can spare some. If it's enough will depend on how many animals you still have alive. I couldn't feed your whole herd. You'll have to drive some to market when the weather lets up. As far as that goes, it's a long time till spring. You might be wise to get them all to market and just keep your bulls. But you have time to sort that out."

Big Bob spoke to Gentry, "I'd appreciate if you'd ride home. Pick up the man from Robb's place and, tomorrow first light, see how many critters you and the other boys can drive to the barn pasture. Dalton will be in no shape to ride but the others of you do what you can. Stick within sight of each other. I don't want any more injured men.

"Keep the horses in the barn and change rides often. I'll get Robb's team from the livery and bring the sleigh out tomorrow. One of you harness that team of bays and lead them to the H-R. I'll need them to switch off for Robb's blacks to get the sleigh to the Circle S.

"And before you go home, go down to the store and see if they have more of this Indian footwear. My feet have never been so comfortable. Buy several pairs and whatever other warm clothes they have, especially hats.

"And you make sure that headstrong daughter of mine stays in the house."

Hamilton and Gentry were soon saddled and on the road. Hamilton had shown the other man how to wrap his scarf over his eyes, leaving just a slight slit for vision to reduce the chance of snow blindness. The sunlight reflecting off the snow was too intense for the naked eye.

It was cold. It was colder than Hamilton had ever experienced and Gentry had no words in his Texas vocabulary that even came close to describing the conditions. Gentry tried to make a comment about it to Hamilton but with his scarf muffling his words and with Hamilton's ears covered, he finally gave it up. They rode in silence the five miles to the H-R.

During the pleasant months of weather, this ride was undertaken with no thought of preparation or problems. The winter ride stretched the endurance of Hamilton and his rented horse and almost reached Gentry's endurance limit. But within an hour and a half they were in the welcoming warmth of the cabin and the horses were stalled in the small barn.

The cowboy who had ridden back with Sam's horse had coffee ready as if he was expecting company. Hamilton hung up his sheepskin coat and unwrapped the scarves from his face before turning to the man. "Heat feels good. Any trouble?"

"No trouble that spring wouldn't put an end to," answered the good-natured cowboy. "I fed and watered the animals in the barn and gathered what eggs I could find. Put the calf in her own pen. Figured you might want milk come morning. Then I walked down to your feeding pasture. Quite a setup you have there. I never saw the like. I threw out some hay and loaded coal into the water heater. Good system. The far side of the tank is frozen some but around the heater the cattle have good access. They drank it down considerable so I filled it from the mill. Hope all that suits you."

"Suits me just fine. If I needed a man, I'd offer you the

job. I just only got Gentry's name at lunch time and I still don't know yours."

"It's Beamer Willard. Most folks call me B but I'll answer to just about anything."

"Alright B. Glad you were here to look after the place. But the afternoon is dragging on and you and Gentry have a cold ride ahead of you. You get yourself ready. I'll go saddle Sam's horse and bring him out. Be good if you boys were to ride within sight of each other just for safety. There's been very little wind so the road will still be clear. Bob said he'd be out tomorrow. Expect we'll have news of the boys' condition then."

After the Circle S riders left, Hamilton rode the livery horse down to his cattle. The cattle experienced snow and cold every winter but still Hamilton worried each fall for the growing weanling calves as well as for the cows that were carrying the next crop of calves. The health of the bulls and their ability to breed was a major concern as well. Hamilton had a large investment in the bulls. They would be difficult and expensive to replace.

The Circle S cowhand who went by the simple name of B had done a good enough job of feeding and all Hamilton had to do was add some coal to the heater. Still, he hung around for nearly an hour looking for problems and riding out from the herd to look for wanderers. Satisfied with what he saw, he rode back to the barn and stalled the livery horse.

Getting water to all the barn animals took another hour and by that time it was getting dark. He took the milk he needed for the house and turned the calf in with its mother. He decided he had done all that could be done to make the animals comfortable so he walked to the house and settled in for the night. Ham and eggs sounded easy so he soon had the pan greased and heating. Ham and eggs was common fare in the bachelor cabin. It wasn't fancy but it would fill the need.

After supper, he sat with his coffee thinking about the day and its problems. His mind went to Wanda and to the first time he saw her sitting up proud on the seat of the spring wagon, driving through a new town, knowing that everyone on the sidewalk was staring at her. She had looked to neither the left nor the right. Hamilton had no way of knowing how embarrassed she had been. He recalled his feelings at that moment and how thoughts of all other possible girls left his mind as if they had never existed. He also recalled how impossible the situation had seemed with Big Bob riding his stallion, entering town like a conqueror, his sons following along behind and the spring wagon pulled by a prancing, matched pair of bays carrying the most beautiful girl Hamilton had ever seen.

His mind went briefly to the evening of the dance and how much he had enjoyed the time with Wanda and then, like a crash of thunder, it went to his declaration just that morning that Wanda would not be returning to Texas but would be staying with him. What a clumsy thing to say. He had never come even close to speaking to Wanda about his feelings or asking about hers. He admitted that the declaration was, indeed, the thought of both his heart and mind but that was hardly the time or the way to reveal his feelings. How many times would he blurt out something foolish before he learned to control his tongue?

"I could write a poem about all the dumb mistakes I've made but I guess maybe I'd better not. Don't know as how I'd have enough paper to list them all anyway."

THE WIND CAME BACK up that night, leaving new drifts in its wake and completely removing some of the older drifts.

Hamilton saddled a horse for the ride to the feed grounds and turned the remaining horses into the corral beside the barn. They needed some exercise and the barn was in serious need of cleaning.

A shout from a rider brought him from the barn, "If you'll open a gate I'll drive these brutes in."

Hamilton hurried to open the gate to an empty corral and the matched pair of bays entered.

"Bob asked me to bring these over to spell off your team. Is Bob and Mrs. S. here yet?"

"No sign of them yet this morning."

"I'll just head back then."

"Do you want to come in for coffee first?"

"We drew straws among us to choose who would make this ride. The others are out beating the bush for horses and cattle that can be driven in. I'd better get back or I'll never hear the end of it. But thanks."

Hamilton gathered a hatful of eggs and carried them to the house, then rode down to the herd. The temperature was still below minus-thirty.

Riding the horse down to the cattle gave him a new appreciation of how cold it still was. "Might have been warmer to walk."

The cattle started to mill around at his approach. It took over two hours of hard work to carry and spread the hay for the six hundred animals and their weaned calves plus the year-old heifers that he kept in another pen, separate from the bulls. He had stacked and fenced the hay into three yards to split the herd and make feeding easier. The snow drifts created serious problems and doubled the time necessary for the feeding.

He set the windmill to filling the water tank. While that was happening, he rode out as he always did looking for drifters. He found none and rode back to the herd. He fussed with the stove until it was burning well and then put in another half-hour walking among the cattle looking for signs of trouble. By that time, he was longing for a hot cup of coffee and the feel of the heat from the open oven door. He rode back to the barnyard and turned his horse into the corral with the others.

He didn't look forward to cleaning the barn but it had to be done. He kept a pair of rubber boots in the barn for this task. It was noon before he was finished and had the horses back in the barn. Satisfied with his morning, he headed to the cabin.

Hamilton hung up his heavy coat and poured himself a pan of hot water. When he finished having a wash, he looked over his supplies and decided on ham and eggs again. 'No one would ever accuse me of being a good cook,' he said aloud to himself, 'no matter what the ladies say about my baked ham. What they don't know is that's about all I know about cooking.' Two other things he knew were how to make biscuits and how to bake a good loaf of bread.

Then he started to wonder if Wanda was a good cook. Didn't really matter, he decided. 'She can't be worse than me. We'll make do.'

He was just finishing his lunch when the dog warned of company coming. Stepping out the door, he saw Big Bob guiding the borrowed sleigh into the yard. Mrs. Stanton was seated in the hay, wrapped in blankets.

He reached back inside the door and grabbed his coat and hat. Big Bob pulled the sleigh to a stop beside the house yard gate. He jumped down and then helped his wife down.

"Warm in the cabin," Hamilton hollered to them. "Step inside, there's coffee and lunch if you want it. You make yourselves at home. I'll be in just as soon as I stall this team."

Mrs. Stanton went to the house but Big Bob took one of the horses and led it to the barn while Hamilton took the other. It was a matter of only a few minutes to stall the animals and hang up the harness. Then the two men walked towards the house.

Looking down the short hill to the feeding grounds, Big Bob stopped. "The last time I was here there was grain growing in that field and an Indian village growing in the hay meadow on the other side of that fence."

He looked the situation over for several moments before saying, "Quite a system you got there. Are those animals all fenced in?"

"Yes, that's my grain field come spring but I feed the cattle there in winter. Holds them close to hand where I can keep an eye on them. It makes it fairly easy to feed. They fertilize the field all winter, too, with no work of mine required."

Big Bob studied Hamilton for another moment. "You've thought this out some. I take it the hay traps are spaced out like that to spread the cattle. And is that water heated? I see smoke. I never saw such as that. I'd like to take a look."

The two men started walking down the hill.

"I just did that this year. You have to understand that most years are not at all like these past few days have been. Never saw the like of this before. We've seen a couple of open winters since I moved here; years when it remained fairly mild with almost no snow. The worst of a normal year was an inch or two of ice on the tank. That was easily dealt with.

"But last year the darned tank froze clear to the bottom. It took me the full of a day with an ax and shovel to clear that mess out of the tank with the cattle crying for water the entire time. I ended that day wet and cold, and determined to not have to do that again. I built a stove out of a steel barrel and sunk it with rocks. So far, it's worked well. I wish I had thought of it before."

Big Bob looked a bit longer and then started back up the hill towards the house.

"Come in," Hamilton said to Big Bob. "I'll put a fresh pot on."

But he didn't have to. Mrs. Stanton had already made fresh coffee and he could smell biscuits baking.

At Hamilton's quizzical look, Mrs. Stanton said, "If you don't mind me saying, this is a typical bachelor setup. I swear you men could starve to death in a field of plenty. I thought you might find use for a couple of day's supply of biscuits."

Hamilton hunched his shoulders and grinned at her. "You're right and I don't mind you saying it. A man alone just eats to keep alive. There's no pleasure in it. The biscuits smell good. Thank you." He didn't bother telling her that he made a pretty good biscuit himself.

As they were finishing up their biscuits and coffee liberally laced with wild honey, Mrs. Stanton cleared her throat, straightened up her knife on top of her plate, fidgeted with the white napkin that Hamilton had never found use for before, and looked awkwardly across the table. "Mr. Robb, you have been exceptionally kind to our family the past couple of days as well as a great help. Thank you very much."

"Just doing what anyone would do. I'm glad it was a help. Now, you haven't told me about Ben and Sam yet, or your rider either."

Big Bob gave a quick hand gesture at his wife as if to say, "You tell him."

Mrs. Stanton nodded at her husband's gesture. "Sam can see a bit this morning and the doctor says he should heal right up in a few days although his eyes might be sensitive to light for quite some time. His feet and fingers were frozen but they'll be alright, too. He's sore and hurting and he won't be dancing for a while but he should see a full recovery.

"Our rider is in some difficulty. The doctor says he came within an hour of freezing to death. He said things I had never heard before. Like that his body temperature was dangerously low. Hypothermia I think he called it. The poor man, he's lost one ear and three fingers. The doctor is still hoping to save his feet but we won't know for a few days. They're black and scarred and swollen and ugly. I do so wish our people had known about that Indian footwear. It would have saved such misery."

Hamilton nodded at that information. "And Ben?"

"Ben is going to live. Mostly thanks to you and that wonderful horse that brought him to your place. He says he was completely lost and couldn't even think straight with the cold seeping into every part of him. We will never know what attracted his horse to this ranch; perhaps he smelled your horses. But with that dreadful wind that seems unlikely. It's more likely he smelled the chimney smoke. In any case, the horse brought him here and you did the rest. Thank you again."

Mrs. Stanton took a few moments to gather herself, then continued, "Ben has lost some toes and two fingers. Hopefully his feet will heal. They look even worse than our cowboy's do. I never before saw anything so ugly. His nose and ears and his cheeks froze but they seem to be healing up. He'll have some skin peel off as he heals but that's a small price. As long as he doesn't lose a foot, he will be alright. He may walk a bit different with the toes gone but he never was much for dancing anyway. None of this will affect his riding or his work. He is very thankful to be alive and we are thankful, too. Sometimes we have to look through the gloom to see the Lord's blessing."

She looked awkwardly at her husband. Big Bob had been almost silent through this entire affair and she wasn't sure what his thoughts were. He had always taken great pride in his accomplishments and had never before shared the credit with God or man. As much as that troubled her, she had never challenged him on it, knowing what his reaction might be.

Big Bob caught her look but didn't respond except to say, "I have work to do at home. Best we were under way. You've been thanked, Robb, but I'm thanking you again. I could live through losing some cattle, as bad as I feel for the poor beasts, but I could not have lived through losing two sons. I have no words for my gratitude.

"If that offer on the hay still holds, I'll be over in the morning with what's left of the Circle S crew. You can show me the stacks then."

"It holds, and I'll be here."

16

THE SUN AROSE THE NEXT MORNING TO LIGHTEN A WHITE, still world. The mercury in Hamilton's outside thermometer still read thirty below but the wind had died down to barely a breeze. As he made his way to the barn, his moccasins gave off a squeak like a rusted hinge with each step, so dry and cold was the snow.

The familiar combined odors of hay, horse and cow, leather harness, manure, and damp wood greeted Hamilton when he opened the door. It was not an unpleasant odor and he welcomed it with thankfulness knowing his livestock were safe and warm in the small building.

The relatively warm air from the interior of the barn created a dense fog as it escaped to meet the frigid outside air. All around the door was a buildup of ice, testimony to the amount of warm air that leaked from around the roughly-fitted door. The dog darted into the barn and took up his usual post, sitting in the manger feed box in front of the very patient wagon team. Hamilton pulled the door shut and reached for the lantern. As that feeble light pushed back the early morning gloom, he spoke aloud to the animals to let them know he was there. There seemed to be an animal in every available space. Before walking among them, he preferred that they be awake, not wishing to surprise a horse and be thanked with a hind hoof.

Hamilton had finished his chores and was shutting the barn door when the sleigh pulled into the yard. He waved a greeting and walked over to the men who were just jumping down from the hay rack. "Morning," he called out. "I'm ready if you are. Just let me get my horse and I'll guide you down."

A series of greetings came from the men and then a female voice said, "Good morning, Mr. Robb, I trust you are well this morning."

Hamilton turned in amazement towards the voice. "Miss Stanton? You're the last person I would have looked for on a hay-loading job in this bitter cold. I didn't recognize you under all those wraps."

"I didn't come to load hay, Mr. Robb. I came to make lunch for all of you. Mother was afraid you would all starve to death by mid-afternoon judging by what she saw in your kitchen. Pa grumbled a bit about me coming but he didn't really mean it. Now if you will show me where things are, I'll get out of this cold and let you men get the rack loaded."

Hamilton walked her towards the porch. "It's not such a big cabin that it's hard to find anything. You just go in that door and you're there. I filled the wood box this morning so you should have a-plenty. The cold pantry has smoke-cured pork hanging in it and that box you see on the north side of the house has frozen cut beef. There's stewing chunks wrapped in brown paper if that would suit you. I haven't dug out the root cellar yet but there's potatoes and carrots in the cabin."

Wanda lifted the lid on the meat storage box. "How very clever of you, Mr. Robb. So you are a butcher and meat cutter, too?"

"Not really. I carried the butchered beef and the hogs to the meat cutter in town. He cut and wrapped it for me. I'm afraid my skills are a little lacking in that area. A whole beef would mostly go to waste with just me anyway so I trade the meat cutter half the beef for his labor. Here's the stew meat but there's steak and roasts, too, if you prefer."

Taking a careful look to see if her father was watching, Wanda whispered, "Mr. Robb, we will have to have a serious talk. I must say, you have a way of springing things on people when they least expect it. Mother and I have kept your words about me staying here with you to ourselves but you know that can't last."

Hamilton looked and felt a bit foolish, remembering his outburst at the Circle S. "I fear I owe you an apology. I'm alone so much that I've taken to talking to myself and sometimes I blurt things out when the smart thing would be to keep quiet. But I meant what I said even though I know I should have bit my tongue."

"Go get your hay, Mr. Robb. We will talk another time."

Hamilton led his horse from the barn and joined the group at the wagon. "I'll show you the hay and you can take it from there. I have work of my own to do but I'll be with the cattle if you need me." He indicated two large blankets he had draped over his saddle. "Take these with you. The horses feel the cold, too, and they have to stand for a while as you load the hay. These will help keep them warm."

They made their way down the grade and into the hay flat along a snowed-in trail through the bush. Big Bob had never driven a sleigh until the trip home from town the day before. He was startled when the wagon, sliding freely on the fresh snow, started to catch up to the team. Afraid the wagon would overrun the team and not knowing what else to do, he urged the team into a trot. Before they reached the bottom of the short slope, the horses were fast-trotting and the sleigh was still close on their heels. When he managed to bring the team and sleigh to a stop at the bottom, he looked over at Hamilton. "There has to be a better way to do that."

"The easiest is probably to keep the sleigh moving slowly. The horses can hold it back when it's empty. In this deep snow, it won't run away."

The stacks were the most of a mile from the cabin. The men shoveled four small drifts but in this sheltered area the snow lay mostly flat on the ground, the wind being dispersed through the bush.

Hamilton tied his horse to the fence and opened the gate to the hay yard. Inside were four huge stacks deeply covered with snow.

"Help yourself. Once you break through the snow cover on top, the loading should go pretty quickly. You can probably make three trips a day if all goes well and after the trail is tramped down a bit."

Big Bob looked at the stacks and then over at Hamilton. "This is a lot of hay. Is it really all extra to your needs? I wouldn't want to short you."

Hamilton waved at the stacks. "Take it all. I have more down in another hay field that you can have, too. I wouldn't short my cattle. They'll be well cared for. Take it and welcome."

Big Bob was clearly ill at ease as he looked from the hay to Hamilton. He had no words ready to mind that could express his feelings. After an uncomfortable span of time, he looked directly at Hamilton. "I don't suppose there's another rancher in many a mile that would do this for me.

I'm as grateful as I know how to be. But I need to ask, what am I paying you for this? It's worth whatever you ask but I would still like to know."

"Take it and God bless," answered Hamilton. "The Lord has taken good care of me and my animals. No reason in the world why I shouldn't share with others. Anyway, this ain't no easy task. Before you move all this cut grass, you'll feel like you earned it. And it's too cold to talk about money. You get to loading and we'll say no more about it."

Big Bob stood rooted as if his feet were frozen to the ground, taking a long study of his neighbor. "Don't think I'm not grateful, for I surely am, but I always pay my way. I'd like to now, too."

"Get those animals fed and take care of my sleigh and I'll consider myself well-paid. Now I have to get back."

Hamilton stepped into his saddle and turned his horse for home, wanting to discuss the matter no further.

Big Bob and the cowboys had very little experience forking hay and the job started poorly with little being accomplished. The first few jabs with the pitchforks did nothing more than bring down an avalanche of snow onto the unhappy cowboys. One of the men finally spotted a ladder leaning on the back side of the stack. He climbed to the top and kicked away enough snow to expose the hay. Working from the top he soon had a steady supply of hay on its way down to the bed of the sleigh.

After an hour or so, they started to get the hang of it and the transfer went more quickly. Still, it was late morning before they turned the first load towards the cabin. The horses were badly chilled from standing for so long in the snow. They didn't pull well until they were nearly back to the H-R headquarters. Big Bob figured that if they were to make three loads a day they would have to improve production by a considerable margin.

When they reached the yard, Hamilton pointed at the house. "It's a little shy of noon but Miss Stanton has lunch ready. Why don't you stall that team of yours for an hour? They'll pull better for having a bit of warmth."

Big Bob led the cold team to the small barn and followed Hamilton inside. The stalls were full and most of the alley also but by nudging a few horses closer together, the two men made room for Big Bob's team in the alley-way. He tied them there and then took a bucket to water them. Hamilton brought a big armful of hay to each one. That done, the men filed into the cabin and the welcoming warmth.

Wanda had made a stew and biscuits. The men tied into it with such force that she feared there wouldn't be enough. The men ate in silence, each taking an extra helping and then mopping the gravy up with the biscuits.

The meal over, she looked at the empty pot and laughed. "Mr. Robb, I had somehow imagined that there might be some stew left over for you for another meal but there's not a drop left. A person would think you men had been working out in the cold or something."

Her father looked at her and leaned back in his chair. "We have indeed been working and it's almighty cold so I guess you have that right. Anyway, that was a pretty good stew. Tomorrow will go faster now that we have a better idea of what we're doing. We should be able to be back at the Circle S for noon tomorrow. That way you won't have to make this cold trip."

"I don't mind the trip."

Everyone in the room understood the unspoken situation, remembering the evening of dancing that they had all witnessed. No one spoke and Hamilton was just as glad, not wishing to have anything provoke the man he hoped would soon become his father-in-law.

The Circle S with the hay wagon was gone about an hour when Hank and Adam Blossom rode into the yard of the H-R. They helloed the house but turned to the barn when Hamilton answered from there.

Hank stepped down beside Hamilton and turned to Adam. "Son, I believe if you were to ask, Hamilton wouldn't mind you going in to the warmth of the house for a bit."

"Go ahead, Adam, warm in there."

When Adam was gone, Hank looked at Hamilton with a serious look on his face. "Don't suppose you heard the news from the Johansson's. Their son Olaf rode over just a bit ago and told us."

As Hank told Hamilton the news, the two men stood soberly, wondering what to do to help their neighbor. Hamilton finally asked, "When did this happen?"

"During the blizzard, two evenings ago."

"Well, it's still almighty cold but at least the wind has died down. I'll ride over there. See what can be done."

After being greeted quietly by Thomas and his family and being seated at the table with coffee, Hamilton asked, "What can we do?"

Thomas sat in silence, wringing his big hands, but Mrs. Johansson said, "The loss is bad enough but it's driving me crazy to know she's somewhere out there under that dreadful snow. We've taken turns looking but have found no sign."

Hamilton drank the last of his coffee and rose to put on his coat. "I'll see what can be done. I'll be back and I'll bring a few people."

Thomas, ever the independent one, looked at his wife and then at Hamilton. "I thank you for your offer but I'll get it done. I'll get back out there again just as soon as I warm up a bit."

Hamilton put his hand on Thomas's shoulder and said quietly, "Not this time, neighbor. Sometimes we all need a helping hand and this is your neighbor's turn to be a help to you. We'll not interfere with the family but we have to do this. We'll never feel right about it if we don't help."

He nodded towards the rest of the family. "You stay and be a comfort to the kids. Leave the other to your friends."

Thomas exhaled a breath and his shoulders sagged a bit. He sat down at the table and put his head in his hands while Hamilton reached for his hat.

He rode first to the Blossom spread. His words were few and his message urgent: "I know you have your own work that needs doing but we have a more important job to do this afternoon. We need to gather as many folks as we can and meet at the Johansson place as soon as possible; these winter days are short and dark comes early. Bring sticks or poles for prodding beneath the snow. Adam, do you suppose you can ride to town and tell folks along the way?"

Adam agreed immediately and went to saddle a horse. Hank saddled up and rode east to call other neighbors.

Hamilton rode to the Circle S. He tied his horse to the hitch rail and stepped through the yard gate and up onto the porch. He was greeted at the door by Mrs. Stanton who stared at him before saying, "My, my, Mr. Robb, please come in. What in the world brings you over here?"

Before he could answer, Wanda and her father walked into the foyer. "We have that wagon unloaded and the boys are just getting warmed up a bit before we head back. The horses are in the barn taking on a feed. Is there a problem?"

Hamilton told them the situation at the Johansson spread as briefly as he knew how. "We're trying to get as many searchers as we can for this afternoon. Can you spare some of your men to help this neighbor?"

Wanda answered for the family, "Of course we can. I'll come, too. Father, how many men are there with the cattle that can be added to the haying crew?"

Bob didn't answer the question but he did pull on his coat and walk out to the bunkhouse.

Before long, a small group from town including Rev. and Mrs. Brockton were on the town road heading towards Johansson's. Mrs. Brockton saw a black speck moving along the side of the road about one-half mile ahead. She studied it closely as they drew near. "Why, I do believe that is Mr. Dillabough. What in the world is he doing out here?"

Rev. Brockton pulled the cutter up beside Smokey. "What are you doing out here, Smokey? You're not dressed anywhere near warm enough for this cold day."

"Heading to the Johansson's. They're going to need a grave. That's my job. I gotta get out there and start digging. Hope they can lend a pick and shovel. The cemetery set is under the snow back to town."

"Climb on the back, Smokey. It won't be any warmer but it might be a bit faster."

Within a couple of hours, there were twenty-six searchers with long poles or cut-off tree branches walking and prodding every foot of the ranch yard. It was a cold and solemn task. Rev. Brockton organized the group into a long line across the yard.

Smokey had found some tools in the shed and went to work on the side hill behind the house. It was tough going but Smokey took the job to heart and, after clearing away the snow, began to dig. Johansson had pointed out the spot. "That will do just fine and thank you. But first you come with me to the barn. I have a warmer coat for you."

It was Wanda walking beside her father who felt something when she prodded a small drift with the pole her father had cut for her. She stooped and brushed the snow away. Pausing, she sat back on her heels and started to cry. Pleadingly, she looked through her tears at her father.

Big Bob went to his knees beside her and brushed off as much snow as he could. Glenda had died lying on her side, her arms tight to her chest and her hands clasped as if in prayer. Her knees were drawn up tight against her body.

She was much farther from the house than where her father had been searching.

Bob Stanton scooped the still form off the ground.

Holding the precious little girl's body in his arms, he turned towards the house. Word of the find went through the group of searchers in moments and all eyes turned to Big Bob and the frozen bundle he was holding.

Mrs. Johansson was in the house with a few neighbor women but Thomas was with the searchers. He slowly walked over, silently took his daughter from Big Bob, and turned to the house. There was no need for words.

As he slowly plodded his way towards the house and his waiting family, the searchers gathered around Big Bob. Hamilton joined them. Quietly he said, "All that can be said, folks, is 'thank you.' You all did real well. Thank you again.

"It's almighty cold out here and that house is too small for us to even warm ourselves in. I suggest we all head for home. Any of you as might wish to are welcome to drop into the H-R on your way home. I'll stoke up the fire and put the pot on."

Big Bob surprised them all. "You're welcome at the Circle S, too, if you're going that way."

Wanda slipped her hand under her father's arm and leaned her head on his shoulder.

It was too cold to linger so the yard was soon astir with men mounting saddles and families turning sleighs for home. Rev. Brockton had been one of the searchers while Mrs. Brockton was in the house with the family. As the searchers slowly made their way from the yard, Rev Brockton stepped into the relative comfort of the barn for a few minutes of lonely quiet, stirring up his faith and searching for words to comfort the family. He then walked slowly towards the house, fearing what the next few sad hours were going to be like.

Smokey refused to leave until the grave was dug. He also refused all offers of help. He said he would ride home later with the Brockton's. Some of the townsfolk who had looked on him with scorn took another, more enlightened look before turning for home.

THE HAYING CREW worked from dark to dark the next day, completing three loads. Wanda came again and made lunch from fixings she brought from the Circle S. She rode home on the last load of hay.

Before leaving, she talked privately to Hamilton, "Mr. Robb, I wasn't snooping. I was looking for a pencil and piece of paper to write up a list of supplies you might want to pick up from town. This kitchen is a bit bare of necessities.

"My suggestion would be that if you are going to write poetry, you should put it where a casual eye won't find it. I can only hope Mother didn't see it the other day. I appreciate the sentiment you wrote but Pa would fly over the moon and might never find his way home again if he were to see it.

"We really do have to have a talk, you and I."

Hamilton had no idea at all what to say so he said nothing, just looked sheepishly at her.

Wanda smiled at him. "We really will have to have a talk."

Before leaving, Big Bob spoke to Hamilton, "If it's all the same to you, we'll take tomorrow to look for more stranded cattle. We have just over one thousand on feed now and they can manage on this load for another day or two. We drove them down to the wintering flat and they're managing to paw out good grass where the snow isn't too deep so that makes the hay go a lot further. There might be other brutes out there alive somewhere and I would like to do whatever I can to save them."

"You come back whenever you can. That hay ain't going anywhere. I expect I'll be here but I have to make a trip to town one of these days. If I'm gone, you can load hay anyway and use the cabin for warming yourself."

The fifty-acre field Hamilton wintered the cattle on was planted to oats each spring. A grain-growing neighbor from east a few miles was hired to do the harvesting. Hamilton bagged the grain and stored it for the horses. He had the straw from the separator blown into a pile in the center of the field. He strung a double-wire temporary fence around the straw and left it for cattle bedding.

After the blizzard had passed, it was only a matter of a few days until the cattle had trampled the snow flat and Hamilton pulled down the fence around the straw pile. The cattle would spread the straw although Hamilton helped them along by throwing forkfuls as far as he could from the pile and carrying other forkfuls further out.

From time to time over the next few weeks he intended to break down the stack and spread the bedding into a larger area. If no more heavy snows fell there should be a fair to middling bed ground for calving season. He would burn the used-up straw in the spring before planting.

The weather gradually warmed but only marginally. Night temperatures were regularly below what had been accepted as normal in past years. With the slightly warmer weather, Hamilton turned his excess horses into the pasture with the cattle and cleaned the barn that had been overcrowded for weeks.

Big Bob and his crew finished their search for cattle. In the end, they found about twenty-five hundred Circle S animals alive but struggling. When Hamilton asked about the search, Big Bob looked up and pointed at the hills on the western end of the ranch. "Never saw the like. Those Longhorn brutes went to browsing on scrub willows and alder bark. How they stayed alive on that feed is a mystery to me. Still, the losses are high. I'm glad the boys talked me into selling off the feeder calves last fall. To lose them would have broken the Circle S. Still, come spring we will have some decisions to make."

Hamilton remembered Big Bob's talk of going back to Texas. Maybe he was rethinking.

The Circle S crew finished hauling hay and Big Bob thanked Hamilton again. "You saved what was left of my herd. I'll not soon forget that. There still isn't enough feed to see the animals to full spring so I'll have to ship some. But that's better than skinning them out for the hides."

THE DOCTOR ALLOWED THE STANTON BOYS TO COME HOME from town but they still needed a lot more recovery time. Sam could see alright in a shaded room but suffered in full light. The doctor had suggested that he wrap his eyes with a dark cloth, leaving just the tiny slit for vision. The sun glare from the snow was almost unbearable for Sam but the head-wrap helped. Overall, he found it more comfortable to stay indoors.

His feet were healing well and, except for his eyes, he was fit enough to get back in the saddle.

Ben was not so fortunate. He had suffered no further amputations but his healing was slow. He couldn't put any weight on his feet except just enough to balance himself while he learned to use the crutches the doctor gave him. He managed to move around the house enough to get to the parlor from his bedroom and to the dining table. Getting to the outhouse was a formidable task that he managed only with Sam's assistance. Such help would normally have included cruel teasing but not under these circumstances.

Both men knew how fortunate they were not to have died in the storm.

HAMILTON WAS HAVING lunch in the cafe in town when the sheriff sat down beside him.

"You hear the news?"

"I haven't been in town for two weeks. Not much news gets out our way."

"A rider left a Denver newspaper at the hotel last night. The storm was worse than we knew. Over two hundred reported deaths so far. There's probably more that they don't know about yet. Hard to get my mind around that. Lots of them were kids sent home from school as soon as the storm struck. The teachers meant well but sending the kids out in the bitter cold and the howling winds was a serious mistake. Paper says several teachers died, too. The paper's calling it the Children's Blizzard. No matter what it's called, it's one we'll all remember."

Hamilton was silent, trying to take all of that in.

The sheriff continued, "Lots of livestock lost, too. Thousands of cattle froze or starved. A rancher was in yesterday telling about how he found dead cattle standing upright in snow drifts.

"Others, drifting before the winds, piled up against fences or tumbled into coulees with more animals piling on top of them. Their suffering must have been unimaginable.

"Some ranchers lost most of their stock. Country's going to be a long time coming back."

TO NO ONE in particular Sam hollered in mock distress, his arms waving in the air, "I've got to get out of this house! I feel like I've been taken captive by a group of warrior women and they won't let me go! My life isn't my own anymore! I've become a slave! Do this, do that, move over there, you're really in the way sitting there! It's more than a man should be expected to tolerate!"

Ben, always happy to help out his young brother, laughed and said, "Why, little brother, this just helps you get ready for marriage."

Wanda turned to her mother with a grin. "What are those two going on about now? I never heard so much grumbling." Not waiting for an answer, she stepped from the kitchen into the sitting room, all set to tease Sam but he was nowhere in sight. She was just in time to see the front door swing closed.

She looked over at Ben propped up on pillows on the couch. "Did Sam go out? Is he crazy? It's twenty below out there."

"He took a blanket."

"Oh, that should help a lot at twenty below."

Wanda's mother guided her back into the kitchen. "Your brothers are adult men, leave them be."

"Adult men and smart is not necessarily the same thing."

A while later as Sam was slumped on a rocking chair on the porch bundled against the cold, his head jerked up at the sound of horse's hooves on the roadway. A smart-looking, red-painted cutter pulled by a trotting gray gelding glided smoothly into the yard. Sam sat upright, shielding his damaged eyes with his hat brim and straining to see who the visitors were. Judging by clothing alone, he could see that the driver was a man and the two passengers were ladies. Other details were beyond his ability to make out.

"Howdy there, Sam," yelled the livery barn owner. "Brought you out some company."

Surprised to hear the town hostler's voice, Sam came to his feet. "Can't hardly see across the yard. Who you got there, Walt?"

"Oh, just some strangers I picked up along the way. Don't expect they're anyone important. You going to invite us in or do we have to sit out here in the cold?"

"Yes, of course. Come in, come in. Warm inside. Come in and we'll put the coffee on."

"I would prefer tea," said a female voice. "That is, if it's not too much trouble."

Sam hesitated, startled to hear that voice. "Is that you, Miss Granet? My eyes still don't like this bright snow but I seem to know that voice."

"That's me, Samuel, and I have Penny with me. Mr. Trimble was kind enough to make this trip for us. But we're a might cold so I'm happy the trip has come to an end."

Walt and the two ladies mounted the four steps to the wraparound veranda and Sam shook Walt's hand. He awkwardly moved to shake Miss Granet's hand, then thought better of it and pulled his hand back not really knowing what was correct in these circumstances. Hoping no one could sense his inward excitement and that his voice didn't betray him, he waved at the big front door. "Come in. Everyone will be happy to see y'all."

Wanda had heard the noise outside and opened the front door. Amazed, she looked at the arrivals and then at Sam. Sam offered no explanation; he couldn't because he didn't have one yet himself.

Sam introduced the ladies to Wanda and then to his mother who had just arrived from the kitchen, wiping her hands on her apron. "We have met before, briefly at the dance and again at the doctor's office. I remember your kindnesses to the boys. Welcome."

Sam had hesitated but Wanda did shake the girl's hands and sounded genuine when she also invited them in.

Sam looked at his mother again. "And perhaps you'll remember Mr. Trimble who runs the livery stable."

Walt touched his fingers to his forehead as a slight nod to the ladies. "Pleased to see y'all again."

He then said to Sam, "We won't be here all that long but that gray will pull better going home if we could shelter him for a bit. Is there space in the barn for an hour or so?"

"Sure, as you know," answered Sam. "We'll take him over there first and then have our coffee."

In the house, Wanda helped the visitors off with their wraps. "Won't you make yourselves comfortable? Pa is out working with the cattle but Ben is in the parlor. I'm sure he will be happy to see you."

"Well, I hope so," said Penny with a smile. "It's him that gave us the invite."

Mrs. Stanton gave the girls a long look and whispered her usual, "My, my."

The three girls made their way to the parlor and found Ben struggling to get his feet under him with the help of the crutches. By his tousled hair and the pillow creases on his cheeks, it was obvious that he had been sleeping. He did his best to stand but still relied on the crutches. He smiled at the girls and looked a bit embarrassed. "Ladies, you caught me napping. Come in. Come in."

Penny smiled her most radiant smile. "You suggested that we come for a visit and since this is Sunday and Mr. Trimble was available to bring us out, here we are. I hope the timing is convenient."

Wanda and her mother looked on, for the first time wondering what the boys had been up to in town besides lying about in the doctor's clinic. Wanda said mischievously, "I'm sure any time would be convenient for

Ben. It's not that he has much else to do these days. Please sit, ladies, and make yourselves at home."

The visitors sat as primly as their bulky winter clothing would allow and smiled at Ben. Ben returned a very uncomfortable smile and turned a bit red in the face.

Again Mrs. Stanton, noticing her son's red face, said quietly, "My, my."

The door burst open and Sam came in followed by Walt Trimble, both brushing snow from their coats and hats. They stomped their boots on the mat at the door and hung their coats on the pegs provided.

Sam, much more outgoing than Ben who took after his father, said, "I'm glad you ladies remembered our invite. We were starting to go a bit cabin crazy around here, what with not getting out and with nothing much to do. Sorry Pa's not here. I'm sure he'd enjoy visiting with y'all, too."

Wanda gave Sam a strange look that might have meant almost anything from 'Are you crazy?' to 'This looks like trouble to me.'

Sam and Walt found seats. Wanda said, "I'll get some tea," and left the room, followed by her mother who was still saying, 'My, my' under her breath.

In the kitchen, Mrs. Stanton looked at Wanda as if to ask, "What's going on?"

Wanda returned her look with a mischievous grin. "Don't look at me. I had nothing to do with any of this. Anyway, they're nice girls and you didn't really think your children were going to stay single and underfoot forever, did you? And you will have to admit that a single visit is a long ways from a lifetime commitment."

"A single visit is perfectly meaningful when it involves a twelve-mile sleigh ride in the bitter cold. Your father is determined to return to Texas in the spring and he won't look kindly at complications."

"Ma, you know full well that Pa is just talking for the sake of having something to say. He's not going back to Texas. And if he should somehow make the foolish decision to really go back, who's to say the two of you won't be going alone?"

This time the look Wanda received was very serious. "Do you have something you need to be telling me about, young lady?"

Wanda flashed her most mischievous grin. "Why, Mother! Why would I want to burden you with worries? You have enough to worry about just keeping father reasonably happy. Your children are no longer children, Mama. I expect you know that we each have a mind of our own and can do our own thinking.

"As for your sons, I am surprised they're both still single. There should be girls out there somewhere who will lower their standards enough to marry a Stanton. And, of course, I'm nearly an old maid so I intend to grab the first live body that comes along. So, what do you have to worry about?"

"Young lady, I'll have you know that I found a gray hair the other day. I shouldn't be the least bit surprised if I were to turn completely gray before all these shenanigans are dealt with. But you didn't answer my question. Is there something you need to be telling me about?"

Wanda took a step back and looked at her mother. She gave a girlish giggle and said, "Why, Mother, I think you might look very regal with silver hair.

"Now, you bring that plate of baking and I'll take this tray of tea fixings. I'll come back for the coffee for the men."

"I'm not going to get an answer, am I?"

Wanda ignored the question.

Arriving in the parlor, Wanda sounded almost too

cheerful as if she found the situation mysterious and much to her liking, "Here we go. I'll get the coffee in a moment. Who would prefer tea?"

Before long, they were all snacking on baked goods and their preferred drink, and the conversation had ground to a halt.

Finally Wanda said, "Mr. Trimble, how would you like to take me for a short ride in that sleigh. I have never ridden in a sleigh like that. I believe it's called a cutter, is it not? We could drive down to the pasture and see how Pa is doing with the cattle. You never know, he might need some advice."

Ben spoke up with a short chuckle, "I'd be careful on that advice thing if I were you."

Walt Trimble nodded. "Good idea. Just let me enjoy this hot coffee and then we'll go."

Wanda smiled at the lady guests and then at her mother. "I'll get my coat and hat. Mother was just saying how much she had to do in the kitchen so I'm sure y'all will excuse her, won't you?"

Mrs. Stanton smiled a strained smile and excused herself.

The whole Circle S had been wearing moccasins outdoors since the cold had struck. Wanda sat on the chair beside the front door and pulled on the Indian footwear, then donned her coat and hat. "Ready," she said to Walt.

Walt jammed the last half of a slice of bread and jelly into his mouth and mumbled, "Com'n."

On the way to the barn Wanda said, "We'll harness our Circle S buggy horse. That will give him a feel for pulling a sleigh and give your gray more rest in the barn."

Harnessing the horse, Walt smiled over at Wanda. "Thanks for getting me out of the house. A cracked coffee mug and a ladder-back chair in the saloon is more to my taste. Can't hardly get a grip on one of those fancy tea cups."

"We're just ordinary folks, Mr. Trimble. We have cowboys tramping in and out most anytime."

They were soon skimming over the snow towards the feeding pasture.

Wanda laughed out loud. "This is great! It rides so smoothly that I don't think the horse even knows it's there. I can hear the runners singing on the cold snow. I love it."

Walt nodded in agreement. "It's a long-ago memory for me but it seems I remember something about a sleigh ride feeling downright romantic. Of course, you have to be with the right person to feel that. You know, some young man with a bright future ahead of him. One who will treat you like a queen." His sly glance at Wanda left no doubt about who was on his mind.

"The less you say about that possibility, the more peaceful our home will be. The girls' visit has mother all in a snit. Please do me the great kindness of not talking any more about me or your long-ago memories, either one. I'd appreciate that."

"I understand but that don't make me wrong in what I'm thinking."

"Think is one thing, saying is quite another."

"Agreed, young lady. My lips are sealed."

Big Bob had no fences to hold the cattle in the feeding yard. He had to rely on their steady feed supply to keep them from wandering. Still, each morning the crew had to dig a few stubborn animals out of the brush and back into the yard.

The ground was too frozen to drive fence posts but the stacked hay had to be protected so Big Bob and the crew had cut alder trees into posts and nailed on sawmill slabs to hatch together a free-standing fence. So far it was holding together and keeping the cattle from the stacks.

Walt pulled the sleigh up at the edge of the herd. Big Bob had seen them coming and rode over to see who it was.

"Morning, Mr. Stanton," called Walt.

"Trimble? What brings you out here on this cold morning?"

Wanda spoke up, "Mr. Trimble brought out some visitors from town, Pa. They're up at the house now. And I wanted a sleigh ride so he was good enough to bring me down."

"Visitors? Who would come visiting in this cold?"

"You'll meet them when you come in for lunch, Pa."

Walt looked over the gathered herd. "Good to see you've saved a goodly lot of animals out of the blizzard. A lot of cattle lost around the country. Troubling time; never saw the like."

Big Bob looked back at the herd and then nodded to Walt. "We saved maybe a bit over half. Can't imagine what the others suffered. We wouldn't have saved any without some help." He did not explain that statement.

Everyone in the district knew about the giving of the hay but it still wasn't openly talked about. A man's dignity was an important part of him. To damage a man's dignity could easily cause a rift that would never be healed. Big Bob had not shown much friendliness to the community but he was still a neighbor and a man of some means.

And then the Circle S joining the searchers for the Johansson girl had broken some of the tension between the Texans and the locals. There was no desire to embarrass him. He wasn't the only rancher caught short in the storm either. If he were to be criticized, that would open a wide path for the criticism of others and that would benefit no one.

Walt looked over at the stacked hay and nodded at Big Bob. "Well, we like to help each other in these parts. Lot of good folks around here. Good neighbors."

Wanda spoke up, "Mr. Robb had some spare hay he let us have."

Those few words put the matter out in the open. Big Bob seemed to take the revelation in stride but Walt, aware of the tension between Hamilton Robb and the Circle S, felt it best to pretend that he hadn't heard about the hay before. He gave a questioning look at Wanda and then at Big Bob. "I'm not surprised. No better man in many a mile than Hamilton Robb. Good neighbor and good friend."

Big Bob nodded, his Stetson tipping a dusting of fallen snow off its brim. He wore his Stetson jammed down over a scarf he had wrapped around his ears. "His hay was a godsend to us, I'll admit that. But, right now, I have work to do. You'll have to excuse me."

Walt stopped him with an uplifted hand. "What's that you're working on? Something I can help with?"

"We just managed to set that stock tank where the windmill can pump water to it. It's not anywhere near level but it will have to do until spring. Now we're trying to rig a stove out of a barrel. An extra hand is always welcome. You can come over if you like."

Wanda asked Walt, "Can I take the rig for a drive across the pasture?"

"You know to be careful so go and enjoy. Don't work a sweat up on that gelding though."

By noon the crew had the tank filled and a fire going in the barrel stove. "This is all new to us," Big Bob told his workers. "We'll have to keep a close eye on it."

Wanda drove the sleigh back to where the men were

working. "Father, this sled is absolutely wonderful. Climb in and I'll drive you to the house. Mr. Trimble will be glad to bring your horse up, won't you Mr. Trimble?"

Big Bob hesitantly climbed aboard the cutter and Wanda had the rig moving before Walt got a chance to answer.

Seeing the girls in the house, Big Bob was too surprised to say more than 'Hello.'

Ben felt that an explanation of sorts might be helpful. "We invited the girls for a visit when they called around to the doctor's clinic. Walt had some time so he brought them out."

Big Bob made that loud grumbling noise in his chest that he had become known for. No one was quite sure what it meant.

The cowboys headed directly to the cook house without seeing the girls or knowing they were there. Somehow, though, the cook knew about the visitors and spread the news. Dalton got up and looked out the frost-covered window although there was no hope of him seeing anything.

He made his way back to the table. "Now what do you suppose…."

No one had anything to add.

At the big house, lunch was a quiet affair with Wanda doing most of the talking.

"Pa, I think you should ask Mr. Trimble if he would sell us that sled. It is a purely wonderful thing and we really should have one. Why, I can see us using it for months every winter. It is ideal for getting to town for shopping or for church or for visiting neighbors. Would you sell it to us, Mr. Trimble?"

Her enthusiasm was contagious but her brothers wisely kept their thoughts to themselves.

Mrs. Stanton, attempting to take pressure off of her husband said, "Mr. Trimble will need his sleigh, dear. And we won't need one when we get back to Texas."

Wanda laughed. "Oh, Mother, we're not going back to Texas. Daddy just said that. He didn't mean anything by it."

Big Bob lifted his eyes from his plate long enough to give her a hard look.

Walt complicated matters by saying, "I have another cutter at the livery. This is a two-seater which you would need were the whole entire family wishful of traveling together. The other is a single-seater. More ideal for a couple who enjoys sitting close together."

Wanda nearly choked on her food. Ben and Sam both sat rigid, their forks held in mid-air. The visiting girls both swallowed loudly.

Walt kept his face averted from Big Bob but he had trouble hiding the beginnings of a grin.

It took a few moments for the words to pass. With nothing more said about sleighs and people sitting close together, Wanda finally relaxed and decided to push the issue of purchasing the cutter.

"Why, it's wonderful that you have a spare cutter, Mr. Trimble. Do you suppose, if I came along to town with you and tied one of our buggy horses on behind, that I could bring the sleigh right back this afternoon?"

"We would have to leave early enough for you to get back before dark."

Big Bob's chest rumbled and Mrs. Stanton quietly said, "My, my."

Ben and Sam were looking from their father to Wanda and back again, not saying a word.

No one had ever seen Big Bob under such pressure. Searching for cattle in a storm was something he knew how to do. Matching wits with his only daughter left him wordless.

Ben, as the oldest sibling, felt entitled to say something, "Little Sister, I don't think you should be out on that road by yourself in this cold. Take one of the cowboys along with you for safety."

"That's a good idea. Daddy, which man can you spare this afternoon? Of course, it's Sunday and we never work on Sundays unless there's an emergency. And now that you have the cattle watered I'm sure you and the crew intend to take the afternoon for rest and quiet reflection." She was in danger of losing the struggle to keep a straight face. "I'll bet Dalton would enjoy a ride to town and back. I'll go ask him as soon as lunch is finished."

Mrs. Stanton laid her hand on Wanda's arm. "But, dear, we don't even know how much Mr. Trimble wants for the cutter."

Wanda wasn't about to let little things like cost get in her way. "I'm sure we can figure out something, Mother."

Wanda continued to carry the bulk of the conversation for the remainder of the mealtime, saying things with a radiant smile that she knew made her brothers uncomfortable. Things about long rides to town, and loneliness, and the long winter months.

"Why, just think, Ben. With that cutter, you boys can get to town just about any time it suits you even if you have to think up excuses for the trips." She looked from Ben to Sam with a grin but avoided looking at either girl.

Her talk turned into a monologue with no one else having anything at all to say.

When it came time for the return trip to town, Wanda again arranged the matter including her talk with Dalton. She shrugged into her winter coat and hat and said, "Mother, why don't you come take a look at this wonderful cutter. Perhaps Father can take you for a short ride through the yard. He and Walt will have the horse out by now and I know you'll enjoy a few minutes of fresh air."

Mrs. Stanton glanced at the girls and then at her sons. Finally, she reached for her coat. As the door closed behind Wanda and her mother, Penny said, "I do believe Wanda has enjoyed our visit as much as we have but for another reason."

"She's a handful at times," answered Sam.

"Be a happy day when she marries and has someone new to harass," said Ben.

Miss Granet smiled at the two men. "I think she's fun. I've enjoyed meeting her. I've enjoyed our visit with you men also. Perhaps you can find time to drop by on your next trip to town."

Sam grinned at the girls. "We may have to try out that new sleigh Wanda forced on Pa. You just never know. Could be Ma will need some kitchen supplies or some other foofraw from town. You just never know what might happen next on the Circle S."

"Well, goodbye then," said Penny. "And thanks again." She offered a handshake to Ben.

He, in his eagerness, let go of his crutch to shake her offered hand and nearly fell. Penny grabbed him and held him until he was steady on his feet again. "Sorry about that," said Ben, blushing.

Sam laughed and slapped his brother on the back. "Well done, Ben. But you're only going to get away with that the one time."

He turned to Miss Granet. "Thank you for coming, Miss Granet. Your visit brightened the day for us. We haven't been out of the house for days on end."

"Well, I think we could drop the Miss Granet thing.

That's for the students. Blizzard heroes and all the young men I visit call me Sophie."

Penny laughed. "Don't take that seriously, Sam. I doubt that Sophie has ever visited a young man before."

With additional thanks and additional goodbyes, the girls made their way to the cutter and Walt soon had them skimming out of the yard on the town road with Dalton sitting beside him, hanging on as if the cutter might try to buck him off at the first opportunity, and the three girls ranged across the back seat warmly wrapped in blankets.

When the family was gathered back in the house, Big Bob looked at his sons. "Well, am I going to get an explanation?"

"Nothing to explain," answered Sam.

Big Bob made that chest sound again. "Might just as well see to the cattle. They make as much sense as what I've seen around here lately."

As he was putting his coat back on, his wife was looking in the gilded mirror hanging on the wall beside the door. "I must admit, that cutter ride was quite exhilarating. I do believe I may have some color in my cheeks."

WANDA, EXPERIENCING A WONDERFUL FREEDOM OF movement, covered a good part of the country with the cutter, loving the driving of the horses and the thrill of the speed over the frozen ground. She had visited the Johansson place a couple of times and found that she very much enjoyed the company of the hurting family. And they seemed to welcome her presence.

Several times her excursions took her near the H-R ranch. She considered turning in but her concern for propriety held her back. The Circle S was already the focus of considerable town gossip following the visit of Penny and Sophie and she didn't have any desire to add to the wagging tongues.

But finally, on one of her trips home from town, she overcame her caution and turned in at the H-R gate.

She drove the cutter to the edge of the hill where she could look down into the cattle feed yard and saw Hamilton working at the windmill. Smiling to herself she turned to the barn, unhooked the horse, led it into a stall and tied it, leaving the harness in place. She then walked over to the cabin and let herself in. The fire had burned down so she shook the grate a bit and added wood. She filled the coffeepot from the pail on the sideboard and put it on to boil. Then, with a quick glance out the window to see if Hamilton was in sight, she dipped up warm water from the stove reservoir and proceeded to wash his breakfast dishes. By the time she finished doing that, the coffee was ready.

She pulled on her coat and walked over to the edge of the yard. She waited until Hamilton was looking in her direction and then waved to gain his attention. Cupping her hands to her mouth, she hollered, "Coffee's on."

Hamilton shielded his eyes from the snow glare in an attempt to see if it was really Wanda. It had sounded like her voice. But what in the world could she be doing on the H-R? After a moment or two, he waved back and moved towards his tethered horse. He stepped into the saddle and was soon at the barn. When he had the horse comfortably stalled, he walked to the cabin and entered.

"This is a pleasant surprise but a might dangerous, don't you think? Between the biddies in town and your father, I seem to see considerable risk in your visit as pleasant as it is."

"Why, Mr. Robb, I thought you might be happy to see me." Her mischievous grin was infectious and Hamilton was soon grinning himself.

"Well, I am happy to see you and to see my dishes washed and the coffee ready. That's all very domestic but there are those around that might not see it in the same light. And I thought we had agreed that my name is Hamilton. Can we drop the Mr. Robb thing, Miss Stanton?"

Wanda slid a cup of coffee across the table to him. "We agreed at one time, Mr. Robb, when our visits were casual, that's correct. But you changed the rules to the game and we had better have a discussion about the new rules. That's why I'm here.

"You said some things a while ago that got my mother's attention and have caused her considerable concern and more than just a little lost sleep. She accused me of being the source of a gray hair she found a while ago. So far, she has not spoken to Pa but I know she's bursting with news that will set off a storm to match the worst Texas blue norther when she can no longer hold it in. None of us will enjoy that."

"Exactly what rules are you referring to, Miss Stanton? And before you tell me, please be assured that I am not playing at any games. I play a game of checkers with the sheriff once in a while but I never play games with life. Your life or mine, either one."

"I get the impression, Mr. Robb, that you are having fun at my expense but I'll let that go for the time being. Very clearly, what you said to Mother when she mentioned returning to Texas and then what you said to me when I came to make lunch when the men were moving the hay, could very easily be taken as a serious intent. Mother is in somewhat of a snit about that. On top of that, there's the visit to my brothers by the ladies from town. I fear that Mother may soon have an entire head of gray hair."

Hamilton knew nothing about the visit from town. "We will talk about my serious intents shortly. But first tell me about your visitors. I've hardly left the ranch since the blizzard and I've heard nothing except some cattle talk. I was in the general store once and if there was news I would have thought Penny would pass it on, but she said nothing."

Wanda giggled her girlish giggle. "She's the news. That's probably why she said nothing. A couple of weeks ago, she and Miss Granet convinced Mr. Trimble to drive them out to the ranch in his cutter. They came to visit the boys. Caused quite a stir around the Circle S. Made everyone wonder what my brothers were up to when they were supposed to be convalescing in town.

"The ladies haven't been back but the boys have been to town more often than would seem needful.

"The good news though is that Pa bought that lovely cutter from Mr. Trimble. It is the most wonderful thing! I have been over half the ranch and most of the roads in it. I would refuse a trip back to Texas just to get to drive the cutter each winter if I didn't have a better excuse to stay."

Hamilton got up to refill their coffee cups. "I baked some bread and I have cold ham. Would you care for a snack? I usually have a little something this time of day."

"I'll have a small snack but you are not going to get away with avoiding our talk. What is it they say? Speak now or forever hold your peace?"

"Very appropriate," Hamilton responded with a smile. "I do believe those words are said at weddings. And, of course, that's exactly what I have in mind, if you wish me to come right out with it. Left for me to make the decision, I would take you in that cutter right now and go find the Reverend Brockton. But I can see how that might set off a considerable storm as well.

"So, what I really wish is for you to allow me to call on you from time to time."

Wanda had a look that suggested that she was choking on something. "Well, I must say, if that is a proposal, it is the first one I ever received. I somehow thought a proposal might be worded a little differently."

Hamilton placed the bread and ham on the table along with a big pot of honey and a dish of butter. "Dear Lady, when the time is right you will receive a proposal as good as any that has ever been spoken. But you won't hear it until I am sure of the answer I want to hear.

"So, what do you say? May I call on you from time to time? Like, say, every evening? Or morning and evening both if that would suit you better?"

"Mr. Robb, I am not at all sure when you are serious and when you are joking. Of course, you may call but certainly not as often as all that. And you will have to speak to Father. That won't be any simple task but you have it to do."

They ate their mid-afternoon snack in silence, eyeing each other from time to time.

Starting on a completely different subject, Wanda said, "Pa sent the crew off to the railhead with a herd. Even with the grass they can scrape up on that bottom meadow plus your hay, they weren't all going to make it through the winter. We probably still have too many animals. The boys talked Pa into selling off the weaned calves when they were still looking pretty good and before the cold hit. I suspect that sale will prove to be the saving of the Circle S even though the calves were still too small for good beef."

"I saw the drive going past my gate. That was a good decision and one that many a rancher has taken this past while. This cold seems to want to drag on interminably. Getting to the haystacks and then moving wagon loads to their feeding grounds is brutal, never-ending, cold work. But even with that work the underfed animals are still suffering. Selling off some stock seems like the best decision.

"The grain growers have long called this 'next year country'. It'll be 'next year country' for some cattlemen now, too."

Wanda nodded and repeated, "Next year country. But not for you. It looks to me like you have a good year coming up. Your calves are fat and you have hundreds of heifers for breeding. Will you be selling some of those?"

"Most of them are already spoken for but I'll have maybe a hundred or so available."

"Pa needs to talk to you about those heifers but I don't suppose he will."

Finally, Hamilton stood up and put the remaining food back in the cold pantry. "I have work to do and you are going to cause more than enough suspicion if you don't get back. Come on, I'll hitch the horse for you and you can get along home."

Later, working around the cattle and stoking the fire in the water tank, Hamilton found himself standing and staring into space, not noticing that a soft snow was beginning to fall. Finally, a cow heavy with calf nudged him out of the way in her desire for water.

Always able to laugh at himself, Hamilton did so now. "Alright, old girl, I get the message. You get your fill of water and I'll get to pitching hay."

Church services had resumed with the partial break in the weather. Hamilton rode in on his saddle horse while Wanda and her mother came in the cutter. After the service, Hamilton sought out the two Stanton ladies. They were sitting in the cutter, their legs wrapped in blankets, ready to leave for home.

"Good morning, ladies. I've been hoping to speak with you. I'd like to ride over your way this afternoon if that would be convenient, Mrs. Stanton. I wish to speak to you and Bob."

Mrs. Stanton paused. Her "My, my," was barely audible.

Wanda spoke up, "I would think a short visit would be alright, wouldn't it, Mother?"

A totally flustered Mrs. Stanton said nothing.

Wanda spoke again with her mischievous smile, "I am

assuming, Mr. Robb, that this would be a fairly short visit and that it is of some importance?"

Hamilton returned her smile. "I would define it as important, yes. May I say mid-afternoon after I care for my animals?"

Wanda's smile widened as she slapped the reins on the horse's back. Hamilton stood and watched them drive away. Wanda made a wide turn onto the road from the churchyard and waved at him as they passed.

Mrs. Stanton was sitting stiffly, staring straight ahead.

After a mile of silence, Wanda asked, "Don't you think these are nice folks around here, Mother? Penny and Miss Granet made a special effort to come and greet us after services. That was quite thoughtful, don't you think?"

After a further silence, Mrs. Stanton said, "It's not those girls I'm thinking of, young lady. And don't you think for one minute that I don't understand what you're trying to do here."

"Why, Mother, whatever are you talking about? If it's Mr. Robb, he probably just discovered another haystack he doesn't need and wishes to offer it to Father."

"I doubt very much if he has cattle feed in mind."

"Well, we'll just have to wait and see, won't we?"

"Stop the word games, young lady, and tell me what's going on. What are we going to hear this afternoon? I expect this visit is totally about you so it wouldn't hurt to hear it from you first. Are you sweet on Mr. Robb?"

"Mother, you act as if your sons aren't supposed to enjoy the company of the girls and as if no man and woman would ever be attracted to each other after you and Daddy met. Do you really think your marriage is to be the last in the line for the Stanton's? Are you trying to stop your family from growing up? The boys are both well past childhood and quite able to plan their own lives and I might have some dreams, too. Why would you wish to prevent those things from happening?"

The rest of the ride home was taken in silence.

At the dinner table, Mrs. Stanton looked at her husband. "You might just as well know now, Bob, we are to have company this afternoon. Mr. Robb is coming over."

There was total silence around the table as everyone looked at her.

Big Bob made a rumble in his chest. "Robb? Why would he be coming over here?"

Ben and Sam looked at each other and grinned, and then looked at Wanda. "What have you been up to, Little Sister? Have you cornered the neighbor into some kind of foolish thoughts?"

Wanda was not in the least fazed by their teasing. "Who's to say which thoughts are foolish and which aren't?"

Big Bob was a good cattleman, if a little stubborn about the matter of winter preparation and cutting hay. But beyond cattle and horses and the men that worked with them, he was often known for missing the most obvious things around him. He had completely missed the purpose behind the girls' visits from town and his sons' interests, and he never once gave serious consideration to the idea of Wanda becoming an adult with her own interests and passions.

Long forgotten was Hamilton's request for permission to come calling, declared on that early spring day when he had driven the Circle S cattle off his grass and water. If Big Bob had understood Hamilton's interests, he would have brushed them aside with little thought, declaring the man as unworthy of consideration as a possible suitor for his only daughter.

He was a big Texas rancher with big ideas. The concept

of a smaller, more controlled ranching operation never once occurred to him. In Texas, he and his neighbors all pushed each other for the free range. To reduce the size of a herd was taken as weakness worthy of exploitation. He intended to be the first and biggest onto the shared hill range in the spring. If the neighbors didn't like it, they could try to stop him. The warning received from Clark Ransom had frightened him at the time but had eventually dimmed in his memory.

Again, he had completely missed the prosperity that his neighbors enjoyed with their better cattle, their more controlled herds, and their fenced pastures.

"I'm going to ask again, why is Robb coming here? Is it something to do with that hay?"

Ben looked at his father and shook his head. "I think the hay matter is behind us, Pa. There are other things altogether ahead of us."

"Speak plain, boy. I don't care for riddles."

Before anyone else could speak the yard-dog announced the arrival of their visitor. "I'll go," said Sam. "I'll stall his horse and we'll be right in."

Sam pulled on his coat and hat and stepped into the frigid air of the veranda. "Howdy, Hamilton. Ride on over to the barn. Best we get that animal under cover. We were just about to have coffee and dessert. Might be some left over if you were of a mind to want it."

"I remember that chocolate cake. Anything like that could tempt me, for sure."

Within minutes, Sam led Hamilton through the front door. They stamped the snow from their moccasins and hung up their coats. Wanda had pulled up an extra chair to the table and directed Hamilton to it. He took his seat and nodded at Mrs. Stanton and then glanced quickly at Big Bob. Seeing no offer to shake hands, Hamilton chose not to push the issue. "Afternoon, folks. Good of you to let me come for a short visit."

"Would you care for a cup of coffee and a slice of chocolate cake, Mr. Robb?" asked Mrs. Stanton. "Wanda scurried around after church and put the cake together. I'm afraid it hasn't had time to cool yet."

"That sounds just fine, Mrs. Stanton, and a cup of hot coffee is never out of place on these cold days."

The group fell into an uncomfortable silence, broken only by the clink of forks on dishes as they ate their cake.

Hamilton placed his fork carefully on the empty plate and looked around the table. "I know you're wondering why I invited myself into your home. The reason is very simple. I have come to ask you, Bob and Mrs. Stanton, for permission to call on Wanda."

Dark realization finally entered into Big Bob's almost closed mind. Mrs. Stanton's, "My, my" was lost in the explosion from her husband.

"Of all the possible reasons for your visit, I never once considered anything so foolish. Now, you know how much I appreciated your help with the cattle feed. If that hay has somehow gotten you to where you think you've earned some right to visit my daughter, we will gladly pay you for the hay and that will be an end to it."

Wanda showed her humiliation. "Pa, that's low, even for you. How could you say such a thing? How can you even think about me at the same time you think of those scrawny Texas cattle?"

Ben spoke up, too, "She's right, Pa. You need to back off here."

"Back off be hanged. No two-by-twice down-at-the-heels nester is going to come calling on my daughter. I'll not have my daughter tying herself to someone who will spend his life putting his feet under a poor man's table.

"Now, Robb, you've come and said your piece and I've said mine. That's an end of it." He turned sideways in his chair and looked out the window as if to dismiss Hamilton and the topic of conversation.

Hamilton looked around the table and smiled at Wanda. He wasn't easily flustered or intimidated; his years in law enforcement had hardened him well past intimidation. "Actually, it's not at all the end of the conversation. And, believe me, the hay has nothing to do with it. Most everyone in this district will help a neighbor in need whenever possible. I'm just sorry that we weren't able to save more cattle, yours and a lot of others, too.

"Now, by most standards, Wanda is considered an adult capable of making her own decisions. She has asked me to speak to the two of you and I'm supposing she wouldn't have asked that unless she welcomed my interest. So, out of respect I sit here speaking to you as a neighbor and a capable cattle rancher.

"But mostly I speak as a man who has strong feeling towards a young lady that I wish to visit in order to see if that young lay could develop strong feeling in return. I suspect that you and Mrs. Stanton went through a similar process."

Bob turned back in his chair. "There's a sight of difference between a shirttail nester and a Texas rancher. What makes you think you could ever keep a woman in any kind of comfort, never mind a family, on that little place of yours?"

Wanda looked like she might start to cry while Sam looked at his father and shook his head.

Ben spoke up, "I really doubt as how a happy future depends totally on money, Pa. I'd give up all the money I've ever seen and all I'm ever liable to see in the future just to have my feet and fingers back.

"And as far as that goes, Pa, what do you really think the Circle S will be worth come spring? Wanda is right when she calls our herd scrawny Texas cattle. The shape those cows are in we'll be lucky to get any kind of a calf crop and you know full well that nearly half our herd is frozen stiff out in those hills.

"Sam and I have tied our futures to the Circle S and from where I sit that future doesn't look so bright. I wish I could look out our window onto a herd of fat Herefords the way Hamilton can."

Big Bob continued to look defiantly at his sons. "Come spring we're going back to Texas. Never should have left."

Ben had more to say, "Pa, you know full well that the Circle S is not going back to Texas. We spent our last dollar buying this place and making the move. And you also know that there is nothing to go back to.

"Do you remember why we left? I'll remind you. Our oversized herd and all our neighbors' oversized herds ate up all the grass for miles around and were starting on the roots. The poor beasts were trying to eat prickly pear, spines and all. We killed the land that fed us. And now we're a fair way along to doing it again here. There's nothing in Texas worth our going back to. And if we don't change our ways, there'll be nothing here for us in a year or two either.

"I'll tell you this, too. I like it here and I'm not going back. Even if I have to take a job in town, I'm not going back. Wanda tried to tell you all of this months ago. It's time you listened."

Mrs. Stanton said quietly, "I'm not sure that Mr. Robb is very interested in our family matters. Perhaps if you have more to say, Mr. Robb, you should do it now."

"Never mind that," hollered Big Bob. "I wasn't going to mention anything because any man should have the right to make a fresh start. But leaving a gunfighting past and trying to start over as a legitimate rancher is too far a leap for me. And I'll not have my daughter caught up in whatever trouble might come upon you."

He looked directly at Hamilton. "And who's to say your gunfighting past won't catch up with you? How many other gunmen are there out there who want to find you? And how many sheriffs? There's no telling what all you might be running from. No, sir, I will not have my daughter visited by a gunfighter and a poor man to boot." His rage was almost overpowering.

The other four Stantons said almost together, "Gunfighter? Who's a gunfighter?"

Big Bob was not to be stopped. "The gunsmith in town told our crew all about it that night of the dance. Even showed them Robb's gunfighting, two-gun rig. Bet he didn't mention that to you, did he, daughter?"

Hamilton looked at the startled faces around the table and started to laugh. "It might have been better if someone had come and asked me instead of stewing about it since last summer.

"I was never a gunfighter. I was a deputy sheriff. That was over in Arizona. My father is still a sheriff and I liked what I saw in him so I followed in his footsteps. I've never knowingly broken a law in my life and don't intend to in the future. It's true I had to use those guns a few times but only in the line of duty doing the job I was hired to do.

"I was a rather good law officer if I have to say so myself but the job was leading me in directions that I didn't enjoy. It got pretty rough at times. I got to where I just didn't want to do it anymore. So I took off my guns, turned in my badge and headed east.

"I moved here because I found I liked green grass better than desert and cactus. I respect my little piece of land and the grass it grows, and it has treated me well. And you have nothing at all to fear from my past. There is no one trying to find me or pick a fight with me."

Wanda had heard all she was going to listen to. She stood up and moved away from the table. "Come, Mr. Robb. We'll go for a walk in the snow."

"I'd love to go for a walk in the snow with you but we had better settle this thing now. Bob, your daughter is an adult and can make her own decisions. I've come here out of courtesy and I hate to leave with anger and misunderstanding hanging between us. You have nothing to fear from my past or my future either, God willing. I am asking again for your approval of my visits."

"Well, you don't have it. Even if what you say about gunfighting is true, that still doesn't mean you can make a living and support a family. I notice that you've avoided the question of money. You can't make a decent living on that little patch of land and I suspect you know that.

"I've wondered a few times why you didn't buy this piece when you knew it was available. You might have had a chance with the two ranches together. I suspect you weren't able to get the loan. You'll probably never get the loans you have now paid off. No, absolutely not, you'll be a poor man all your life and Wanda deserves better."

Sam looked ashamed. "Pa, I never thought you could be so narrow in your thinking. I'm finding it a bit difficult to sit here. I think I'll go for a walk in the snow, too." He pushed back his chair and reached for his coat.

Ben said, "If I could walk, I'd join you."

"It's OK, Sam," said Hamilton. "I can fight my own battles. Bob, I never talk about money. I don't care if a man is rich or poor. It's what he is inside that counts and that will quickly enough show itself. I've never gone hungry or cold or poorly dressed and I expect that will continue.

"I take that for your final word, so here's mine. If Wanda will welcome me, I will come calling on her. You have my promise that all of my intentions are honorable and will stand up to your examination. I won't impose myself into your home again but if she's willing to, Wanda and I can walk or ride and get to know one another. I also promise that never will Wanda and I be alone together at my place. I hold great respect for her and will do nothing to ever cause gossip. But I will call on her as long as she welcomes me.

"Thank you for the coffee and cake, Mrs. Stanton. I'll be taking my leave now."

Within a few minutes, Big Bob found himself sitting alone at his dining room table. Wanda had put on her coat and gone to be with the barn animals, one of her favorite places on the ranch, Hamilton standing beside her but with neither one speaking. Sam was outside in the cold and snow walking aimlessly along the ranch road. Ben had gone to his own room. Mrs. Stanton had sat quietly looking down at the table and had finally gone to start the dishes. Big Bob took another drink of his cold coffee.

After a considerable wait, sitting alone, Big Bob sought out his wife in the kitchen. Walking into that room, he was startled when his wife turned her back on him. She did it quickly but not before he had time to notice that she was crying. He stood awkwardly for a moment and then walked into his den, alone.

19

THE WEATHER REMAINED VERY COLD FOR THE NEXT THREE weeks. During the first week, Hamilton drove to the Circle S in a cutter. When he knocked on the door, Mrs. Stanton invited him in but he simply said, "May I speak with Wanda, please?"

Wanda joined him in a minute and again invited him in. "Pa's out with the cattle. Come in."

"I'll wait here. I'll do nothing behind your father's back. Would you like to take a ride in my new cutter?"

Wanda squealed with delight. "Where did you get a cutter? They are the absolutely most wonderful inventions. I'd love to take a ride."

They were soon skimming across the snow, warmly wrapped in blankets and sitting close together in the cutter. Again, Wanda asked, "Where did you get this lovely thing?"

"I ordered it late last summer from the general store catalogue. I'm surprised Penny was able to keep her mouth shut about it, she's been that curious since the Circle S bought that rig from Walt. It just arrived yesterday."

They rode in silence for several minutes. Finally Wanda spoke, "Hamilton, I don't know if it is possible for one person to apologize for another person. But you need to know that none of us are happy with Pa. He's always been loud and a bit gruff but since the big freeze, he's been totally out of control.

"And then the thing with the Johansson girl really shook him up. I'm so sorry for the things he said to you. I think he's worried half to death. I know you said you don't talk about money and I'm not asking you to. But I will just for a moment.

"The Circle S is deeply in debt. We had debts back in Texas and had to sell a large part of our herd to pay them off. Then we had to borrow again to buy this place. I really don't know how much it all totals but I know Pa is not sleeping well and he's worried about it all. And then to be proven wrong about his preparation for winter has embarrassed him more than anything in his life. His pride is near the breaking point. Add to that the loss of half the herd or more and the help he had to accept from you, and it all makes for a weight he's not sure he can carry.

"But his concern for me is genuine. Pa remembers the grim start he and Mother had, and he doesn't want anything like that for me."

Hamilton studied on that short speech for several minutes, saying nothing. Wanda could see his mouth working but no words were coming.

Finally, half ready to explode, Wanda said, "Hamilton, speak to me. I can see your mouth working and the gears going around but I don't hear anything."

Hamilton laughed and reached for her hand. "I told you before that I've taken to talking to myself. That's a really bad habit that I'm going to have to work on. So I'm trying to choose my words carefully.

"The thing is, I don't have any financial worries. The ranch does very well and I have everything I want. For the first few years I went into the hills after freeze-up and caught wild horses with my Indian friends. I spent the winter months breaking them to saddle and sold them in the spring for a good profit even after paying the Indians. I didn't go after horses this year for two reasons. The first is that there aren't many left worth catching and the second is that I don't need the extra work or the extra income. The H-R is really doing quite well.

"As Mrs. Robb, you might find some things to worry about. Like if our children were to look like me. Or if I got caught up in the chores and forgot to come home at dinner time. Or if I were to come home from town and forget to bring you with me. You know, those kinds of worries. But you wouldn't have to worry about money."

Wanda laid her head on his shoulder with her mittened hand lying on the blanket. "I think it would be delightful to have sons that look like you. And I think I can fix it so you won't forget I'm there."

Hamilton put his hand on top of hers, "Then we really won't have anything to worry about at all, will we? Of course, you will have to milk the cow and gather the eggs and muck out the barn. And keep the garden watered and help feed the cattle all winter. But other than that, I can see you having a mostly leisurely life."

She gave him a friendly punch on the shoulder and laid her head back down.

20

About a week later, on a bitterly cold February morning, Hamilton looked up from his feeding yard to see about a dozen Indians sitting their horses on the brow of the hill. The men were wrapped in old clothing, blankets, scarves and whatever else they could find to ward off the penetrating cold.

Johnnie carefully rode his horse down the slope to the cattle yard while the others waited at the top. "Hello, Hamilton. How do you like our foothills winter so far?"

"Worst I've seen, Johnnie. How have things been in the village?"

"Many of our cattle froze. All we have left are the breeding cows, and now the people are experiencing hunger. I have come to see if you have a few steers you could sell us."

"I would sell you some animals before I saw your people go hungry, Johnnie, but I shipped all my heavy steers in the fall and all I have left besides the calves and bulls are bred cows and breeding heifers. I could let you have some calves but they still need a lot of growth before they'll make real beef. How many head do you need?"

"It will not be enough but the agent gave permission to deal for one hundred head. I have a form with me guaranteeing payment."

Hamilton thought about the situation at the Circle S and wondered. Finally, he asked, "Can your men ride another few miles?"

"We'll ride."

"Let me saddle a horse and we'll go over to the Circle S."

In less than an hour they were all sitting their horses in the yard of the Circle S with the cowboys glaring at them and with Sam stepping out of the house onto the porch. Hamilton walked up to Sam. "Sam, I need to talk with your father. It's about cattle."

Big Bob stepped onto the porch, showing no friendliness. "What's this about cattle?"

"These men just arrived at the H-R. Johnnie tells me that so many of their cattle were lost in the storm that there is near starvation on the reserve. I shipped all my steers in the fall and I thought if you sold a hundred head it would relieve your feed situation. The men would take them right now."

"I don't know as how I would trust Indians to ever get around to paying once they had the animals."

"Johnnie has a government chit with him that any bank will honor and if that isn't good enough, I'll pay for them myself and collect from the government."

Ben had hobbled slowly onto the porch in time to hear most of the conversation. "I don't see any problem with that, Pa. We surely need to sell off a few head."

Big Bob was becoming stubborn as if he had to

somehow make a point. "I'm only worried about getting paid."

Ben said, "I'll tell you what. A part of this ranch is mine. We'll get the men down there right now cutting out the hundred head and we'll call them mine. You go back in by the fire, Pa. This no longer concerns you."

"Everything on the Circle S concerns me," hollered Big Bob. "I'll still want to see the money."

Hamilton said, "If you'll let me in and loan me a pen, I'll give you a check for the cattle. You can go right in this afternoon and get it cashed."

Big Bob stepped aside and glanced at his eldest son. "Ben, you take care of this and I'll get the men to cutting out the animals."

Ben asked, "What do you figure to ask for the cattle, Pa?"

"Come spring they'll be worth twenty-five dollars but we won't make it to spring." He looked at Hamilton. "Will the government pay ten dollars?"

Hamilton nodded. "I'll write you a check for a thousand dollars. But that includes a hot meal and coffee for these men. You tell the cook to get some food together and get the men in where it's warm, and I'll get to writing the check."

Big Bob stood there looking stunned. "I'm not sure the cook will want Indians in his cook house. Not sure I do either."

"They're men, Bob, just like you and I are men. God created all of us. The difference now is that they're cold and hungry and so are their horses. But if you want something extra for the meal, tell me how much and I'll add it to the check. But whatever it is, let's get it done quickly."

"I have serious doubts about the bank honoring your check but I'll take the chance. I ain't forgetting about the hay and what you did for the Circle S. Get the thousand, Ben, and I'll talk with the cook."

Ben said, "If he argues about it, fire him and send him packing right this afternoon."

The men were soon filing into the cook house and the cook was grumbling at his big cast-iron stove. Sam piled a load of hay in the yard and the Indian horses grouped around it.

The cowboys weren't happy about having to leave the warm bunkhouse but Big Bob rousted them out and they saddled their horses.

Sam hollered at the men, "Don't you men drive any culls up here. I want to see good steers or you'll be going back after more."

Wanda met Hamilton inside the door. "I heard. That's a good thing you're doing for the Indians. It's good for the Circle S, too, but I doubt anyone around here is smart enough to figure that out." Ben gave her a troubled look.

Hamilton fished in his shirt pocket and brought out a blank check. "My hands are too cold to hold a pen properly. If you'll make this out to the Circle S for one thousand, I'll sign it and then go help the men."

Wanda wrote it out and, after Hamilton signed it, she placed it under a paperweight on the table. She then asked, "Do the Indians know about driving cattle? Of course, you'll be with them to the H-R. Will they be alright after that?"

Hamilton answered, "They know some but maybe not enough. I'll go with them and try to guide them along."

"You can't leave your ranch for that long. When would you be back?"

Hamilton was pulling his mitts on. "If all goes well, I should be back by noon tomorrow. My animals can wait that long. I'll swing off the road long enough to pick up a spare horse for myself. We should make pretty good time. There's too much snow for the cattle to stray."

By late morning, the Indians were back in their saddles. The Circle S crew was holding one hundred head of recently fed and watered steers in a loose group in the big ranch yard although it really didn't require much holding. The steers had little desire to wander.

Ben hobbled out into the yard on his sore feet. He spoke to the crew, "I want to see some of you men volunteer to go along with the drive. I know it's cold but it's only twenty-five miles. You know why I can't go myself. Now, some of you have strong feelings about Indians. But these are men, too; men with families in need. And I would remind you that the Circle S was in great need just a few weeks ago. Help came from a neighbor who didn't have to help but did anyway. And you all volunteered to help when that little girl was lost in the snow."

Sam, dressed for riding, interrupted Ben, "I'm going along, men. Who'll come with me?"

The crew looked at each other and then some looked at the ground. Finally, Dalton spoke up, "It's just another job of work, boys. Don't much matter who it's with or for. I signed on to drive cattle so I'll go along."

He looked over at Hamilton and Johnnie who were sitting their horses side by side. "Let's move em out."

Hamilton smacked the closest steer with his coiled rope and got the small herd moving towards the town road. The Indian riders fell in behind. Dalton and six more Circle S riders crowded the sides as much as the drifted snow would allow. Hamilton looked at the Circle S men and nodded his thanks.

The reluctant steers covered the distance to the H-R in good time and Hamilton swung into his yard. He hollered at Dalton, "Keep them moving. I'm going after a spare horse."

He was soon back, driving three spare horses. After crowding the horses into the drive, he took up a place on the drag. He spoke to the Circle S man beside him, "Ever take the drag before without eating dust?"

"Not that I can remember, except in Oregon. I spent a couple of years out west but didn't like the rain. But I have to admit that the green grass kept the dust from forming. All things considered, though, I might prefer dust or rain to cold and snow."

Another Circle S rider ventured his opinion, "When you sign on to work cattle, you sign on to take what comes. I sometimes wonder if I'm even as smart as the cattle. I know I'm not as smart as my horse. My horse didn't volunteer for this ride."

Wanda was worried about the chores that would be left undone at the H-R while Hamilton was away. She decided to take control of the situation.

A couple of hours after the cattle left the yard, Mrs. Stanton walked into the front hall of the big house to see Wanda pulling on her mitts. She was dressed warmly and ready to go out. "Where in the world are you going in this dreadful cold, dear?"

Wanda gave her a defiant look. "I'm going to the H-R. There will be fires to tend and animals to care for. It's the least I can do. I'll be home as soon as the men get back. Probably by noon tomorrow."

"I notice that you chose to wait until your father was down with the cattle before stepping out. I doubt very much that he would approve."

"And how about you, Mother. Do you approve?"

Mrs. Stanton hesitated. "You're a smart young woman and I don't see the problems with Mr. Robb that your father sees. And it would be best if you didn't remind your father of this but I did something very similar when we were courting."

Wanda flashed a mischievous smile. "Why, Mother! I would love to hear that story."

"Well, you're not going to, not now or any other time. I only mentioned it so that you would understand why I'm not stopping you from going. But the bitter cold does worry me. Take Ben with you. He can't do the barn chores on those sore feet but he can be a help in case the cutter tips or an animal acts up."

"I never thought of Ben coming. That's a good enough idea. I'll ask him."

Ben spoke from the doorway to the sitting room, "Ask him what? I heard my name. What are you two up to?"

Wanda explained and Ben nodded in agreement. "You get a horse on the cutter while I get some warm clothing on. Take that dapple gelding. He's the steadiest harness animal we have. Better put a small valise together, too, in case you get wet and need to change clothes."

The brother and sister were soon at the H-R with the dapple gelding crowded into the small barn. Before putting the horse away, Wanda had driven him down the short hill to the feed yard. There she stoked the fire in the water tank heater and threw some hay over the fence. Ben drove the cutter from stack yard to stack yard while Wanda did the work with the pitchfork.

In the cabin, pulling off their outer garments and stamping the snow from their moccasins, Ben said, "It's starting to get cold in here. I'll build up the fire if you'll fill the coffeepot."

With that done, Ben hobbled through the rest of the cabin. He came back and sat down at the kitchen table. "This is a nice cabin. Cold in that back bedroom though.

That night when Hamilton pulled me from the storm he bedded me down on that cot by the fireplace. I expect that's where he sleeps and that I was putting him out of his bed that night. There's a stove in the back bedroom but there's no sign of recent use. Tonight, you can have the cot. I'll be fine on a pallet on the floor. Too cold in the other room for me."

Wanda looked at the choices in the cold pantry, shook her head, mumbled something about starving to death, and went out to the meat locker. She soon returned with a small package of steaks.

Ben looked at the package and grinned in wonder. "Where did you get those?"

Wanda explained as Ben shook his head. "We have a lot to learn about cold country. Never once thought of keeping meat frozen over winter."

They worked together to make a lunch of beef steak and grease-fried potatoes and then sat over their coffee for a while. Wanda went back out to the meat locker and brought in a packaged-up roast of beef. She busied herself during the afternoon with the slow roasting of the beef.

"She looked at Ben and grinned. "I believe most bachelors would starve if it wasn't for eggs, stew and biscuits. A roast of beef with potatoes and carrots might be a treat for Hamilton when he gets home."

"Stew and biscuits sounds good enough for me if there's a bite of side meat to go along with it once in a while."

Hamilton had shoveled out the entry to the root cellar so Wanda pulled open the sloped door and entered. Ben held a lantern high over his head while he made his way with considerable difficulty down the steps.

Wanda hesitated at the bottom of the stairs. "I hate root cellars. If there's a snake wintering down here...."

Ben chuckled, "Any self-respecting snake is hibernating right about now so you have nothing to worry about."

Wanda looked for a long time at the bins of potatoes and carrots before she reluctantly started placing them in the bucket she had brought with her. "Are you sure snakes even have self-respect?"

"Grab the vegetables you want and let's get out of here so we can close that door. We're letting all the heat out."

The days were short in mid-winter and dark came early. As afternoon waned into early evening, Wanda made her way to the feed yard to stoke the fire for the night. Worried about her, Ben hobbled to the top of the hill and watched her the whole while.

They went together to the barn. Ben managed to find a few eggs while Wanda threw down some hay from the loft. She then struggled from animal to animal with pails of water. The cow and calf were together so no milking needed to be done. With nothing else required, they closed and latched the door and headed back to the warmth of the cabin.

Ben lit a lantern and hung it on a hook he found on the porch. There was still some daylight left but Ben was being cautious. "In case one of us has to go out later."

Wanda chuckled, "That's nice. But I don't hardly think I'm going to get lost in this small yard."

"The Johansson girl did," was Ben's answer and he showed no sign of humor as he said it.

THE CATTLE WERE SLOGGING STEADILY WESTWARD BUT THE pace was slow. The lead steers ploughed through the drifts and the piled-up snow, becoming exhausted in the process. The animals following had a somewhat easier walk as the snow became trampled down. The men made an effort to rotate the lead steers but finally gave it up as the animals showed no willingness to move from their place in the herd. No amount of pushing and encouraging from the drag changed the pace for long. A few humped backs and quickened steps of the rearmost steers had no effect at all on the leaders and the riders had to adjust their desire for speed to the listlessness of the cattle.

The Indian riders, having already made the trip one way, were showing signs of fatigue, mostly from the penetrating cold. Their horses were suffering even more than the men. They had passed the turnoff into Canyon View but still had fifteen miles to go. The truth was evident to all the men: they would pass much of the long, cold night in the saddle.

A couple of townsmen heading home on the road

stopped what they were doing, nodded a greeting to Hamilton and watched the cavalcade go by, then turned to spread the news. They had noticed the Circle S brands.

One Circle S rider swung quickly into town to purchase a pair of woolen mitts and some more scarves which he passed around to the other riders.

Hamilton rode over to Johnnie. He had to shout to be heard through the scarf wrapped across his own mouth and the one tied around Johnnie's ears. "What would you think about sending some of your faster riders to the village? They could send back fresh riders and fresh horses."

"Good idea," Johnnie hollered back. He rode to the rear of the drive where most of the Indians were bunched and spoke to them. Six men were soon riding past the strung-out cattle and heading to the village as quickly as their exhausted horses would allow.

Johnnie rode back to Hamilton. "When the fresh men arrive, they can take over and these others can ride on ahead. We'll be close enough then to go the rest of the way ourselves and you and the Circle S men can turn back."

On the Circle S, a quiet lunch was eaten with neither Big Bob nor his wife having much to say. Stepping away from the table, Big Bob began struggling back into his heavy coat. Mrs. Stanton saw from the kitchen and walked to help him. As she pulled the collar up over the bulky shirt and sweater, she asked, "What are you up to now? Surely the cattle don't need more attention. You've been down there all morning and we have men to do most of that work."

Reluctantly Bob answered, "I'm going into town."

"What on earth would cause you to make a ride into

town on a day like this? The temperature hasn't risen above thirty below zero all day"

"I need to see if that check is any good." He knew how foolish that sounded given the fact that the cattle were over three hours down the road already and far out of his control.

His wife shook her head at him. "Bob, I love and respect you but there's many a time I don't understand you. You and I both know that check doesn't matter on this bitter cold day. Let it go. We'll get to town soon enough after the weather breaks."

Bob pulled on his mitts, looking stubborn. "I stated my case to Robb and now I have it to do. If it turns out that he's written a bad check, it will prove my point to Wanda."

"And if the check is good, what will that say to Wanda?"

Bob reached for the doorknob, ignoring the question. "I have to hurry if I plan to get back before full dark."

Mrs. Stanton tugged on his arm, giving him a loving look. "Bob, you're a good man and I know you love your daughter and want the best for her. But this crusade you're on could well tear our family apart. We have all suffered this winter, you most of all, and our losses are great. But your determination which I have always admired has turned to pride and stubbornness which I don't admire even a little bit.

"Are you sure that having to accept help from Mr. Robb hasn't eaten away at you to where you want to find anything at all to hold against him?"

Big Bob stretched to his full height and looked defiantly at his wife. "Not even you have a right to talk to me that way." He had never spoken that roughly to his wife before and immediately felt shame but didn't admit it. "Let go of my arm. I'm going to town."

Mrs. Stanton stepped back. "Alright, Bob. I'll have supper ready when you get back."

THE EARLY DARKNESS was threatening to envelop the H-R but Ben and Wanda were ready for it. They had gone out to check the animals again and Wanda had built up the fires to hold for the night. She had struggled mightily to lever the windmill into the neutral position knowing that, left on its own, the tank would overflow during the night and the cattle would find themselves slipping on fresh ice in the morning.

Finally, with all the outside work completed, Ben topped up the oil in the lantern and re-hung it on the porch. He smiled at Wanda. "Just in case."

As an early dusk descended on the ranch yard, Hamilton's dog growled and a desperate holler was heard out of the cold evening.

"Hello the house!" Bone-weary and near collapse, his jaw and lips so cold he could barely move them, Big Bob had trouble with the words but Ben and Wanda somehow understood.

Ben laughed and Wanda showed an exasperated look. "That's Pa. Can't leave anything alone."

She hollered, "Come in. The door's open."

The door opened and Big Bob all but collapsed onto the kitchen floor.

"Pa," hollered Wanda. "What's happened? You look half done in."

Ben leaped to his sore feet and grabbed his father's arm, easing him into a chair. "You're near frozen, Pa. Where have you been?"

Big Bob said nothing. He slowly pulled off his hat and

unwound the scarf from his face. Ben helped him pull his coat off while Wanda poured him a cup of hot coffee.

Big Bob managed to gasp out a few words, "Coming from town. My horse slipped on some snow and broke a leg. Fell on me. Must have taken nearly an hour to get free. Cold, almighty cold. Had to walk here. Didn't have a gun so the poor beast is still suffering down the road a couple of miles."

Ben reached over the doorway and picked down Hamilton's old carbine. He checked it for shells and then leaned it against the wall beside the door. He pulled on his coat. He had never looked grimmer.

"Wanda, I need you to help me harness the horse to the cutter. I'll be alright after that. It will just take a short while to get to that horse and back. You sit here and get warm, Pa. When I get back, I'm going to expect a really good explanation as to why you rode to town on a day such as this." Right then Ben sounded more like his father than he knew.

As Wanda was pulling on her mitts, she gave her father a stern look. "Pa, I'm going with Ben. We won't be but an hour or less.

"You have some terrible hard feelings towards Mr. Robb, Pa. Can I trust you to not do anything foolish while we're gone? I wouldn't like to see this cabin accidentally catch fire."

Big Bob looked more hurt than Wanda had ever seen him. His eyes showed the beginning of tears and his cheeks were quivering. He formed words on his mouth as if he was speaking to himself. Finally, he managed to say, "Is that what you think of your father? Do you really think I would stoop so low?"

Wanda saw his hurt but didn't relent. "Pa, a few months

ago I would never have thought anything like that of the man I love most in the whole world. You've always been strong and determined - hard almost - with the ranch, driving the men and yourself relentlessly. But you were kind to the family and your friends. Now, since the storm, you haven't been yourself at all. You seem to be the only one who can't see that. Your family sees it and your crew sees it.

"Mr. Robb has shown you ranch-saving kindness and still it's as if my seeing him personally is about to drive you crazy. I hardly know what to expect of you anymore."

Bob looked at the floor, the coffee cup clutched between work-hardened hands. "Go harness the horse and get back here as quickly as you can. The cabin will still be here."

Wanda made her way to the barn. Ben had already led the dapple to the alleyway where the harness was hanging. Between them they got the harness on and Ben led the horse to the cutter. Wanda swung the barn door closed and dropped the latch into place. She was already feeling the cold.

Ben drove the cutter to pick up Wanda. She stepped into the rig and took her seat. She swung her arm in a semicircle as if to take in the whole countryside. "I don't really know how men work out in this kind of weather but somehow they do. I'd rather bake bread in a warm kitchen with the cast-iron stove belching out its heat."

Ben had no comment, his mind firmly on the suffering stallion.

The drive to the injured horse took less than twenty minutes.

Ben had been silent during the drive. Arriving at the place of the accident, Wanda gave a cry of alarm and Ben recoiled in horror at the sight of the injured animal. It had been thrashing in the snow, trying to stand on its three good legs. Clearly in terrible pain, the animal whinnied as the cutter drew near as if crying for help.

With the arrival of Ben and Wanda, four coyotes each took one final grab at the horse's torn flesh before scurrying over the closest snow drift and disappearing from sight, chunks of bleeding meat hanging from their jaws. The horse cried out in pain again and thrashed its head against the piled-up snow.

Wanda buried her face in her woolen mittens and cried.

Ben let out a startled oath and cursed the coyotes. "Scavengers. Unfeeling, miserable scavengers. Couldn't even wait for that poor stallion to die before tearing into him."

Ben carefully slid out of the cutter and stood in the snow at the head of the suffering stallion. He jacked a shell into the carbine and raised it to his shoulder. "Hold the reins, Wanda. I don't want a runaway with you in this cutter when I pull the trigger"

Wanda was crying in great, gulping sobs and Ben had to speak a second time. Finally, she picked up the leathers and held on tight.

Ben took another look at the suffering stallion. The pain and misery was plain in the animal's eyes. The horse lifted its head a bit and then dropped it back into the snow. A faint whinny, almost a cry, came from its throat. It was as if the animal was pleading for help or perhaps that was just Ben's imagination.

When he pulled the trigger, the stallion jerked once and then lay still. The echo of the shot lost itself in the surrounding snow drifts and was finally heard only in Ben's and Wanda's ears and hearts.

The dapple gave a startled leap, moving the cutter a couple of feet but Wanda held fast. She didn't look at the stallion again.

Ben let out a breath that he seemed to have been holding forever and lowered the gun. A trickle of blood was running down the stallion's forehead and into its eyes. Ben stared as if mesmerized. He spoke quietly to himself, "Pa, you're paying a heavy price for pride."

Wanda lifted the reins and in a very small voice pleaded, "Let's go back, Ben, I don't want to stay here any longer."

"Just hold that horse steady a bit longer. I want to get the bridle and saddle." He reached to unfasten the bridle. The horse had died with his mouth open so the bit slid out easily and he soon laid the bridle in the back of the cutter. He unfastened the cinch on the saddle and then stepped to the cutter and lifted down a rope he had brought along. He tied this to the saddle horn and the other end to one runner on the cutter. "Alright, move forward slowly until I tell you to stop."

Wanda guided the dapple along the road until she felt the tension in the rope pull the cutter sideways on the trail.

"Keep going," hollered Ben. "Just a bit further. Gently."

The dapple had to dig in and pull harder but Wanda knew by the sudden freeness of the sleigh that the saddle was loose. She pulled the cutter to a stop at that point. Ben untied the rope and hollered, "I think I see a wider clearing just ahead there. See if you can turn the rig around and then come back for me and the saddle."

Wanda made the turn and had the cutter heading back to the H-R almost before Ben had a chance to throw the saddle in and get seated himself.

He glanced back at the dead stallion in time to see the coyotes already there, growling and tearing at the warm flesh of the horse. He chose not to say anything to Wanda about it.

Wanda passed him the reins and again buried her face in her mitts.

Ben said, "Interesting that Pa was riding his favorite stallion. Losing that horse will hurt him almost as much as losing the cattle. I've shot a horse or two but I purely hated to shoot that one."

Arriving back at the H-R, Ben said, "Pull up at the door. Pa can take the rig home. We'll get back somehow tomorrow."

The two of them walked into the cabin and stamped their feet. Ben did it very gently, his feet still a long way from healed. Wanda hung up her coat but Ben kept his on. He replaced the carbine on the pegs over the door. "I don't know where Hamilton keeps his cleaning equipment. I'll have to clean the gun for him after he gets back."

Big Bob was just finishing up a bowl of Wanda's stew. He looked at his two children but had nothing to say.

Wanda had a lot to say but she wasn't sure just where to start. She hung up her hat and scarf and turned to her father. "Pa, I expect you went to town to cash that check. I can't think of a single other reason for you going. So, tell me, was the check good?" Her anger and hurt had only increased after the ordeal with the stallion and the coyotes.

Her father looked at her and answered, "We'll talk at home. I'll take the cutter and come back for you in the morning."

Ben passed his father his coat and hat. "It's pitch dark out there now and we've all had enough trouble and to spare for this one day. You getting lost or in more trouble in the cold isn't something I want to contemplate. I'll go with you.

"Wanda will be alright in the cabin for the night. I'll go with you and we'll both be the safer. Anyway, I've been sizing up this floor and decided that my own bed looks mighty welcoming by comparison."

Big Bob had no arguments left in him. "Let's go then. Wanda, you stay inside. The animals will be fine until morning. And I want you to promise that you'll wait for me in the morning. I'll come and do up the feeding. I don't want you in the barn or down with the cattle, either one, by yourself. Those brutes aren't as wild as Texas Longhorns but they're not yard pets either. You stay away from them. Can I have your word on that?"

Wanda agreed and Ben and his father walked out to the cutter. "Bar the door," Ben hollered as they pulled away.

DOWN THE ROAD to the west the drovers were within about ten miles of the reserve village. Normally a ride of this distance would be undertaken with no concern for strength or staying power of the ridden animal. But the bitter cold over many days had sapped the strength of man and beast alike. Hamilton's spare horses were put into service to relieve the weakest of the ridden animals.

The cowboy's horses were still walking strong but the Indians' horses had made the trip both ways and were showing signs of fatigue. The cattle, having survived on short rations ever since the big storm, were walking slower every mile. A few had staggered to a stop. On a big summer drive, the men might have left them, hoping that they would catch up in the cool of the evening. But to leave them in the dark and snow and bitter cold would mean their suffering and death. Even if the urge to leave the stragglers behind was strong, the knowledge of hungry families in the village was stronger. The weary men hollered through their scarves and slapped the staggering rumps with their coiled lariats.

Everyone was suffering in the thirty-below night but no one voiced a complaint. As each weary mile went by, the Circle S riders gradually gained more respect for the toughness of the Indians riding at their sides. There was no talk. There was no bantering as is common with cowboys. There was only the cold and the snow and the dark and the miles covered and yet to be covered.

An Indian rider's horse fell, the rider nimbly jumping free, landing in the snow in front of the steers. Dalton pushed his horse between the rider and the cattle and reached his hand down. The rider swung up behind Dalton and they rode to safety. The cattle were moving so slowly that the danger was soon past. The fallen horse rose to its feet and followed along, limping.

Dalton shouted to be heard, "That was a pretty good leap off that horse. I don't know as how I could do that with all these clothes on and as cold as my legs are."

The Indian spoke only broken English, "Man have to, man can do."

Dalton shook his head and laughed through his frozen scarf. "Ya, I guess you're right but I'm glad I didn't have to. Now you need a new horse. Sit tight; we'll catch that bay over there."

Riding up beside the bay, the Indian made a graceful leap and took a position bareback on the new horse. He guided it over to his limping mount with his knees and a handhold on the mane. He soon had bridle and saddle switched over and was riding along as if nothing at all had happened.

Johnnie had been watching. "Everything alright?" he hollered at Dalton.

"Alright except your rider is showing off a bit."

Johnnie laughed and said, "Thanks for picking him up."

It wasn't planned and it wasn't organized but somehow

the two groups of riders had become one. Where two men rode together it was Indian rider and Circle S man as often as not. They were no longer Indian and white. They were no longer civilized and savage. They were no longer victors of the Indian wars and the vanquished. They were simply men suffering through a long day and night of work. Nor did any of them really have to be there. They were volunteers all, doing what they knew to be right at the time and, once started, gave no thought at all to not completing their task.

Prejudices were set aside that night, at least in this small group of men. Prejudices long held but little understood. An Indian rider looked astonished when a Circle S rider passed him his scarf and indicated that he should cover his ears and nose. The Indian was clearly suffering with his inadequate clothing but had said nothing. He nodded his thanks and reluctantly accepted the scarf.

To say that the men became friends on that long cold day and night would be going too far but they at least were no longer enemies.

The wind had died down a bit, allowing the blowing snow to settle. The clouds thinned out and started to break up. A few stars cast their cold light onto the reflective snow. The night was not as dark as it had been but it was still a long way from bright. The moon was hidden behind cloud, offering no light at all.

A chorus of whoops rose from the road ahead and a group of riders came into view. Hamilton hollered at Johnnie, "Yonder comes your new riders."

The arrival of a dozen Indian riders on fresh horses brought new hope, seeming to impart new energy into the long-suffering riders and animals alike. By then, they were within eight miles of the reserve. Under good circumstances, that distance would be taken in stride but it loomed ahead on this cold night as a challenge to the very souls and determination of the men.

The new riders swung into position and the original Indian drovers pulled out for their homes. Their horses were staggering with weariness and cold and there was no run left in them but they outpaced the plodding cattle by a considerable amount. After the first curve in the trail, they were seen no more.

The Indian who had been passed the scarf brought it back before he rode off. He said something in his own language and nodded his thanks again. He touched his nose and smiled at the Circle S rider and then headed for home.

Johnnie rode up to Hamilton. "We can take it from here if you feel you should head back. Or you can come to the village and get some rest."

"These horses aren't going to make it home were we to turn around. They're about done in and so am I. We'll stay with you."

There was no way to reach a timepiece under all of Hamilton's winter clothing or any way to see it if he had fished it out but he knew it was well past midnight when the light of the first lantern came in sight. Johnnie was riding beside him. "That will be the agent's office with the light showing. We turn into the village just this side of the office. The people will meet us with lanterns to direct the herd to the corrals."

It took another full hour with the staggering cattle but it was as Johnnie had said. Hamilton looked at the gathered people and all the lanterns held aloft in mittened hands and chuckled to himself through his weariness. "Looks like the entire village is awake and waiting."

The cattle were soon in the corral. It took them only moments to discover the pile of hay laid out for them.

The ridden horses stood with heads hanging as the riders stepped to the ground. More than a few of the men reached for a grip on the saddle horn to keep from staggering or falling.

Johnnie spoke to Hamilton, "The men will put all the horses in the other corral and feed them. Come, the women will have food ready for us and pallets laid out for sleeping.

"Tell the Circle S men. They will eat at my home and then spread out to the other homes for sleeping. I will speak our thanks to them in the morning but for now let's get out of this cold."

The Indian riders went to their own homes while the Circle S riders joined Hamilton at Johnnie's cabin. His wife and two other women had food ready. The men were almost too tired to eat but the smell of highly-seasoned beef stew and coffee woke them up. They loosened their coats and removed hats and scarves and sat on the floor, ringing the walls of the small kitchen.

The women served them, coffee first, and then bowls of stew and hot biscuits. The slurping of coffee through half-frozen lips and the smacking of mouths on the stew would have been a social disaster at a box dinner. But on this night, no one thought anything of it or, if they did, they said nothing.

The riders were taken to the other homes for sleeping while Johnnie kept Hamilton at his home for the night or for the few hours that were left of it. Johnnie's wife had prepared a pallet for Hamilton in an unused room. When she came to explain it to him, she found him sound asleep with his coffee cup and stew bowl lying on the floor beside him. He hadn't even stretched out. He had simply lain over sideways where he had eaten. She spread a blanket over him and left him there.

Going into her own bedroom, she smiled at the sight of Johnnie sound asleep on top of the bedcovers and still in his riding clothes.

She looked at her husband and thought about what Hamilton and the other riders had done, and the hunger in the village. "You're better men than you know."

A rifle shot awakened Hamilton. Startled, he sat bolt upright on the kitchen floor just in time to hear a second shot. There was just a faint promise of daylight.

Johnnie's wife saw him sit up and answered his unasked question. "Just the men beefing out a couple of those steers."

Still half asleep, Hamilton made his way to the door and stepped out. There was a great deal of excitement in a clearing beside the corrals. As Hamilton made his way towards the gathered people, he could see two steers hanging from a timber that had been wedged between the branches of two poplar trees. The men had shot the animals and then pulled them up onto the timber with ropes that they then tied off around the base of the trees.

Now it was the women's turn. While Hamilton watched, a woman stepped forward and slit the throats of the dead animals, allowing them to bleed out. She then, with a single quick slice, opened their bellies. She stepped back quickly as the entrails poured out like small steaming avalanches. Other women carrying baskets dug through the innards and picked out the hearts, kidneys, livers and a few other delicacies. As these were carried away, more women pulled out the intestines and after squeezing them almost empty, put them in other baskets and went to clean them.

Hamilton pictured the women making sausage with the intestines as casings although he knew that it was more likely they would stuff them with a combination of dried meat and berries as a way of preserving the food. They called it pemmican and commonly carried it during their travels. Johnnie had given some to Hamilton and he found it quite to his taste although, given a choice, he preferred hot, cooked food. Unless it was chocolate cake. That he could tolerate most any time.

Four women stepped forward with skinning knives and Hamilton was fascinated by their efficiency. The knives seemed to flash in the rising morning sun and in no time at all the steers were hanging there naked with their hides rolled up for tanning at a later time.

The carving of the meat began immediately and soon women were making their way to their own homes, each with a ration of freshly-killed beef.

"They're good with their knives, aren't they?"

Hamilton turned around at the voice to see Johnnie grinning at him.

Hamilton shrugged. "Kind of makes me wonder what other uses they've put those knives to in the past."

"Best to leave it alone. Anyway, both you and I are standing here with no coats on. Let's get back to the house before we freeze."

Hamilton and the Circle S riders were served coffee and fresh-baked biscuits with honey for breakfast along with strips of fresh beef fried in lard, and were soon on the road home. With no cattle to worry about and only Hamilton's spare horses to drive, they hoped to be home in four or five hours. It was only a three-hour trip in the summer.

Passing Canyon View, Sam asked, "Anyone need to go into town?"

No one spoke up so they moved on. An unscheduled visit with Miss Granet would have to wait.

A northeast wind blew up as they traveled, blowing loose snow from the accumulated drifts into their faces.

Gradually, over the next half-hour the wind moved from the northeast to the southwest. They could feel a distinct difference in the temperature and the feel of the air.

Hamilton stood in his stirrups, held his arms outstretched to the breeze and laughed. "Do you feel that wind? That's spring on its way. Take a deep breath and you can smell the Pacific Ocean and California orange blossoms. You'll be hanging your coat on your saddle horn before you get home. And if you need more proof, take a look at the sky over that mountain. That big blue arch under the clouds is called a Chinook arch. You see a Chinook arch like that, you can start to plan for melting snow and full creeks and mud, lots of mud."

Sam chuckled. "I ain't never seen an ocean, Pacific nor any other. And I never seen or smelled an orange blossom, nor saw California. You may be right in your prediction but I'll keep my coat on for just a while yet. As far as that goes, I don't see you taking yours off."

"The world is full of doubters." Hamilton shook his head and feigned a hurt expression. "It's sad really, what this world has come to."

Dalton, riding ahead but still within earshot, pulled up on his reins and held out his hand to bring the group to a stop. "I'd say that one of the things that's happened in this sad world is that Big Bob got in trouble and it cost him his stallion."

He was pointing to the coyotes running off and the dead stallion lying in the snow.

The riders gathered around. Sam spoke, "That was Pa's special horse. I wonder what he was doing out here with it. Yesterday was no day for riding without there was a good reason. We'd better step it up in case there's trouble at home."

Hamilton stepped to the ground and said, "Two or

three of you throw me your ropes. We'll drag this carcass off the trail."

It took three horses to pull the dead stallion into the bush a distance from the traveled road.

It was a solemn group of riders that Hamilton spoke to, "At least it's out of sight and I expect the coyotes will have no trouble finding it again. The crows and hawks will feed on what's left and by summer nothing but hide and a few bones will be showing. Let's ride on."

At the cutoff to the H-R, Hamilton said his goodbyes to the Circle S men and thanked them again. The men pulled out for the Circle S and Hamilton turned down the short trail to his ranch.

As he entered the yard, he saw Wanda just coming from the barn with a basket in her hands. She heard him and turned his way. Seeing the loose horses, she stepped quickly towards the corral and swung the gate open.

Hamilton drove the horses in and as Wanda closed the gate he stepped off his riding animal. "What in the world are you doing here?"

Wanda made a face at him and tried to look serious. "Well, that's a fine greeting! But I might have been happier with - oh, I don't know - perhaps hello?"

Hamilton knew she was having fun at his expense but he still wanted an answer. "Yes, well, hello. It's good to see you. But the question still stands. What are you doing here and do your parents know where you are?"

"Why, Mr. Robb. Do you suppose I would do anything behind my parents' backs? Shame on you for such thoughts." Her smile gave her away.

"I'm clearly not going to get an answer so I'd better care for this horse. He's had a rough few hours, last night and today." With that he led the animal towards the barn.

Wanda hurried ahead and opened the door. The barn

was empty except for the milk cow and the chickens. "When it started to warm up, I thought the animals could do with some outside air. I left the doors open for the same reason, knowing they were closed tight for weeks. It was starting to smell like a barn in there. I finally closed the doors because the stupid chickens insisted on going out and I didn't know if I could catch them again or not.

Hamilton looked at her and laughed. "Smelled like a barn, did it. Well, that will never do. Guess it could do with some cleaning, couldn't it? I'll get around to that but there's other things more important.

"I have to get the cattle looked after but first let's try this again. What exactly are you doing here? Not that I mind. I'd like to have you here all the time but that's another matter for another time."

Wanda figured she had pushed the fun about as far as was wise so she told him the short story about Big Bob's accident and her night alone on the H-R. She finished with, "So your cabin is warm, there's the remains of a roast of beef on the stove and the cattle are fed.

"I'm not sure how you men can enjoy so much stew but I made a big pot anyway, besides the beef roast.

"Ben forced me down that dreadful root cellar. Claimed he couldn't do it himself with his sore feet but he can do most everything else so I expect he was falling a little short of the whole entire truth on that. Anyway, I brought in more carrots and such.

"Pa came over and fed the cattle again this morning. Made me promise to stay away from them. Made me promise to stay away from the barn animals, too, so the less said about that at the Circle S, the better. I can't think of a single thing stopping you from coming to the cabin and telling me all about the drive and the things in the village."

Hamilton hung his coat and headgear on the peg beside the door and dipped hot water from the stove reservoir for washing. He rolled up his sleeves and turned his shirt collar in. When he carried the pan and a towel to the wash-stand on the porch, Wanda said, "My goodness, it's too cold for washing outside."

Hamilton laughed. "It's invigorating."

Wanda folded her arms across her chest and gave him a strange look. "You need to know that I have some serious doubts about you."

Hamilton soaped and scrubbed and splashed water on the porch floor and then reached for a towel.

Wanda looked on in awe. "My goodness, if I had known that you were going to spread water and soap from here to the barnyard I would never have suggested that you do it in the house. Outside is starting to look like a good idea. I can't imagine the mess when you take a bath."

Hamilton threw the pan of water into the snow beside the porch and wiped the pan out with the towel. He then hung the pan on a nail on the wall and carried the towel inside. He grinned at Wanda. "You're too young and inno-cent to know all the secrets of life."

As he drank a cup of coffee, Wanda more fully explained the situation with the dead stallion.

"So why did your father ride to town?"

"He wouldn't say. Just said that we would discuss it as a family when we are all together."

"Speaking of family, I'd better get a horse on the cutter and take you home. As much as I enjoy having you sitting in my kitchen, I made a promise to your father that we wouldn't be alone here. I intend to keep that promise or at least as much of the promise as is left after the work you've done. I do appreciate your concerns, and the work. Your father's, too, with the cattle."

As he reached for his coat, Wanda reached for hers also. Within a matter of minutes, they were seated in Hamilton's cutter and headed for the Circle S.

Hamilton pulled the rig to a stop in front of the house and Wanda stepped out.

"Thanks again for looking after things. I hope to see you soon, perhaps on Sunday. It's going to warm up now with that Chinook wind blowing. Time to get back to normal life including church."

Wanda said her goodbyes and headed for the house as Hamilton turned the rig towards the H-R.

22

HAMILTON HAD NO VISITORS NOR DID HE SEE ANYONE UNTIL he made his regular trip into town on Saturday afternoon. He did some shopping and deposited the Indian Agent's draft for the purchase of cattle. He ate supper at the hotel dining room where he greeted several old friends whose single topic of interest was the blizzard and the losses sustained. He then found his way to the saloon, hoping to find the checkers players gathered. He wasn't disappointed. The group was larger than normal as if they had been waiting for weeks for an opportunity to get to town. Each man again had a single thought in mind: the blizzard.

Since their first meeting, the checkers players had made up a happy, fun-loving and teasing group, easily guffawing at each other's expense. The blizzard had changed that. The men were playing checkers and whittling as before but there was little laughter. Each man told how things had been on his ranch and estimated his cattle losses. They were sobered by the losses but even more sobered by the potential loss of good friends and neighbors who had given up and were talking of moving out.

The sheriff sat back in his chair and looked around at his friends. "Family in this afternoon. Some of you might know the Temples although they live in a remote corner of the hills and don't come down often. Lost a child, same as the Johansson's did. Unclear just what the child was doing outside. His body ain't been found. I offered our help but they turned it down. Independent folks, I guess."

Tiny finally spoke so quietly it was difficult to hear him, "Can't imagine that or what the Johansson family has gone through. Hurts to even think about it. Sure glad our kids were held in the school overnight although I will admit to dread anxiety all of that night, imagining the worst. There were a lot of relieved families the next morning when that bunch of kids was found safe."

Walt, showing up after his livery business had slowed for the evening, picked up on Tiny's thoughts and told about Sam Stanton and his night of rescue at the schoolhouse. Most of the townsfolk already knew the story but there was no stopping Walt.

Clark Ransom mentioned the talk going around about the Circle S and the hay. "Not worth talking about," was all Hamilton had to say.

The men studied him, knowing there was a story there but that they would have to get it from the Circle S. Hamilton wasn't talking.

The following morning, Hamilton made his way to church on horseback. The cutter had been put up on blocks for the summer. There was still snow around but there were lots of bare patches, too, where the wind had scoured the ground. Some of the larger drifts would be several weeks melting off. Again, he went to the hotel for lunch and then left for home.

Hamilton was unsure of what his next step should be with Wanda. Neither she nor her mother had shown up for church. The image of Big Bob's anger was strong on his mind and, while it was good of Bob to feed his cattle while the crew herded the steers to the Indian village, he figured that was entirely to keep Wanda from attempting the task.

To knock on the door and ask Wanda to go for a ride or a walk when he knew he wasn't welcome on the Circle S seemed somehow demeaning to the entire process of courting although he had done it the once when he took out his new sleigh. Between the sale of cattle to the Indians, the controversy over Hamilton's check, and the loss of Big Bob's stallion, the situation had become very confusing.

Mrs. Stanton had prepared a full midday meal while Wanda had baked two dried apple pies. This would normally have caused an exuberant discussion and much family teasing and laughter. But the meal was taken mostly in silence.

The pie finished and the coffee served, Ben looked at his father. "Alright, Pa. We've had a big, unnecessary fight with a neighbor, shown serious misjudgment towards the Indian Agent, and questioned the integrity of that same neighbor, a man who has done nothing but show great friendliness towards the Circle S and honorable interest in Wanda. You managed to kill your favorite horse and nearly froze to death in the process and I am not at all sure just why we did any of it.

"We are all adults here. There are no children anymore in the Stanton clan. So it's your turn. Talk to us like adults and tell us just exactly what's going on and what the outcome of your foolish ride to town was."

Mrs. Stanton scolded Ben quite harshly and completely out of character, "Ben, please remember that you are speaking to your father."

Ben ignored her and the silence deepened for several

moments.

Bob's voice was quiet, "I am deeply sorry about a couple of things and man enough to be thankful for others. The issue with the hay is something I have no explanation for. I know of nothing like it now or ever before. I can't explain or understand why anyone would do a thing like that but, without that single act, we would have lost the entire herd and I am well aware of it.

"Selling off the weaned calves turned out to be a good decision although I admit it seemed like we were selling off our future at the time. Selling that hundred steers to the Indians was a godsend, too. Driving part of the herd to the railhead had to be done to save the others although it produced mighty little income. We still won't make it through to green grass without selling off more animals but all the sales were a big help.

"Still, Robb is a small rancher and my experience told me that to make it in ranching you have to be much bigger than the H-R. Your mother and I fought our way out of poverty over several years and I don't want to see any of you having to do that. To think of Wanda struggling the way your mother did makes me want to fight its cause. I'm not saying that Robb isn't a likable young fellow but I'm left with serious questions and concerns.

"The issue with the guns makes me wonder if we know that whole story. Robb says he was a sheriff and maybe he was but that's a gunfighter's rig sitting in that showcase in town. I can't help feeling a bit uneasy about that story.

"And the only Indians I ever saw before were either shooting at me or trying to escape my shots. I can't help wondering about that connection with Robb either, just like the gun story.

"At first I thought it would be best if we were to head back to Texas come spring and forget this entire sad episode. I saw it as a mistake from the start."

Wanda was all set to say something but Ben held up a hand to stop her.

"Pa, you as much as called Hamilton a liar and killed your best horse riding to town to prove it. You need to tell us about that."

The response was slow in coming, "Yes, I guess I do. I'm sorrier than I can tell about the horse but even more sorry about doubting Robb's word. Many and many a fight has started over slights such as that. I let my feelings about Wanda get in the way of my good judgment.

"I did take the check to the bank and talked with the banker direct. He barely glanced at the check and confirmed that he would honor it. I don't mind telling you that I was pleased to hear it. He deposited the funds into the Circle S account right then and there. And we needed those funds."

As the eldest son of the family, Ben was leading the discussion, "You're not telling it all, Pa. I can tell by the look on your face. You owe us the whole story."

Big Bob looked around the table again and then sat back in his chair. "I don't know if Robb has pulled the wool over the banker's eyes or if he has the straight of it but he thinks a lot of Robb and of his management of the H-R. Without me asking more than just about the check, he started in to telling me things he thought I might want to know. No man has ever talked to me like that but I guess because he's the banker he felt he could take the liberty. I need that bank right now so I sat there and took his words."

Big Bob couldn't bend enough to tell the family everything that was said in the banker's office but his mind went there and he remembered the banker's words with a feeling of bitterness, never having been spoken to like that before but knowing he had no choice but to sit and take it.

"Bob," the banker had said. "You've had this country wrong right from the start. You came in here showing Texas pride and arrogance. You bought out a good ranch but you brought in more cattle than your range could support and more riders than you needed or could afford. Then you bought still more cattle and bulled your way onto the public range, taking the grass your neighbors had shared on a friendly basis for years. They didn't fight you, knowing that you wouldn't last out the first winter.

"You walked around town with heavy heels but what you didn't see was that people were laughing at you and shaking their heads at your actions. Your neighbors are good folks, Bob, honest and hard-working. And those that have been here for a few years have learned how to live with the country, not against it. Many of them have done very well and your neighbor, Robb, has done better than most.

"The whole country knows about the hay that saved your ranch but I can tell you that Robb has never breathed a word about it, nor will he. The whole country also knows that Hamilton is sweet on your girl but I can promise you that he would have given you that hay whether you had a daughter or not.

"Now you came in here with his check. Word gets around quickly out here, Bob, and the sale to the Indians is already a well-known story. That story hit town as soon as the herd was seen heading towards the reserve this morning. One of your riders swung into town to pick up some warmer clothes. He talked some so your refusal to accept the government chit from the Indian Agent is also well-known. Those that know Robb are surprised that he let you get away with calling him a liar, or near enough to it, about his check. There was a time back when he first came to this country that he would have beaten you into the ground for even hinting at his integrity. He's changed some since that time.

"You've been heard calling Robb a nester and a man fighting poverty. I'm going to break a banker's confidence for the first time in my life because I like Robb and he won't stick up for himself. I'm prepared to like you too, Bob, but so far you haven't made it easy.

"Robb is far from a poor man. He came in here with some money and he's increased his net worth every year since through hard work and good management. He has no mortgage and no loans and his herd and machinery are paid for. He pays cash for everything he buys and he carries a substantial balance in this bank. Further, if there was ever anything he asked for, this bank would give it without any hesitation.

"And if you ever repeat what I have just told you, I'll call you a liar and I'll call your loan, too. You don't want either of those things to happen.

"I don't act as the town matchmaker, Bob, but if your girl should choose Robb, you could never ask for more. Now, get out of here. I have work to do.

"Go home and think it over. Go shake Robb's hand and start again."

No, Big Bob could never repeat all of that to his family, especially to Wanda.

Even knowing he had been wrong in some of his thoughts, Big Bob wasn't big enough to repeat all the banker had said. He settled for, "I'm not always completely right but I'm not always completely wrong either."

Thinking now of everything that had happened in the

previous few weeks - the blizzard, the near loss of his sons, the gift of hay, the loss of his cattle, the suffering throughout the county, the loss of the Johansson girl on top of all the banker had said - Bob Stanton, for the first time in his life, was truly humbled.

He looked around the table at these people who were more important than life to him. He wondered what to say; how far to go. He had laid awake most of the night thinking about what was best for the family and for the Circle S. Towards morning, he had come to some decisions.

Finally, he continued talking and, as he talked, his thoughts seemed to become clear so he put into words what he had been thinking about since the ride home from the bank.

"More important than what the banker said is the memory of finding that little girl under the snow. When I picked up that frozen child, I thought I wouldn't be able to bear the feelings that came over me even though I never saw her before or met her family. When Johansson walked over and I placed that dead child in his arms, I was trembling with feelings like I can't really explain. That poor man took his lost child in his arms and then just turned and walked away. I have never experienced anything even close to what happened that afternoon.

"We came awful close to losing you two boys this winter and looking at that little girl, all I could think of was one or both of you dead under the snow. I looked at Johansson's suffering and I saw myself and knew I wouldn't have been man enough to take the loss.

"It made me remember again how much my family means to me and what I would do for any of you.

"I always had big plans for this family.

"So I wanted a prosperous ranch to turn over to you

when my days are done and, by Texas standards, that means big acreage and big herds.

"I wanted to protect you so I didn't like the girls coming out from town or you boys going in there. And when Robb showed an interest in Wanda, I panicked and fought it with everything in me, knowing that my daughter deserves the very best.

"But what I missed in all of this is that my children are no longer children. You are all adults and people your mother and I can be rightfully proud of. So we're going to correct some things, starting right now.

"First thing your mother and I are going to do is trust your judgment. We've done all the teaching we can ever do so now you can put that teaching into your lives without me watching every move you make.

"The next thing we're going to do, after we make some basic changes, is turn this ranch over to the three of you to run and manage as you think best. Even though you will one day be gone from here, Wanda, still you own your fair share of the ranch. I will hold final decision on important matters but as long as you're doing well you won't hear from me.

"As soon as the roads are fit for travel, we will pay off the riders. The payroll has been a serious drain. The three of us can do what needs doing if we keep our fences up and build some new ones.

"We're going to start replacing the Longhorns. You boys can figure out how best to do that but my thought is that we could sell the bred cows off as replacement animals to those ranches that suffered blizzard loss. We should get the best prices that way. I wouldn't mind if we sold them all off and leave the land to grow back while we find better animals.

"We're going to start a feedlot and buy corn or other

grain to finish out our own animals. Might finish some animals for other ranchers, too.

"We're going to be ready for winter. And in case you think any of this sounds easy, know this: You're going to do most of the work. Your mother and I are going to go to town a bit more often and visit a few neighbors from time to time. I'll work with you when you need me but first you try to do it yourselves.

"Now I need to come back to Robb and the banker. I'll say no more here or ever again. What he told me does not affect you boys in the least and is not your affair.

"Wanda, what you and Robb talk about is between the two of you, if it comes to that. That's a part of our trusting you. There'll be no more talk about money."

The family sat in stunned silence, hardly able to take in the changes in their father or in the plans he had outlined for the Circle S. Ben finally pushed his chair back and hobbled to the door, picking up his jacket on the way. Sam followed after a few moments.

Wanda stood up and reached for her coat. "I promised the Johansson's I'd drop over for a cup of tea this afternoon. I won't be long."

Entering the barn to shelter from the cold, Ben and Sam leaned on a stall railing and looked at each other. Ben finally spoke, "Never thought I'd see the day nor hear the words."

Sam nodded. "You alright with all of that?"

"I doubt as how Pa's willpower is quite as strong as he thinks it is but it's a start. I somehow think he'll have considerable to say and say it louder than he plans once his memory of this day fades a bit. But were we to do a few things before he starts to go back on his word, there wouldn't be much he could do about it."

Sam grinned at his brother. "I like that. What did you have in mind?"

"Let's saddle up and check the herd. We can talk along the way."

23

EARLY SUNDAY MORNING, WANDA AND HER MOTHER WERE dressing for church. Big Bob had harnessed a team and drawn the spring wagon up to the house yard. When the ladies were ready to leave, they were startled to see Bob come downstairs in his best suit and with his new white Stetson in his hand. "Ready to go?"

Wanda spoke first, "Pa?"

Bob tried to sound casual without much success. "It's a free country. A man can go to church if he chooses to."

As he walked out the door, the two women looked at each other. Wanda smiled and Mrs. Stanton said, "My, my."

Ben and Sam were walking up from the barn. They stopped dead in their tracks when they saw their father dressed for church and helping their mother into the wagon. Wanda took a seat in the back.

Bob turned the wagon in the yard and the ladies offered casual waves to the boys. Ben and Sam stood in silence for several moments until finally Sam looked at Ben and grinned.

"Well, why not? We can change and catch up to them before they reach town."

Ben slapped his younger brother on the shoulder. "Big changes on the Circle S. Don't know as I really understand it all. Are we going to just walk up to the church door bold as brass and give everyone heart failure or should we slink in the side door hoping no one see us?"

"Depends. I'm hoping to spot a lady who usually wears a red hat."

Following the service, where everyone was friendly if a bit reserved and no one had heart failure, Wanda sought out Hamilton. He had still been holding back, keeping his distance, not knowing how things lay between himself and Circle S.

"Good morning, Mr. Robb. I enjoyed the choir music this morning."

"Good morning to you, too. Is it alright for us to be talking?"

Wanda ignored the question. "Is that your buggy I see over there, Mr. Robb?"

"It is. I'm still hoping for the day when I can take you home in it after church and all other times as well."

"If you'll pardon my boldness, Mr. Robb, I would suggest that you invite me to lunch at the hotel dining room and then we will see about the buggy ride."

Hamilton looked at Wanda, then over at the rest of the Stanton family and then back at Wanda. "That's a mighty big change. Care to tell me what happened?"

"I still haven't heard your invite for lunch, Mr. Robb. But if you were to do that, we would have a chance to talk."

Hamilton, in mock seriousness said, "Miss Stanton, I would be most honored if you would join me in the dining room for lunch."

"I thought you would never ask."

He helped her into the buggy and grinned as he turned the horse towards the dining room.

Mrs. Stanton watched them drive off and predictably whispered, "My, my!"

THE END

A LOOK AT MAC'S WAY

Raised in poverty in Missouri, Mac is determined to find a better life for himself and the girl who is still a vague vision in his mind. Work on the Santa Fe Trail, and on a Mississippi River boat give him a start, but the years of Civil War leave him broke and footloose in South Texas. There he discovers more cattle running loose than he ever knew existed. Teaming up with two ex-Federal soldiers, he sets out to gather his wealth, one head at a time.

While gathering and driving Longhorns, Mac and his friends meet an interesting collection of characters, including Margo. Mac and Margo and the crew learn about Longhorns, and life, from hard experience before they eventually head west. Outlaws and harrowing river crossings are just two of the challenges they face along their way.

AVAILABLE NOW FROM REG QUIST AND CKN CHRISTIAN PUBLISHING

ABOUT THE AUTHOR

REG QUIST'S pioneer heritage includes sod shacks, prairie fires, home births, and children's graves under the prairie sod, all working together in the lives of people creating their own space in a new land.

Out of that early generation came farmers, ranchers, business men and women, builders, military graves in faraway lands, Sunday Schools that grew to become churches, plus story tellers, musicians, and much more.

Hard work and self-reliance were the hallmark of those previous great generations, attributes that were absorbed by the following generation.

Quist's career choice took him into the construction world. From heavy industrial work, to construction camps in the remote northern bush, the author emulated his grandfathers, who were both builders, as well as pioneer farmers and ranchers.

Quist's heart was never far from the land. The family photo albums testify to how often he found himself sitting on a horse, both as a child and into later life, when he and his wife owned their own small farm, complete with kids and horses.

Respect for the pioneers, working alongside skilled, tough workmen, and learning from them, marrying his high school sweetheart and welcoming children into the world, purchasing land for the family to grow on, and riding horses with the kids, all melded together to influence Quist's life and writing. Over, and under, and wrapped around his life is Quist's Christian heritage. This too, shows itself in his writing.

Quist's writing career was late in pushing itself forward, remaining a hobby while family and career took precedence. Only in early retirement, was there time for more serious writing.

Quist's writing interests lie in many genres including children's work, short lifestyle stories, cowboy poetry, western novels, plus Christian articles and novels.

Woven through every story is the thought that, even though he was not there himself in that pioneer time, he knew some that were. They are remembered with great respect.